FIRE DANCER

Susan Slater

Books by Susan Slater
THE BEN PECOS MYSTERY SERIES

The Pumpkin Seed Massacre
Yellow Lies
Thunderbird
Firedancer
Under A Mulberry Moon (summer 2018)

A Way to the Manger (a Christmas novella)

FIRE DANCER

Ben Pecos Mysteries, Book 4

Susan Slater

Secret Staircase Books

Fire Dancer
Published by Secret Staircase Books, an imprint of
Columbine Publishing Group LLC
PO Box 416, Angel Fire, NM 87710

This book is a work of fiction. Names, characters, places and
incidents are either the product of the author's imagination or are used
fictitiously. Any resemblance to actual events or locales or persons, living
or dead, is entirely coincidental.

Book layout and design by Secret Staircase Books
Cover illustration © Melanie Kowasic

First trade paperback edition: April 2018
First e-book editions: April 2018

Publisher's Cataloging-in-Publication Data

Slater, Susan
Fire Dancer / by Susan Slater
p. cm.
ISBN 978-1945422454 (paperback)
ISBN 978-1945422461 (e-book)

1. Pecos, Ben (Fictitious character)--Fiction. 2. Navajo
Indians--Fiction. 3. New Mexico--Fiction. 4. Christmas--Fiction.
I. Title

Ben Pecos Mystery Series : Book 4
Slater, Susan, Ben Pecos mysteries.

BISAC : FICTION / Mystery & Detective.
813/.54

Heartfelt thanks go out to Stephanie Dewey, my new, talented, publicist/web maven and never-tiring, go-to, idea person who was the impetus behind bringing out these new editions of my entire Ben Pecos series.

Chapter One

She winced and caught her breath. The pain was sharp, but fleeting. Breathe in, one, two; breathe out, one, two. There, that was better. She smoothed her skirt and glanced out over the audience. Autumn shadows crept across the first two rows of seats, casting a dappled grayness. The end of the Indian summer was near—a metaphor for her life? Possibly. It would be one week tomorrow since she'd known—known that the lump in her groin heralded a far more pervasive, insidious illness than the muscle pull she'd thought it to be. She had leukemia. And she had very little time. The exit was cast in stone—four months without an aggressive round of chemo. A treatment she soundly refused. Or the long shot. A bone marrow donor. No. She had no right to ask. There was one person, one possibility, but hadn't she burned that bridge forever?

The crispness of the breeze made her pleased she'd chosen the black nubby wool suit. She loved fall in New Mexico. Sitting on the dais overlooking the crowd of perhaps a hundred well-wishers, the wind ruffled the scarf at her neck, but the sun warmed her face. And then the ever-present jolt—this would be her last season. The reminder of time evaporating shadowed her every move. Like a specter she must address. Meet head on, resolve— make decisions that would affect so many. She was being recognized today for her contributions to the University of New Mexico. When one had money there were always countless ceremonial thank yous. The obligatory gatherings to celebrate good deeds—an ostentatious show to, perhaps, encourage others to share their largess. She would be expected to say a few words.

The Chancellor droned on about expansion and research—attracting the best to be had to lead the University in competition with other top schools—all this made possible by caring individuals like herself. He turned from the podium to acknowledge her. She nodded, but already her mind was skipping away, ducking into the reverie which paraded her past across her memory. She smelled crushed maple leaves—as if she'd just walked across a lawn kicking up the slightly sweet earthy dampness of muted reds and oranges. Something she hadn't smelled since her youth at school in Vermont. But there it was. As real in the moment as if it had just happened. And it was this olfactory memory that repeated itself. The scent of lilacs out of season, rain on parched desert in October, sopapillas sputtering in hot grease in her office—her nose deceiving her with a rush of places and times past.

Sixty years seemed both a long time and as fleeting as a second. There should be no regrets … but one. One regret, one irreconcilable action taken … but she'd been given a brief time to make it right. She had put out feelers, discreet inquiries. Hired someone who came recommended. She was dying—give her this last wish. Would it work? Would she come face-to-face with her past? Sit down and say, "I should have never let this happen. Forgive me. I've loved you with every breath I take."

"Consuelo Bigrope CdeBaca." Her name. She bumped back to the present. The Chancellor beamed while most of the hundred guests were on their feet in polite applause. How sweet. She acknowledged the audience with a wave, thanked the Chancellor, reiterated how dear the University was to her and her late husband, spoke of its future in safeguarding the state's youth, how the state university must remain the leader—no, the initiator in protecting the brain trust so needed to encourage industry to choose this state and establish employment opportunities for all. How the school should provide the national labs with top-notch candidates, those prepared with solid skills and a mission to maintaining the competitiveness of our great country. How her modest contribution should be used to retain the youth—offer scholarship opportunities to minorities, Native Americans who otherwise might not have a bright future.

Her words—nothing new or earth-shattering— brought vigorous applause. The Chancellor jumped to his feet when she'd finished and encouraged the audience once again to stand. She smiled, nodded slightly and waited at the podium while the Chancellor approached her with a large box, a rainbow-hued bow dripping over its sides.

"This token barely expresses our deep gratitude for your thoughtfulness, your magnanimous contributions over the years. Your gift of two million dollars comes at a time when …"

She tuned out his officious droning and turned to smile her thanks at the five people sitting behind her—the Chancellor's wife, the head of educational research, the Provost, acting Dean of the Medical School and his wife.

The Chancellor stopped and politely withdrew, leaving her to acknowledge their gift. She lifted the lid of the box and placed it beside the podium before digging into the layers of tissue. Her fingers touched a rounded surface—a pot, of course. They would know of her collection. Something from Acoma, or Jemez, or San Ildefonso. A tasteful addition to what she'd gathered for years. With both hands, she scooped the vessel up, letting the box fall to the side.

She brought it to eye level and gasped. She was looking into the vacant eye sockets of a skull. A hole, bullet-sized, squarely between those orifices was outlined in red—in the shape of a heart. She turned toward those sitting behind her. Their plastic smiles looked at her expectantly—not realizing, of course, what she held. Because not for one minute did she believe anyone on this distinguished panel had anything to do with what was happening. She could hear her breath coming in short spurts. There would only be one skull anyone would send her. But from a time so long ago … why now? Who would need to let her know that her secret was shared? The man who had held the gun? Held her finger to the trigger? He was gone. Well paid to stay away. Could greed have brought him back?

She swayed, struggling to focus, at least to stay upright, but it was the private knowledge that she knew whose skull this was that brought the terror to the surface, brought her fear in all its starkness and laid it bare. She had once loved this man more than life itself, and now someone was threatening exposure. Please … not now, not when so much was at stake.

She swung back, clutching the skull in one hand and grasping the edge of the podium only to have it collapse with her weight and topple over the edge of the narrow stage. The skull popped from her grasp, and the screams of those in the front row barely drowned the clanging of metal chairs pushed into one another as the audience scattered.

Chapter Two

A prank. I'm convinced that it was nothing more."

She was reclining on the sofa in her own study, thank God. She'd prevailed and had only spent an overnight at University Hospital. There would be enough of hospitals soon enough. The tumble from the stage resulted in a few bruises, nothing broken. She felt much more up to the obligatory questions in familiar surroundings. And though irksome, the discovery of a human skeleton—even a part—necessitated exhaustive investigation. A quick call to her lawyer stemmed the inevitable media frenzy. She had barely filled a half dozen sentences on the ten o'clock news. Still, persistent reporters might doggedly try to pursue an answer. Would they be able to figure out who—no, she couldn't think that way.

"Ms. CdeBaca—"

"Connie, please. May I call you Ryan?"

"Hmmm, yes, well, you have no reason to suspect someone is trying to scare you? Threaten you?"

"None." She knew the young detective wouldn't be comfortable using her first name.

"Is there any chance that you might know the deceased?"

Had her intake of breath given her away? She shrugged, exhaling slowly, seeming to search her memory. "My husband and I have had hundreds of workers on the ranch over the years. Because of his time in public office, I've made countless thousands of acquaintances. I currently employ fifty people in my construction company. Of course, it's possible I've known the person. Will you be able to come up with a date? Some idea of time when the …" She couldn't finish.

"Yes. I expect answers by the end of the week. About all we know now for certain is that it's male. We're treating this as a homicide but haven't ruled out a self-inflicted wound. We'll be looking at a time frame—they can get pretty close. Then we'll try to match it with any remains from the same period—unexplained partials found in the vicinity. Actually, not just the vicinity, our scope is pretty broad."

She knew he was talking about the countless bones— bits of femurs, metatarsals, clavicles, that appeared on the mesa, in someone's garden, or when excavating a landfill. Good for a story in the afternoon paper and speculation, then forgotten. Unless they identified it, found the match and made the connection. But wasn't that impossible? A missing person, a few paragraphs on microfiche in some archive—but not a body. Hadn't the ashes been scattered in the Sandias … the body assumed to be complete, decapitated in life but whole in its final journey? But what if they reconstructed … first by computer, then putty until he emerged as in life. How common was that practice? Would forensics spend that kind of money? Maybe, if they thought the stakes were important enough. She could never handle the questions—the relentless questioning. But she would be spared. Death seemed comforting somehow.

"There's a computer listing of unsolved murders—where only parts of a skeleton have been found. But that doesn't explain the heart, does it? That would seem to indicate a more intimate knowledge." She snapped to the present; he was watching her.

"Certainly, a rather bizarre touch." She reached for a cigarette. Funny how the minute she'd found out she was dying, she'd bought a carton on the way home from the clinic. Twenty years a non-smoker and then back in a second, the cravings, the need for menthol. She clicked the lighter shut. The smoke curled upward, dissipating before reaching the domed ceiling of stained glass. The cigarette gave her something to do with her hands. Kept them from trembling, she hoped.

"I'm sorry. I didn't mean to upset you."

"It's all right. Really. I just find it a bit gruesome. I admit to waking up last night after dreaming I was holding it in my hands again." She shivered then admonished herself to collect her thoughts. No tears. She couldn't let him see the wound, the fear … "You know, the skull might have been meant for the Chancellor."

"We've thought of that. But because of the presentation, it seems someone went to great lengths to make certain you received the skull. The original gift was purchased from

Wright's Gallery. We've interviewed the store owners." He referred to his notes. "Mr. and Mrs. Bobrick. Both were instrumental in choosing the gift—an Acoma pot—I believe they are familiar with your collection?"

"Yes. Over the years they've always called when something they knew I'd like came into the store."

"A graduate student picked up the gift—watched it being wrapped and brought it to campus, leaving it with the Chancellor's secretary. The switch apparently happened while it was in the Chancellor's office. I understand the university sent a replacement this morning? It seems the Bobricks had a difficult time choosing between the original gift and its replacement, in the first place. In fact, Mr. Bobrick indicated that he thought this was the appropriate choice all along."

Connie walked to a lighted glassed cabinet and took out a clay Indian corn maiden. "I agree with him. Beautiful, isn't she?" She turned the ten-inch figure so that he could see the corn pattern intricately displayed down one side of her mantle. "I've collected Maxine Toya for some time now. This is really some of her best work. I'm honored, frankly." The sun played tricks with the polished rust-red cloak that covered the figure's head, causing the clay to look like shimmering cloth. The black accents had been polished to shine like obsidian.

"Here. Beautiful, don't you agree?"

She handed the figurine to him and sank back down beside him on the leather couch. Ryan gingerly turned the figure over in his hands before placing her on the glass and iron end table. He paused for a moment, then, "You're isolated out here. I think I'd give some thought to moving closer in. Just in case what happened was meant as a threat."

"The daughter of a friend is coming to stay for a few weeks. My friend is recovering from surgery or I'd have the two of them. I'll be fine. Besides, I like being close to the site." She didn't add that she had servants. Of course, until their quarters were finished, there would be no one staying the night. She couldn't have them there at night anyway, not for a while. But a cook, a housekeeper and grounds man were there during the day.

"Ah yes, the construction site. Millionaire row—isn't that what it's being called?"

"The houses will be—are large—all a minimum of five thousand square feet with natural accents. They are not cheap—I don't have to apologize for that." Why was this man making her feel defensive? The exclusive community was just another part of her legacy.

"Choosing to build at the edge of the land grant encroaching on sacred Indian land has caused concerns. Six months ago a house was burned."

"A house under construction. The investigators traced it to faulty wiring." She believed that. A simple explanation is often the true one.

"There was a letter if I remember correctly. Some eco-terrorist group took responsibility—claimed victory?"

"So much easier for those groups if they don't have to do anything. It was an accident—one we've made certain won't happen again."

"How many houses are occupied?"

"This one, of course. Only one other is close to completion. Five have been started. The fire slowed us down a bit."

She wasn't admitting to the lawsuit. She couldn't talk about it even if she wanted. The detective was correct in saying a neighboring pueblo was disputing her claim to the ten thousand acres left to her husband's family and then to her. One of those details she needed to give attention to. Sandwiched between forestland and Indian land, the strip was of interest to a number of groups. Her husband had kept it stocked with elk and treated visiting dignitaries to a private, herd-thinning hunt once a year. She was certain more than one felled elk had bought her husband the favors he'd needed in the state house.

"Ma'am?"

"I'm sorry. Did you say something?"

"Did your husband have enemies?"

She stifled a laugh. Did he have enemies? Was there anyone who hadn't wished Skip CdeBaca dead at one time or another? His own children fit into that category. And didn't she? Didn't she still berate herself because money and convenience made her turn her back … accept the fear, the heartbreak, do something that she regretted every minute of her life in exchange for everything around her, including her own life.

"He's been gone two years in December. He would have been eighty-one. I think he simply outlived a lot of ill-will." She gave a short laugh. "I can't imagine any grudges that might have lasted beyond the grave." Only because those players were also dead. Except one. Didn't the very skull she had held in her hands prove it? And her … but hadn't her anger just turned to bitterness?

"Sometimes answers are right under our noses. It's a matter of examining things. You might want to make a list of possible trouble-makers, grudges, that sort of thing—"

"You like what you do, don't you?" She said it kindly. The young man was trying—probably had a promotion riding on some sort of swift closure to this case. And she knew she was still celebrity enough to warrant the time spent—meaning a far more heinous crime would lack manpower.

"If I think of something, I'll call. Do you have a card?"

He took the hint and, putting a card on the table, got to his feet.

"Rosa? Oh, there you are. Could you show Detective Salas to the door?" Connie rose and extended her hand. "I appreciate your concern. Thank you for stopping by."

"You take care. I don't think you should just dismiss this."

Once again a shiver prickled across her shoulder blades, and the hand she held out in parting was ice cold. "I'll be careful. I promise."

She heard the heavy front door thud shut and waited for Rosa to walk back through the study.

"Miss Consuelo? This is my early evening. Can I get you something before I leave?"

"If you have time, make a plate of sandwiches and leave them covered on the kitchen counter. I won't go out this evening, but I may have guests." Not a lie, really. She was expecting someone. But not someone who would come into the house to eat.

"Yes, Miss. I could stay. I do not mind sleeping in the study if you—"

"No, I'll be fine alone. I just need to rest. I'll go to bed early. But thank you, Rosa."

Connie walked to the bar, filled a glass half full of ice and a generous couple splashes of Herradura. Running a lime quarter around the rim, she dropped the spent fruit into the liquor. Thank God for the blue agave. What would she do if the plant became extinct? And then that familiar jolt … would she care? Death was far more difficult to become accustomed to than she would have imagined. There was a part of the human being that clung desperately to life … refusing to believe. How easy it would be to slip into denial. Was it all that wonderful to have a warning? To know when her time of departure would be?

She carried the drink into the living room and stood by the wall of glass that practically brought the Sandia Mountains into her patio. The green of the sloping foothills stood out in stark contrast to the desert floor. As always, the vastness of her view from this spot filled her with awe. She'd worked closely with the architect. Every detail was designed with care, with feeling for the land.

She started this house the year after Skip died. She had discarded the plans he'd drawn up and replaced them with her own. The heavy masculine touches had given way to sunken tubs and ponds of Koi and lilies, Italian marble and natural granite, greenhouses combined with bathrooms, a lap pool—everything she'd ever wanted. Skip would have built a fortress; she built an open invitation for the surrounding mesa to become a part of her living area. She replaced or moved every desert plant other contractors would have destroyed. The result garnered her Albuquerque's House Beautiful award and assured her a permanent spot on the City's Parade of Homes every fall. Sadly, she'd be able to enjoy it less than six months.

Sometimes she would wander her house and let memories of poverty intrude. A childhood of few extras. The kind of poverty that resulted in wanting what was around her now, no matter the cost. The opulence was born of a problem marriage but one that erased the struggles of a young child. The reservation was painful, but she shrugged off the memories. Hadn't she overcome all that? Hadn't she paid dearly for all that was around her?

November with daylight savings time meant shortened days. It was barely five, but already a smoky haze spread across the hills, and the dying light turned the Watermelon Mountains a brilliant red-violet. She sipped her drink as night slipped across the mesa, chiseling the mountains into black silhouettes against the dusky blue evening sky. Would he come? Was tonight the night she'd been waiting for? Yes. It had to be. She'd watched the pile of piñon wood grow against the outside wall of the patio. Stick by stick, log by log. In the cover of darkness. And then, a discreet distance from any structure, the logs were placed in a tent pattern.

Ramon, who cleaned the pool and fountains, asked if she had ordered the wood. She said she had. But she declined his offer to bring it in or chop it into smaller pieces for use in her fireplaces. This wood was not meant for a fireplace. It had a greater calling in its life. This afternoon dried grass had been stuffed into the cavity formed by the triangle of logs. The grass would explode into flame and ignite even the most stubborn gnarled pole. The result would be spectacular.

In times of great sickness or distress, the Mountain Gods would come to her people, the Mescalero Apache. Men from her tribe would impersonate these gods and perform the dances handed down over the centuries. She knew the songs. They were coming back to her. Bits of them floated through her head now like everything else. Just snatches. A phrase long forgotten, a chant that seemed to reverberate through her body.

"The sandwiches are on the sideboard, Miss. There's a tossed salad in the fridge. If there's nothing else, I'll see you in the morning."

"That's fine, Rosa. Thank you. Have a good evening."

She listened as Rosa backed her car out of the garage and turned down the long lane to a county road that would take her back to civilization. She was alone now. He would know. The ceremony was meant for her eyes only. She had anticipated tonight's visit and, digging through box after box of stored clothing, she found her shawl. Squaw shawl as her husband called it. She reached for the folded square of material at the end of the couch. Pale aqua with foot-long fringe knotted every eighth of an inch around its large perimeter. She shook it out, then refolded it into the triangle that would form two points to gather around her torso. The fringe shimmered and danced on its own at her every step.

She gave an excited giggle and watched her reflection in the wide expanse of glass, twirling as the shawl hugged her hips and unwound to curve around her once again when she turned the other way. Slight of frame, she was almost dwarfed by the material. Then she reached up and let the shawl slip to the floor as she pulled two large pins from her hair. Mesmerized, she watched the cascading wave tumble to her waist. She looked young. The silver threads were muted by darkness.

She stood, squarely facing the window-mirror. Tentatively she touched the glass and traced the curve of her cheek. Consuelo Bigrope. The most beautiful girl in her tribe. Crowned Indian Princess at the Gathering of Nations when she was sixteen, national barrel racing champion at eighteen on a horse loaned to her by the man she would marry. Too early, too soon, too young for a man like Skip CdeBaca. But would she *ever* have been ready to join a family of children who were barely younger than she? Was it any better now that they were all middle-aged? Of course not. Hatred surpassed all else. If time was not a healer, it was an instigator. People could thrive on hate as easily as on love. Didn't the lawsuits attest to that? Two of the three children still contesting their father's will and soon her own. Unless … she had hope, didn't she? One last chance of life if he agreed? But she shouldn't count on it. Better to go ahead with her plans.

They would be shocked by her will. She wished she could witness their outrage when they were told where her millions would go. She only lamented the innocent soul they would turn their venom on.

She had given their father everything but what he wanted most—her love and a child who would show the world his virility and give him a hold over her. But it was not to be. There had been no child. But for forty years of marriage, she had played by the rules—only once straying, starved for a love she'd never had. And this one time not to be found until she was in her forties. By then, far too late to start over. One more unhappiness. A young man who captured her heart—the only man she'd ever loved.

When she had been a child, before she married, before there had been a lover—had she been happy? She was happy at school. The two years of high school made possible by the nuns. The cloistered two years in Vermont, half a world away. Those austere women who wanted her to better herself, perhaps find a life in Christ. Connie smiled. It was difficult to think anyone would have thought that would be her calling. But she came back.

New Mexico was her home. Yet, life was difficult on the reservation. The poverty, the drinking, her mother dying before her eighth birthday. Her grandmother was her salvation. A woman determined that Connie should learn about her heritage. She remembered the great fire of her puberty ceremony. Six young girls celebrated their womanhood on an evening in early summer. The Mountain Gods danced against the fire's redness, approaching, blessing, backing away, circling, inviting the girls to join them in a wider concentric ring of rhythmic motion.

She would dance this evening after the great fire had been blessed and bits of the ground where it had been built was offered to the gods. The crown dancer would wait until well after dark. But he would come. She smiled and laid both hands flat on the glass, then placed her cheek against the coolness. She must be patient.

She would carry the plate of sandwiches and a soda to the far wall. He would need to eat something. He would not come in the house. That she knew. She found the sandwiches on the sideboard in the dining room—roast beef with horseradish, a couple ham and Swiss, one plain Swiss on rye. Would they meet with his approval? There was no way of knowing. She continued into the kitchen— commercial stove, Sub-Zero refrigerator, butcher block island twelve feet square, open cabinetry with glass fronts, pots and pans gleaming overhead from enormous hooks on a steel rectangle twelve feet long above the island. Rosa had put white gladiolas in huge clear glass bowls on the tile counter and on top of the wine rack. Of course, there was a wine cellar. Not of her choosing, a remnant from Skip's house plan, but she did entertain; the architect talked her into keeping it.

She walked quickly across the brick floor and opened the fridge. She chose an herbal iced tea instead of a soft drink. Would he like her choice? She thought so. She carried everything back through the study, into the living room, then out the side door.

The early evening was still, moonless; everything had soft fuzzy outlines in that black velvet way the desert had of casting stark silhouettes across the landscape. The patio was a vast flagstone stage, sunken kiva-like in the center with tiers of steps fully surrounding it. Had she anticipated this miniature amphitheater's first performance? Hardly. But she couldn't have designed a better setting if she had thought about it.

She set the plate of sandwiches on the far wall, retraced her steps to the living room, and let herself in the side door. It would be awhile. The fire had to be lighted and then fed until it towered into the night sky.

She sank onto a chaise lounge facing the expanse of window. Night's curtain of black bounced her reflection back. She waited. A half hour? An hour? She lost track of time. Suddenly a whoosh of flame illuminated the room. Leaping skyward, the brush burned brightly, igniting the logs. She shivered. Not from cold or fear but from anticipation. He would let the fire settle, placing more logs on the mound before retiring to begin his prayers—chants that would beg the gods to cast a favorable eye on what he was about to do.

She rose to scoop up the shawl and gather it around her. She would wait here until he had finished the blessings. Then she would go out to join him, circle the patio as he danced around the fire. It would be just the two of them. One on the rim and one near the fire below. Two people moving in rhythm—alone, yet together. Two people who had been shadows to each other all their lives. She risked bad luck, death even, if she recognized the face of the dancer beneath the mask. But she knew who this was. This man was her one regret. A reason not to die. Would there be time now to make amends? Could her money make things right? Could she offer this man enough to save her life?

He was approaching the fire from the back, loading log after log onto the pyre. It wouldn't be long now. When he finally appeared in headdress and mask, his body painted with white and ochre, she stared at his height, over six feet, the additional three feet of the crown gave him majestic proportions. The crown reached beyond his head—at least a foot and a half on each side and three feet above—white, flat pieces of wood forming an E on its side. Knee-high buckskin boots were bleached golden by firelight. He averted his face, made sinister by the black hood-mask with two round eyeholes and kerchief covering his neck.

Suddenly she was aware of drums and chanting. A tape? Or some recollection from her youth now playing through her memory? Did it matter? She opened the side door onto the patio and stood by the edge of the flagstone. She wanted to run to him, hold him, tell him all the things he had a right to hear from her. But she didn't. She couldn't. This ceremony was sacred. He was performing it now at great risk. Possibly without the tribe's blessing.

She stood, then began swaying, bringing the shawl around her head. She was vaguely aware of the shimmering fringe as her feet moved in half-steps carrying her clockwise a discreet distance above the Mountain Spirit— the fire dancer—who could bring such joy to her life. Who now, after all these years, sought her out in a time of need, came when she had called out to him. And he offered the only thing he knew, which was his to share—a heritage that might save her or, at least, make her next journey less complicated. Or maybe, just maybe, a part of himself that would give her life.

But what would he say if he knew she had held the skull of his father in her hands? That she knew his murderer and had said nothing. She had robbed the son of his parentage and suffered every day of her life. And now, if the terrible disease inside her body didn't kill her, someone else most surely would.

+ + +

He watched from the rim of an arroyo that cut high above the back side of the game preserve. He'd promised the old man that he would live and let live. For a price, of course. But now, with the old man gone, him out of money, and the bitch fixing to destroy God's little slice of paradise? Building a secluded compound of multi-million dollar houses where only elk roamed—all she ever cared about was money. And now her hocus-pocus witchcraft. It didn't fool him, this fire dancer; it gave him an idea, though—a brilliant idea. Was this fire dancer the one who was bedding her now? Maybe she'd like to receive another skull. Just a little threat, a little insurance. A reminder that he meant business. He wanted what he was owed and maybe a little extra. He was worth it—hadn't he kept his mouth shut all these years? Yes, he could be trusted. But he needed to act soon. She'd gotten his message; she would know he was back.

He carefully wiped the lens of the binoculars and raised them again to stare down at the fire. She was dancing now. If ol' Skip had ever thought he could take the squaw out of her, he should see her now. Funny how the old man considered her a trophy, let beauty blind him to just about everything.

As an employee, so to speak, he'd been Skip's right hand—knew a lot of things he wasn't supposed to. But he had been willing to lay down his life for his employer. And now that the money'd stopped, he needed to renew his pension—up the ante while he was at it. She was so hell-bent on taking away his livelihood, then let her pay. Maybe this time a lump sum that would be a ticket out—a permanent ticket. He was glad now that he'd known her secrets. Secrets he could use—secrets that would be worth a lot to the family. If he couldn't make her pay, there were others. But first he'd make her believe he would do what he threatened.

And who was to say he couldn't accept money from two sources? He laughed at this. It was brilliant. He held the answers and he could offer his services. No, sell his services. His brash laugh startled a doe partially concealed in brush. He watched her bound away. He wouldn't let the squaw-woman ruin this.

Chapter Three

Julie had no patience. She had meant to surprise Ben at the hospital and then whisk him away for a really fantastic lunch—maybe Scalo—before she drove up to Connie's. She was lucky he was even in Albuquerque. They had both been living in Gallup before her mother's operation, but he'd been offered this fantastic opportunity to help out IHS in Albuquerque and do some research. He would still be driving back and forth—Gallup on Mondays, Tuesdays, Wednesdays and Albuquerque on Thursdays, Fridays, and the weekends. He was so excited about the opportunity; she couldn't really nag about the tough schedule. She'd find him an apartment in the city—unless he'd be willing to take Connie up on her invitation and stay with Julie at the house. From what her mother said the place was big enough. They could have separate rooms or they could be together. She really didn't think Connie would mind. Free lodging was about all their budget could handle until she turned in some work. She hoped Ben wouldn't have some attack of Puritanism just because Connie was her mother's friend.

Julie had called the Indian Hospital when she got in. Gloria, Dr. Sandy Black's receptionist, answered and assured her that Ben was taking care of a crisis and had only one other patient before being free for lunch. Gloria said she'd mark him out for two hours, then she giggled and said she'd mark him out for the whole afternoon. This was before lapsing into small talk, trying to catch up on the last few years.

So, Julie had rented a car and driven from the airport to sit in the waiting room connected to the basement office Ben was using. It was the poorest excuse for a waiting room she'd ever seen. Three file cabinets squeezed out any furniture except four folding chairs and a magazine holder. There was a "Do Not Disturb" sign on Ben's door and she found herself fighting the urge to just ignore the sign and rush in. It would be a cardinal sin, even though they'd been apart for over a month while she babysat her mother in Scottsdale. Her mother's surgery probably wasn't even necessary—at least, not urgent—the straightening of two toes, removal of a bone spur on her heel. But her father was in Los Angeles and Mom decided she needed attention— attention barely disguised as a chance to talk Julie out of her engagement to Ben. Julie sighed.

Finally, the chance to escape. Connie—her mother's best friend in boarding school—had called to invite her friend to come stay with her. The invitation fell to Julie because her mother was still incapacitated and hobbling around on crutches. After her special on Southwest fetishes for *Good Morning America*, Julie had been offered a chance to freelance a piece about warrior tribes in the Southwest. The money was great and she had a two month timeframe. Wasn't Connie a Mescalero Apache? This seemed the perfect chance—escape, have some fun, be with Ben, and get paid for it.

Connie had also hinted at the possibility of needing someone to help with marketing. She had been vague but wanted Julie's ideas for advertising the one-of-a-kind custom homes for the very wealthy—the special community Connie was building in the foothills. Julie would help with the business and manage the office for a while until her wedding. Wedding? Was she really going to get married? Julie held out her ring finger. The diamond winked back at her. Looked like this time it was going to be the real thing. The fact that Ben was able to wrangle two days a week at the Albuquerque clinic made it perfect.

She looked up as the door to the hall opened. A young man hesitated, then pushed between her and the magazine rack and took a chair on her right. She tried not to stare but looked sideways when he reached for a magazine. His choice was a much-thumbed *Good Housekeeping*—a vintage copy, no less, some three years old. But he seemed intent on reading it. He was strikingly handsome—no, beautiful was a better word. Tall, graceful, perfectly layered black hair reached to mid-back; he slipped off a lavender suede jacket to reveal a deep wine silk shirt a shade darker than his suede silk slacks. His shoes were suede pumps with a two-inch stacked heel in the exact same wine shade that matched his shirt. She secretly wished they were hers.

Feigning choosing a magazine herself, she leaned forward. He was shifting in his seat. He seemed nervous but was pretending, at least, to read. He absently flattened one side of a straggly mustache with the underside of his thumb, long graceful fingers sticking straight out. And his fingernails were painted a bright cherry red. She suddenly realized he had looked up. She caught the smirk. His eyes were beautiful—made more luminous by eyeliner—permanent, she guessed. She knew she could never draw a line that thin or that straight. She supposed she shouldn't be surprised. A transgender Native American was more a sign of the times than an anomaly. And s/he was singularly beautiful—mustache and all.

"Someday I'll have bigger boobs than you do. What do you think?"

She caught herself before she laughed and offered with a straight face, "A good idea—maybe a full cup-size bigger?" She could play along but something told her he was being dead serious—he really wanted her opinion.

He pulled the wine silk taut across his chest to reveal the budding beginnings of breasts. "I'm considering a boob-job. On my frame I'm thinking C cups. What do you think?"

"At least. I'm not an expert and I'm not saying bigger is better but you could carry it off." She smiled. What an interesting conversation. Certainly one she wouldn't forget. "I'm really interested in where you got your shoes. I love the color."

"Online. I'm lucky I can still squeeze my foot into a woman's size twelve."

She stole a look at her own size sevens. "Well, you won't have to worry about my wanting to borrow them."

He laughed and returned to the ancient *Good Housekeeping*. Then he closed it, slipped it into the rack, and scooted his chair out to face her. "Speaking of shoes, do you have a brand of pantyhose that you could recommend?" He tucked a strand of long black hair behind his ear and earnestly leaned toward her.

"Pantyhose?"

"Uh huh."

"Do you know your size?"

"Queen." Laughter danced behind his eyes.

"Then L'eggs." She bit back a comment on queen. "But with slacks you should consider knee-highs. They're so much more comfortable and last a lot longer."

"Really?" He seemed to consider the idea. "I'm getting tired of investing a paycheck on pantyhose every week. Sometimes I put on three pair before I'm run-free."

Julie nodded knowingly. "I'll be honest, I can't remember the last time I wore pantyhose. I try to keep a good tan on my legs and go bare-legged."

"Potawatomie?" he asked.

"What?" She was still thinking pantyhose and the discussion had taken a turn.

"Your tribe. You could be a quarter Potawatomie to be eligible for treatment here. That's all it takes. I had a friend once who had red hair and he was Potawatomie."

"Oh. No, I'm just waiting on Dr. Pecos. He doesn't know I'm here—it's kinda a surprise."

"I like Dr. Pecos."

"Me, too." She held up her left hand, her engagement ring turned outward.

"Beautiful. When are you getting married?"

"Our plans are a little up in the air." Julie shrugged. No

need to go into detail here, but the lack of a date was a bit of a problem.

"By the way, I'm Emma but I like being called Em. I think one-syllable names are star-makers. You know, like Cher. You'll remember Em someday."

She nodded, then added, "I'm Julie," realizing she'd just taken herself out of the star competition. Had the singer, Jewel, started out as a Julie? Maybe she still had a chance. But she couldn't help wondering how he was going to become famous.

"You look familiar. Have I seen you on TV?"

"Maybe. I've done some work for *Good Morning America*."

"I knew it. Last month you did that thing on fetishes."

"Yes."

"You're famous."

Julie laughed. "I don't think so."

He scrutinized her then pushed his chair back. "Well, thanks for the tip on knee-highs." He reached for the same magazine he'd put in the rack and reopened it.

The conversation seemed over, so she reached for a magazine herself. The two-year-old *Newsweek* featured an insert of Skip CdeBaca on the cover—New Mexico's premier statesman, dead at seventy-nine. The picture showed an elderly but still dapper man with a black cowboy hat pushed back on his forehead. Dear Uncle Skip. She flipped to the article and paused to look at a snapshot of Skip and Connie being greeted at the White House. Connie looked absolutely gorgeous—silver sequined gown setting off her tanned skin, dark hair caught at her neck in a thick braided bun, those luminous eyes outlined perfectly with long black lashes. Julie mentally counted up the years—

wow—Connie was 58 in the picture before her. Thirty years older than Julie was right now. She fleetingly thought of her own mother who looked good for her age, but it came out of a jar with help from a scalpel.

The article was a good tribute. There were more pictures—Skip and his children. Julie searched for their names; the oldest son was Byron. She remembered him. And yes, Cherie. How could she forget the daughter? And the youngest—still twenty years older than she, at least— was Jonathan. According to the article, all were prosperous. Cherie and Byron looked out from the picture with plastic smiles, all corporate America in suits. Byron was swinging a leg off the edge of a large modern glass-and-steel desk while Cherie sat behind it. The setting was opulent Wall Street. There was some reserved reference to Byron being a broker and Cherie having her own cosmetic company.

It was Jonathan who caused her to pause. Bearded and scruffy, he seemed totally out of place in the one picture that had captured him on a bicycle, his sinewy body leaning over the handle bars, helmet in hand. No smile here. He was almost scowling at the camera. If the other two children were artificially attractive, he was simply naturally ugly—a real string bean, too gangly, face too narrow for the shock of hair that poked out at all angles. She caught herself. What a terrible thing to think. She glanced quickly at Em as if he might have read her mind.

"Do you know them?" He was watching her.

"Well, yes, I do. My mother is an old school chum of Ms. CdeBaca."

"She's beautiful." Em leaned in for a better look and pointed at an insert of Connie in soft gray cashmere, black pearls at throat and earlobes. The caption extolled her philanthropic endeavors, listing several charities and foundations she chaired. The CdeBacas were generous. Certainly being very, very rich hadn't hurt Connie's beauty. She appeared to glow even in newsprint.

"She's a head-turner, even today. You know, I always thought my mother was somewhat jealous." Now why had she said that? To a stranger? Even if it might be true, she wasn't in the habit of gossiping about her family with just anyone.

"I can understand that." He leaned over to study the photo of Connie. "She's Indian."

"Yes, Mescalero Apache."

He seemed about to say something else when the door to Ben's office opened.

"Julie?"

There was no hiding the absolute joy in his voice. Her first inclination was to rush to him—all two giant steps, that is. Leap into his arms, smother him in kisses—maybe one long, teasing promise of what she had in mind for the evening. But she felt Em's eyes boring into her.

"Hi." God, how romantic. Didn't that just say it all? She could kick herself, but still, in front of a patient she needed to give some semblance of propriety.

"Want me to push a couple chairs together?" Em's meaning wasn't lost on either of them.

Julie laughed. Guess there was no need to worry about being proper.

"Emmett, why don't you wait for me in the office?" Ben stepped to Julie's side. "This will only take a minute or two."

"Hey, take all the time you want. Don't let me stand in the way of true love." Em nudged Julie. "You go, girl. And you," he turned to Ben, "practice calling me by my real name." He gave Ben's shoulder a playful punch and closed the office door behind him.

Julie pointed to the closed door and whispered, "We had a good talk—"

Ben whispered back "Later" and drew her to him. The kiss wasn't chaste and Julie was a little breathless when he released her.

"This is the best surprise I've had in a long time. But I'm going to be tied up for an hour. I don't want you disappearing."

"Don't worry about me. I'll go bother Gloria."

Ben kissed her on the forehead and held her for a moment. "Maybe I'll just mark off the afternoon."

"Already done." She snuggled against him then forced herself to step back. "I'll meet you out front at noon. Blue Impala."

He nodded, bent down for one last brush of lips and went into his office.

For the first time in a month, the ring felt right. She wiggled her finger and maneuvered the stone to catch the light. Yes, being Mrs. Dr. Ben Pecos was exactly what she wanted.

+ + +

She'd had a chance to talk with Gloria and pick up toothpaste from a nearby Walgreens before Ben was ready. She pulled the Impala under the wide portal in front of the hospital and took the Employee of the Month slot. As long as she waited in the car, it shouldn't matter and would get her out of the way of deliveries. The portal that covered a dozen coveted parking spots had been added recently—in the last ten years or so. The architect had done a great job of blending the old with the new, retaining the trim around the roof, matching the stucco color to the original.

The hospital had been a tuberculosis center in the 1930s—one of many when it was discovered that the high, dry desert climate offered relief, if not a cure. She remembered pictures of men and women lounging on the hospital's flat roof in white robes. The scattering of deck chairs always made her think of a cruise—some sort of inland *Titanic* with doomed passengers roaming around topside. Treatment centers had been a going business back then. And hadn't she read that tuberculosis was on the rise again in third world countries?

Em came out first. She watched as he strode purposefully out the sliding glass door, wine suede pumps and all, then stopped and primped—fluffed his hair, put on the lavender suede jacket before opening an envelope purse Julie hadn't noticed before. Now a mirror and lipstick. She couldn't see but could only imagine how great any color would look beneath that straggly mustache. She watched as he unlocked a pickup parked at the end and swung up behind the steering wheel.

Ben came out next and stopped to wave to Em before glancing to his right down the line of parked cars. She loved the grin when he spotted the Impala.

"So what's with Em?"

She didn't even wait until he had settled into the passenger-side seat.

"Emmett, Emma, Em—guess its Em this week. Interesting case. This was our fifth meeting. I'm going through the required preliminary workup before he gets a sex-change operation. He's one of the reasons I'm in Albuquerque two days a week—the counseling is intense."

"You're kidding." Julie stopped in the middle of backing out of the parking space. "He's doing the whole thing? I can't imagine anyone wanting to change sex—do something so irreversible."

"I agree, it seems extreme. The process has a number of roadblocks before any action is taken. He'll have extensive therapy, hormone treatment, additional transition counseling with the end result an evaluation that might nix the deal even after a year or two's investment."

"If he passes, where will he go to, um, have it done?"

"Trinidad, Colorado or Galveston, Texas."

"You're kidding. Not some major city clinic?"

"Those are the two best known treatment centers. They've been around for a long time."

"Unbelievable."

"I'm sure all this sounds like the possibility of a story, but I'd rather get some lunch."

"Me, too."

+ + +

"I think we need to run by Connie's. I called her from the airport and she insisted I bring you out if you could get away." Julie set her crème brûlée aside. "She even offered to let you stay. Now, before you get paranoid about living three days a week with my mother's friend—think of the savings. It's a little far out, but gas still costs a lot less than an apartment—"

"Yeah, you know, exactly what I was thinking—gas money and driving distance—those are a couple things that will keep me away from you every time." He grinned and reached for her hand. "I think it's a great idea. I even admit to hoping she'd offer."

"Really? I was so worried that you'd have scruples or something."

"Nope. I've been inoculated—haven't had a good case of scruples since junior high."

"Be serious." But she was laughing.

"Okay. I can't think of anything on earth I'd rather do than come home to you three nights a week, sleep with you, get up in the morning, have breakfast with you—I missed you. I don't want to be apart any more than we have to."

She loved the huskiness of his voice and the earnest way his eyes explored her face. And somewhere between her navel and her knees, there was a certain warmth.

"Let's get out of here." Julie put her napkin on the table.

"Isn't it un-American to leave a half-finished dessert?"

+ + +

"You're Ben. You absolutely redefine handsome, don't you?" Connie had thrown her front door open and grabbed both of Ben's hands, then stepped back to give him a scrutinizing once-over. "And you look perfect together—light and dark. Well, your almost-aunt totally approves. Remember when you used to call me that? Auntie Connie?" She turned to include Julie.

Julie was feeling a little left out, but Connie dropped Ben's hands and hugged her.

"Please, come in. I cannot tell you how I've looked forward to this."

Julie always felt a little overcome by Connie. Her

beauty? Her perfect manners? Her million-dollar settings? She totally understood her mother's reaction. She marveled at how Ben seemed to take this in stride. He turned to wink as they were being ushered into the vast living room, but he never missed a beat as he answered questions about Indian Health Service.

"So tell me, when is the date?" Connie leaned back on a forest green leather couch, pulling her long dark braid over her shoulder. Even in casual clothing, a lime green velour sweatshirt and jeans, Connie looked spectacular. This woman made Julie's outfit seemed wrinkled.

"Spring, probably. We had thought Christmas but that didn't work out."

"No date?"

"Depends on good ol' mom—"

"No, it doesn't," Connie interrupted. "If you wait until Bev Conlin is ready, then Julie Conlin will never ditch that last name. Listen to me—and I'm sure this is nothing new—no one will ever be quite right for you. One of the drawbacks to being an only child, I suppose. But enough of that. I'll intervene—if you want. We have plenty of time to talk strategy. Let's take a look at your rooms. "

And it was rooms, plural. Connie had put them at the back of the house in a bedroom/living room suite with a private entrance. But Julie wasn't sure whom they would disturb; the house had to be over ten thousand square feet.

"This is perfect." And it was. The furniture was new but comfortable—lots of leather, overstuffed and plain, heavy with wood accents. The room was really unisex and just oozed good taste. Lamps were stained glass and rugs were Navajo. All, of course, works of art. Julie looked down at the large Two Gray Hills she was standing on and realized it was worth at least ten thousand. This part of the house was adobe, judging from the irregular white walls. Building with mud never ceased to amaze her—bricks of mud finished with ceilings of wooden beams and latticed wood sticks in between.

"Here's keys to your private back door and the front. And here's a key that will let you in from the garage and the electronic opener. There's an alarm but, frankly, I find it a nuisance. I think you ought to ditch that rental and borrow one of the cars here. I've kept three. I've taken the liberty of assuming that you'd want the BMW. So, here are two sets of keys. House keys, car keys." She handed a key ring to Ben and then to her. "You can park your truck out here—the driveway extends to just beyond the wall—or in the driveway at the front. I hope that will be all right. There just isn't garage space. Skip had planned a six-space garage. It was one of the first things I changed."

"My truck wouldn't know what to do if I put it inside at night."

"Connie, I don't know what to say—this is all so perfect." Julie took in the computer and twenty-one-inch monitor in the mini-office to her right. Even a space to work.

"Don't say anything. I've looked forward to having you here. It's my treat. I have a couple appointments this afternoon, but let's have dinner here tonight. Seven thirty?"

Julie looked at Ben who nodded. "That would be great."

"Oh, I hope you don't think it's presumptuous of me, but I've hung a few designer dresses in the closet. I must pare down—I've collected far too many things over the years. You'll see some still have their original wrappings. If there's anything that you'd like, I'd love you to just take it."

"I couldn't—"

"Yes, you could. With Skip gone, I have very little use for dressier outfits. There's a lovely off-white vintage Chanel, dress and jacket, that might just work for that very special occasion we just discussed." A wink and Connie turned to leave the room.

+ + +

Julie took Ben back to the hospital to pick up his truck and belongings—all of which seemed to fit into two cardboard boxes and one grocery sack.

"Indian suitcase." Ben teased and pointed to one of the boxes.

Did he even own luggage? Julie wondered. Funny how there were still lots of little things she didn't know about him. It wasn't as if they were planning a cruise—because of work, a honeymoon might be totally out of the question. And if he did bring his clothes in a box, would she mind? She smiled. Her mother would, but she wouldn't.

Ben followed her back to the airport to return the rental. It felt good to climb into the cab of the pickup and snuggle against him.

"I've missed this."

"I could probably say the same thing."

"Probably? A disclaimer?" She playfully punched him in the shoulder.

"Hey, you know any good shrink is going to hedge his bets." But he laughed and threw an arm around her shoulders. "I've missed you." Anything else he was going to say was lost as he kissed her.

+ + +

"I'm going to admit to being a snoopy old lady. But when I took towels back to your room this afternoon, I saw the most marvelous storyteller. Is one of you a collector?" Connie opened an intricately carved liquor cabinet and withdrew a bottle of pale gold liquid.

"My mother's work," Ben replied.

Connie turned to face him, "I didn't realize you knew your mother. Knew who she was."

"I was adopted at four—the summer my mother died. The memories are not the most pleasant."

Something in his tone made her drop the subject. They were in yet another small sitting room off the dining room that had nothing but glass for its fourth wall. Dinner had been perfect—duck salad, potato pancakes, a pâté to start, twisted cheesy bread sticks hot from the oven—Julie knew she could get used to this life. Rosa had probably been stolen from some five-star restaurant.

"Would anyone like a fire? Ben, if you would do the honors, it's as easy as flipping that switch. I think the room is a little chilly."

The wood was piled teepee style in the corner horno— three up and two crosswise on a raised hearth that offered a close-up banco-style seating arrangement to each side. The gas lighter took the work out of wadding paper and praying the fire would take off. Julie watched the burst of flame as Ben ignited the gas element and savored the air now scented with piñon.

"Can I get you something? I'm having a pear wine— almost a liqueur but not quite. It's exquisite."

"No thanks," Ben said.

"Julie?"

Julie shook her head, "The view from this room is my after-dinner treat."

"I agree. I congratulate you on situating this house to complement the landscape and vice versa." Ben walked to the window-wall. "This house is exquisitely done."

"Thank you. It's the one thing I'll leave behind that will outlive me. The Consuelo Bigrope house. One up on Mabel Dodge Lujan, don't you think? Or Millicent Rogers?"

The reference to the two heiress's houses in Taos was apt. New Mexico liked to honor its eccentric dowagers, writers and poets alike by preserving their habitat. D.H. Lawrence also came to mind.

"How old did you say you were when you were adopted?"

The question was abrupt. Julie looked quickly at Ben. This was not something he readily talked about. How strange for Connie to approach such a sensitive subject.

"Four." Ben swiveled an overstuffed leather armchair so that he could enjoy the view and sank into its soft comfort. "My mother died and my grandmother thought it might be best for my ... my what? Chances, I guess. She sensed the importance of an education off the reservation."

"So you really don't know much about your history?"

"My parents let me visit during the summers if I wanted to. We used to call it pueblo summer camp. There were some summers that I chose not to go. The church camp my friends went to had an Olympic-sized swimming pool. As a child I thought it was superior to swimming in the Jemez River. So, no, a few scattered summers weren't enough to learn my language or know the ceremonies. I'm an outsider."

"Would you change things, if you could?"

"You mean go back?" Julie sensed Ben's reluctance to continue as he paused a moment. A buttermilk gold moon appeared above the mountains. He waited until it had cleared the nearest rounded peak. "Congress passed the Indian Child Welfare Act in 1978 because of what was perceived as problems. Indian children losing their heritage, going back as adults and being shunned."

"Is that what happened to you?"

"More or less. I went back to live with my grandmother and complete an internship in the Tewa Pueblo a few years back. I lost my grandmother that summer after just a couple months together."

"I'm sorry to hear that."

"One of my uncles has her house now. There was no way that I could stay there. I'd been gone too long."

"Do you feel strongly about outsiders adopting Indian children?"

"Very little of it's done any more. Child Welfare League of America, National Indian Child Welfare Association, Lost Bird Society—very few Native American children are allowed to leave their extended families today. I'd often thought of organizing a group for adopted Indians who were taken from their tribes as children—for some, the trauma is devastating. It would be easy today with the internet. Maybe I should follow up."

Julie was amazed at how calmly Ben was retelling such a painful part of his history. And more amazed that Connie would probe.

"But the question was, would I have wanted things done differently." Again, Ben took his time in answering. "I suppose not. I can't not be appreciative of what my adoptive parents did for me. I was the late-in-life baby they could not have had any other way. My mother was well into her forties, the survivor of one bout with cancer. She was gone before I entered high school."

"Did you think of going home then—I presume you called the res home?"

"It wasn't really an option. My adopted father needed me. And, yes, the res is home."

The silence in the room was deafening—or whatever the saying was, Julie thought. The moon's light rippled across the brick floor; the fire crackled, casting dancing shadows across the furniture in a yellowed light. Connie switched off a reading lamp and then remotely dimmed the ceiling lights.

"Sometimes I just like to enjoy the moonlight inside. Moonlight and firelight—a combination difficult to beat."

Julie agreed. This natural light, funneled through an expanse of glass, gave the viewer the best of two worlds— on a night like tonight, the warmth of being inside and the front row spectator seat to the desert world surrounding them.

"Would you be Dr. Ben Pecos, Ph.D. psychologist, if you hadn't left?" The sound of Connie's voice intruded on the beauty, Julie thought.

"It's a good question. Studies today seem to indicate high achievers will attain full potential no matter what the obstacles. This includes environment. But I don't think the studies have included kids on reservations. It's damned hard to leave."

"Did you ever think of adopting?" Julie was curious about Connie's acute interest in Ben's childhood. "Skip's children must be very close to your age."

"I thought about it, but it wasn't an option for Skip. He

could not have accepted someone else's child." Abruptly, Connie rose and placed her glass on the sideboard. "It's bedtime for me. Thank you for so gracefully playing twenty questions. I'm curious about life on the reservation—I'm a contributor to Lost Birds and hope I do the right thing by uniting families who've been separated." Connie brushed Julie's cheek with a kiss. "I'm sure you'll be up and about before I will. Rosa will be here at six. Just tell her what you want for breakfast. It's so great to have you both here. Thank you for agreeing to come."

Julie waited until Connie was out of earshot. "Any reason we couldn't do the same?"

"Go to bed? It's only a little after nine." Ben feigned surprise. "Surely, you have some reading to do …? Maybe we should just sit here and enjoy the fire."

Julie made a face, grabbed his hand, and pulled him toward the door.

+ + +

Julie awoke with a start and an uneasy feeling that a noise had intruded on her subconscious. But she couldn't recall what it had been or where it had come from. She lay perfectly still, keeping her eyes half-lidded, willing her breathing to sound even, and then she took inventory. She slowly moved her eyes to the right, the left, then straight-ahead and up as far as she dared. Nothing seemed out of place. Not that she had perfect vision through half closed eyes in a darkened room; in fact, this was probably stupid. These were new surroundings. There was a man beside her snoring softly in a post coital stupor. It could have been anything; the drying of the new pine vigas supporting the ceiling could have made popping or cracking sounds—that would be enough to wake her.

But some sixth sense made it necessary to continue to control her breathing. What was it researchers said about a sixth sense? That really your peripheral vision had picked up some potential danger—something subliminal that sent a warning to your brain? And the brain dictates the flow of adrenaline.

Movement. Another rush of adrenaline. To her far left coming toward her. Maybe twenty feet away. The shadowy figure hesitated, then rapidly faded from her line of sight. She kept her body rigidly still and strained to hear any sound, breathing evenly as if asleep. There it was—the faint click of the side door being pulled shut. The very click which awakened her when it was opened? Probably.

This was not some duck-salad induced moment of indigestion. She threw back the covers and hurried barefoot across the Italian tile. The door was unlatched. She slipped the deadbolt into place and paused. There was the distinct lingering of scent in the air. A perfume she knew well. Guerlain's Champs-Élysées. Her mother's favorite but also Connie's. Last year for Christmas the two women literally traded large bottles of the stuff—each sending the other her favorite as a gift. It had become a joke but attested to their closeness.

But why would Connie sneak into their room at 3:17 in the morning? Julie forced herself to walk around the large sitting room/bedroom combination. Nothing was amiss. She checked the bathroom, a huge room with sunken tub and glassed-in wall that continued the architect and owner's penchant for bringing the desert inside. At least there was no shower curtain à la *Psycho* but could she ever bathe in front of that kind of openness?

She sat in a desk chair, far too awake to go back to bed. Should she wake Ben and tell him? But tell him what? That she suspected Connie of voyeurism? Maybe Connie had just remembered something she'd wanted to tell them. But how could it be important enough to sneak into their room in the middle of the night? And why would she use the side entrance? That would mean walking outdoors most of the way around the house. Julie knew one thing for sure— she'd check the lock on the door next time.

Chapter Four

Her nightgown's filmy silk stuck to her perspiring body, her nipples chafing against its whisper softness. The memory of his caress lingered; a finger sliding down between her breasts, tracing an aureole on the left, then on the right, mouth encompassing one then the other, lips tugging gently before his tongue circled and began flicking, quickly teasing each nipple into aching erectness. She arched her back as his hand slipped between her legs and she turned toward him, crying out his name. And her arms gathered in the emptiness of air. A dream. One more in a parade of dreams, real, hauntingly real, but of another world. Did she believe she would join him soon? Yes. She had begun to hang onto that. It was her solace. She was going to meet him and he would be waiting. Wasn't the message not to fear? He had crossed and now it was her turn. And he had forgiven her.

Connie pushed to a sitting position and fumbled for her cigarettes in the dark. The flare of the lighter brought the room into stark unreality. She held the flame to the tip of the cigarette. Weren't there jokes about smoking after sex—she couldn't remember any that delivered a punch line about smoking instead of sex. She bunched the covers around her legs and balanced an ashtray on one knee.

Would people think she was crazy if she told them that he talked to her? Read her poetry, his poetry filled with images of their time together—time which was far too short, time that evaporated. A brief four months. But still a time she lived and relived over and over all these years. She could still feel his touch as though it were yesterday and hear the huskiness of his voice, "My darling, we are meant to be together. Promise you'll come with me."

She had longed to leave Skip. They would have gone away and been a family. There could have been other children. But how stupidly naïve she had been. Skip CdeBaca owned people and bound them to him with money and favors, letting go when he wanted and not before. She pressed the switch at the head of the bed and a bank of spotlights came up slowly to illuminate the artwork that stretched around to circle the bed. Gorman, English, Peña, Shoulter—originals, old now, created when the artists were struggling to be recognized.

She walked to the closet, using the rugs as stepping-stones even though water circulated beneath the floor to warm the bricks. She pulled open the hand carved doors to her closet, another room with a vaulted ceiling, its domed glass top now showcasing twinkling stars. If you want to know how you really look, study yourself in natural light—the light that never lies. If you have the nerve, that is. And she did. Time had been kind. She studied herself in the bank of mirrors that framed a fitting room—really an alcove with step-stool and dress mannequin. Had twenty years changed her that much? Not really. But what good was her beauty now? She shivered and reached for a dressing gown.

She knew what she was looking for and, parting a rack of eveningwear, she pulled the large box from a hidden shelf and carried it back to her bed. When she had been diagnosed, it had come to her what she should wear to be buried in—what was proper. Yes, that was the correct word. Proper. Cheated in life, she would not be cheated in death. She lifted the lid and gently unfolded the simple, high-necked ivory satin floor-length wedding gown. There were a hundred tiny pearl buttons that reached from hem to high, stiff collar to accentuate her long graceful neck. The circle of matching satin which anchored a shoulder-length veil would soften the severity of the bun laced with pearls, or maybe she'd wear her hair in a single braid. Pearls at her earlobes and a cascading, matching rope that reached to her waist. The instructions for her burial would include a viewing.

Chapter Five

Julie sat up. Nine o'clock. How could she have slept so late? There was a note on the pillow beside her—love from Ben, he'd call later. She threw on jeans and a sweatshirt then pulled her hair back, barely getting all the bright red wisps not to defy capture and spring out from under the confines of a velvet band. A splash of water to clear her head and she was off to the kitchen. It was obvious from her stomach's growling that dinner wasn't even a memory.

"Good morning. I let you sleep. I'm a great believer in our bodies dictating needs." Connie was sitting at a stool at one end of the butcher-block worktable with papers spread out in front of her. "Help yourself to waffles and sausage. I have two offices and yet this is my favorite place to work. I think it's the light here. The skylight gives me perfect overhead illumination without glare."

Julie had to admit the kitchen's domed overhead skylight—bigger than any she had ever seen—showed off the natural wood and gleaming appliances to good advantage.

"Is Rosa here this morning?"

"She's in some part of the house with the cleaning crew. Once a week she brings 4 or 5 relatives to do the heavy cleaning. I'd like to show you around after you've eaten. I even thought we might go over to the land office later."

"That would be great." The waffles and sausage were gourmet, but she wasn't here for an extended all-expense-paid vacation, Julie reminded herself. She'd agreed to step in as marketing consult for the land development company. She would design brochures and media packages and represent Land of Enchantment Realty to the public—even record a couple TV spots.

"Do you have any servants who stay here at the house?"

"Not yet. There are two guesthouses under construction. Rosa will move in when the first is completed."

Julie thought of mentioning that someone had come into their room last night, but somehow that seemed ludicrous in broad daylight since there was the possibility it had been Connie herself. The scent of Champs-Élysées hung in the air.

+ + +

The ten-thousand-square-foot house, impressive and almost overpowering, was not half as awesome as the gardens and terraced landscaping surrounding it, Julie thought. She was always most impressed by what someone designed for the exterior and, in most instances, this was an afterthought. Yet, Connie had planned every inch.

Perfectly marked Koi, bright red-orange and black spots on glistening white, lazed in deep pools or swam along connecting moats that circled the house and paralleled the driveway. A stone amphitheater, fireplaces, natural rock walls, and arched gateways connected the outside living areas—and everything blended with nature. Color was provided by six-foot tall urns and squat, five-foot-diameter round pots in muted clay tones of tan and green and mauve. Some of the groupings were fountains with bubbling sprays of water cascading over their sides. Bronze statuary—life size figures of Apache women and men drawing water, riding horseback, and gathering wood—formed a silent community on a raised stone dais a quarter acre square.

To some, the desert was just one unending dull, crisped-brown panorama. Others could see the beauty and enhance it. There was a starkness about Connie's landscaping that supported the cholla, prickly pear, juniper and piñon that crowded the edges of her property and stretched to the base of the mountains—at least her style wasn't in competition with nature. No false ironwork or, worse, razor wire on chain link.

Their walk took them full circle and back to the garage. Connie left her to pull out the Range Rover, and they were both seated in the car before Connie turned to her.

"What did you think? Will I rival Mabel?"

Another reference to leaving a legacy. Odd, Julie thought, but added, "There will be no comparison." It was the truth. What she had just seen would make a perfect museum—outdoors and in.

"Before we go to the office, I'd like to show you the project. I've taken a thousand acres from the original ten thousand acre land grant and planned it for an exclusive community. My house sits outside the compound but less than a mile from the entrance. We have six houses under construction at the moment—one nearing completion that's sold. My house is the prototype. Each house will have five to ten acres of land—a good amount of separation between residences and landscaping that will carry out the theme of shallow canals, stonework and statuary. I have the architect on retainer—and his designers. The community is guaranteed to be exclusive."

"Where is the lodge from here?" As a child, Julie had spent a few summers and one Christmas vacation at Skip's infamous retreat where it was rumored the land was "salted" with elk and every hunter had to push animals out of the way to get a shot at the one he wanted. People stood in line to get invited.

"About two miles beyond the project. I'm thinking of razing the lodge. Old plumbing, drafty construction, someone vandalized the kitchen—it would take too much to restore it, and it's not the image I want for the subdivision. Tranquility, not the bloodshed of hunting, is what I'm striving for."

The arched entrance with the Land of Enchantment logo loomed up out of the desert floor, a combination of rock and bronzed plaque. Shiny green piñon clustered to each side, trees some twelve to fifteen feet high.

The first house on Julie's left was set a quarter mile back from the road and appeared to be the one near completion. The vast red-tiled roof seemed to stretch forever.

"How big is the house?"

"Approximately 6,500 square feet."

Connie turned into the winding drive. "I should have neighbors before Christmas, if all goes well." She slowed the Rover. "I should tell you there's a lawsuit pending. A neighboring pueblo is claiming this land and some of the federal forest adjoining as sacred tribal land."

"But this land has been in your family for years."

"Tribal offices came forward with new evidence that this ten-thousand-acre strip was originally part of the government's gift to them."

"Can they do that? I mean after so long?"

"They can and did. I expect there will be a hearing and, in the meantime, my hands are tied. It's not going to stop me from advertising. This is just something that will slow us down—not shut us down."

+ + +

The land office was on Juan Tabo, a street that once marked the easternmost perimeter of Albuquerque but not any more. Connie's endeavor held the first floor of a modest faux-adobe building stuccoed a sandy brown with red brick trim around the top. Plainness proved to be on the outside only—the furnishings were exquisite. Hand carved doors, conference tables, credenzas, beaded cradleboards, framed early photos of Apache life, a buffalo rug with its leather side painted covered one wall. What surprised Julie was that Byron CdeBaca came out of the executive office to greet them.

"Byron is chairman of the board. You remember Julie?"

"Of course. Welcome. I've set up one of the offices for you. Great to have you with us."

Bullshit. This was not a man doing somersaults over her joining the group. This was a man who barely met the laws of civility. The smile was pasted on and the handshake forced. Byron was probably mid-fifties, the oldest of Skip's children and a lawyer, if she remembered correctly. And the child that looked most like his father—dark hair slicked straight back. A tie tack and two rings sported diamonds of a carat or more. Jeans, a leather bomber jacket, and hikers completed the "look." Must be casual day, Julie mused.

"When will you be joining us?"

No time had been set, but the sooner the better. "I thought I'd be here in the morning."

"I'd like you to brief Julie on the suit," Connie said.

"Sure." Byron turned and led the way to a large office at the back of the complex.

This was where good taste stopped and garishness took over. The office suite was brightly varnished golden knotty pine with a cherry wood floor. Furniture was black leather and the desk teak, yet another color of wood—expensive, modern, with svelte tapered lines and an inset of bird's eye maple crisscrossed the top. Nothing could be less right for a room that looked like the inside of a barn. The conference room adjoining the office was dominated by a long carved oak table—yet another color of wood stain. Looking like the hand-carved door to a monastery, the twelve Stations of the Cross were preserved under glass. A built-in espresso machine, liquor cabinet and glassed-in, locked corner cabinet filled with silver jewelry made the room with its twelve roller-adorned chairs oppressive. Julie took a deep breath—it felt as if even the air was crowded.

Byron grabbed a folder of papers off his desk and flopped it on the table before taking a seat at one end. There was no invitation, but Julie rolled out a chair and sat about halfway down the left side. She had some kind of instinctive need to distance herself from this man.

"Haven't the boundaries of this land been cast in stone?" Julie wasn't an expert on reservation boundaries but knew most had been in place for a couple hundred years or more.

"The people in the Sandia Pueblo have been living in the Rio Grande Valley north of what became Albuquerque for centuries. Actually the crown of Spain set up the land grant in 1748, giving the Sandia Pueblo certain acreage and a 10,000 acre packet to the CdeBacas. A little over a hundred years later in 1859, the area was resurveyed under the terms of the Treaty of Guadalupe Hidalgo. It's this survey that's under dispute. Supposedly, the government surveyor, Reuben Clements, couldn't get anything right. All three tracts of land surveyed under the treaty had errors. In our case, whether the error was misunderstanding the pueblo's eastern edge as the foothills of the Sandia Mountains rather than its crest is the crux of the argument."

"What can be done now?"

"The pueblo is asking that Clements be judged incompetent and the survey set aside."

"After more than a hundred years?"

"Exactly. One Reuben Clements has cost us a lot of money from the grave."

"But the very top of the crest is government land—a national park—under the jurisdiction of the Forest Service, isn't it?"

"The suit names the government as well. It seems the

Indians have been charged for permits to harvest ceremonial plants. Dad used to just look the other way. Nothing was ever disturbed. It wasn't like they were stripping the land, but you can imagine the Indians are a little pissed—hasn't helped our cause, believe me."

"What would happen if the pueblo was given back the land? The lodge, the houses that you've built?"

"They've indicated that they might overlook the six houses under construction and Connie's. But who wants to live literally inside the jurisdiction of another government—new rules, new taxes—they would be under the jurisdiction of the tribal courts."

"What about the one house that you've sold? How does the owner feel?"

Byron fiddled with a pen, screwing the point in, then out, then in—"the deal falls through. Dr. Swanson has a clause in his contract."

"But what are the chances of the courts awarding the land to the pueblo?"

"I wish we had a feel for it. There was a time when I would have said, no way; now, frankly I don't know. The climate is different." Byron turned to pick up a newspaper clipping off of his desk. "The New Mexico Conference of Churches has just come out supporting the pueblo. Free front-page space for their diatribe on equality and supporting Roman Catholic interests. They get attention and make us out as the bad guys—the ones holding out, depriving the Indians."

"We're not giving up." Connie leaned forward, opened the folder in front of Byron and pulled out a map. "Earlier this year we offered them a plan that gave them veto power over any new building. It was suicide for our plan of a special community. But it would get things moving again. We offered to let them use our land, tolerate the six houses, grant us an easement to run electrical power across the reservation, and they would have the final say as to how the land was to be used."

"That seems generous under the circumstances."

"A couple state senators stepped in and objected, said it would lead to more lawsuits," Byron added. "We're back to square one."

"How many houses were you planning to build originally?"

"Our plan calls for fifty. Look." Connie slid a map toward Julie. "Right now, the six we've started are here. We had hoped to place the community no further east than this." She pointed to a boundary barely making a dent in what Julie assumed was a map of the entire ten thousand acres.

"We could reduce the size of the lots, but we wouldn't be offering the kind of exclusive development that Dad and Connie envisioned," Byron said.

"There's another hearing tomorrow. Julie, I want you to attend," Connie added.

That made one person in the room who did. Julie hadn't missed the frown that lingered as a crease between Byron's eyes.

"I'll be there." Was it her imagination or was there a twitch of muscle in Byron's right cheek?

The rest of the tour included a stop at Julie's office—a small but wonderfully tasteful room with three narrow floor-to-ceiling windows showcasing an inner courtyard filled with sculpture and fountains—obviously, Connie's touch.

"As long as we have the time and the Range Rover, let's go take a look at the lodge on our way back to the house," Connie suggested.

+ + +

People who had never been to New Mexico couldn't understand that the desert had mountains and thick forests. Julie marveled at how quickly they were above the city and off pavement, heading upward through the pines. The Rover was a blessing and didn't falter as Connie took the off-road vehicle higher.

"Is all this part of your land?"

"Every bit of it. Beautiful up here, isn't it?"

The road wasn't much more than two tracks, but the Rover made it seem smooth as it effortlessly climbed over chunks of rock and rough dirt embankments.

"We're almost there. I'm going to get out at the next turn. It's that time of year—I need to check the propane tanks. If they need to be filled, I'll get the truck out this week. Byron still invites friends to hunt. Drive the Rover down about a mile and a half. There's a turn to the right and then another immediately to the left. Stay on the road; it winds back to the lodge. I'll meet you on the front porch in twenty minutes."

+ + +

Connie hurried along the path to the lodge. The tanks were just an excuse to go in alone. No one used the lodge anymore, and the tanks had been emptied and disconnected years ago. But the lie served a purpose—she'd bought enough time to find out what he wanted. No. Amend that to how much he wanted. He wouldn't hurt her, knowing Julie was close by. Actually, he wouldn't hurt her because he wanted money. If her suspicions were correct, he was here. And probably expecting her to come to him.

Only one person could have sent that skull. The man who had set her up—found her with her lover. The man hired by Skip CdeBaca to find them and put an end to what he couldn't tolerate. Art McNamara—Mac, to her husband—grounds man, gamekeeper, guide, bodyguard, driver, confidant and murderer. When Skip died, she looked at the books, and she'd seen the withdrawals. And let them go until the last two were returned undelivered. She'd hoped he'd either died or developed a conscience about taking payoff money, but does the tiger ever really change its stripes? Her answer was looking down at her from the porch.

"Hey, squaw-lady. Good of you to come for a visit."

She almost laughed. He hadn't changed. Insolent with a streak of meanness. Worn cords and a flannel shirt, both threadbare at knees and elbows, his once-pale straw-colored hair now streaked silver. He would be in his mid-forties, possibly a bit older but still over six feet without a slouch or pound of fat. Whatever he'd been doing, he stayed in shape. Heavy-lidded eyes and a full mouth that would be sensual on someone else just made him look pouty. But his eyes, deep-set, dark and small gave him a feral look that made her shiver. A peccary or javelina. Would she be this brave without Julie—knowing she'd be there in minutes? She didn't think so.

"Hi, Mac. I figured you were back."

"Didn't you like your present? The heart was my little

addition just in case you didn't recognize who it was."

Connie stopped at the bottom of the wide expanse of wooden steps—four up to the porch that circled the lodge's front. She loathed this man and the depth of her hatred shocked her. Maybe she hadn't been ready for confrontation. Funny how impending death gave one a false bravado.

"Was there supposed to be some special meaning? I'm sorry if I missed it."

"Oh sure, bitch, like you didn't know whose skull you were holding in your hands. The head of the man sleeping beside you that night. The man who made a fool out of you. The man who needed to be taken care of."

Connie reached out to a banister and steadied herself. She wanted to clap her hands over her ears to shut out the memory of the screaming—her screaming, begging Mac to spare him. But Mac dragged him off the bed, struck him as he tried to stand, staggered him and punched him again for good measure. She remembered Mac holding the gun to his head, her jumping onto Mac's back only to be flung aside. And then Mac saying he had a better idea—"I'll make you kill your own lover."

He grabbed her hands, wound the cord from the blinds around her wrists and with his hands over hers held the gun in place. And then the shot—point blank. The gun in her own hands. Her index finger held to the trigger. A pocket gun, small and innocent, all chrome and blackened grip; until the blast, she'd actually thought it was a cap pistol, that it was all an act. Mac would rough them up, put the fear of God into them and then go away. Just something to scare her? And him. Teach them a lesson. But never murder. Too brazen, too final ... too incriminating. But couldn't anything be covered up with money?

Over and over, she heard Skip saying, "You can't do this to me; you belong to me. You'll have nothing. I'll take it all away." The shot preserved her world, kept her by her husband's side and the bullet never even came out the back of his head. A 25 caliber short that burned through the pulp of that brilliant mind and erased it.

"What do you want?"

"Gotta admit that it takes guts to come out here alone."

"First, you're not going to kill the golden goose and second, I have a friend who will be bringing a Range Rover up that drive in about ten minutes." She thought there was a flicker of surprise as his eyes darted to the drive and beyond. "So, why the calling card?"

"I figure you and me need to do some business. I don't think you want anyone to know the particulars about that skull," Mac said with a sneer. "I still have the gun with your prints."

"And the cost for withholding the information?"

"Two years advance salary—let's say, $150,000—and leave the lodge standing. I'll move back as caretaker."

"I'll think about it."

"No, we're going to get this settled now." He jumped to the ground, clearing the four steps, and towered over her. "The deal was for the rest of my life."

"You know what they say—you should have gotten it in writing."

"Skip wouldn't have screwed me."

"You got paid to dispose of the body. And you didn't do a very good job of that."

He was quick. She felt rather than saw the hand grab her throat and tighten, then release.

"It would be easy to kill you."

"I think my being alive better fits your needs."

"Maybe I should just kill your new lover."

"Lover?" What was he talking about?

"Your fire dancing man. You think I don't know what goes on down there?" He flicked a hand in the general direction of her house.

"If you so much as touch him—" She grabbed the banister for support, her knees threatening to no longer hold her upright.

That laugh. One of pure pleasure at winning. "I guess I know what's important to you. Put the one-fifty in the mailbox, Saturday afternoon, four p.m. promptly. And that'll be cash. I won't come begging. If I don't find it, you'll have another skull for your collection." This time the hand at her throat was a caress, a thumb lightly pressing her carotid artery.

"I can't get the full amount by Saturday. Give me two weeks. I'll leave fifty thousand in an envelope—a good faith down payment. You'll have to wait for the rest."

"I'm not good at waiting. Two weeks is tops. And don't forget your fire dancer lover—get smart and he's toast."

They both turned as the Rover appeared at the end of the half-mile driveway accelerating toward them.

"I'll check the mailbox at four." And he was gone, a leap up the steps and a jog down the long porch around the corner of the kitchen.

Panic. She had to take long, deep breaths to steady herself. Had she been stupid? No, it was better to know he was watching; she had placed her only salvation in danger. She had to warn him. Had to snatch the babe from the wolves and save him—at all costs, save him. And fifty thousand? She'd have it by Saturday.

Chapter Six

Listen to me for God's sake. It's right here in the newspaper. She gave two million dollars to UNM so that a group of damned Indians could go to college. Two million of our money, brother dearest."

Byron clicked her off speakerphone and picked up the receiver.

"Calm down, Cherie."

"Are you forgetting that you buried your father? We're his flesh and blood—not Pocahontas. I don't think there's any reason to believe he expected this throw-away to continue."

"Dad gave to charities all his life. Don't overreact. We need to maintain our cool."

"I'm launching Lavender and Lilacs next month. I need money. This line of sachets is killing my reserves.

The advertising alone—my crew is meeting with Martha Stewart's people. If I'm lucky she'll mention the product in her column."

"You know as well as I do that until Connie dies, our hands are tied. We have our allowance, but it's looking like that's it for awhile." He interrupted an expletive on the other end of the line. "Patience. First things first. We need to make sure the land stays in the family for now."

"How's that coming? The lawsuit by the pueblo."

Byron CdeBaca didn't try to cover the sigh.

"That good?" His sister's voice sounded hard. "I think we need another family powwow. The sooner the better."

"I like your choice of words."

Cherie ignored his chiding about the reference to her stepmother's heritage. "And have that lawyer of yours give us a rundown on what he's doing for two-hundred-fifty dollars an hour. Screwing us out of it, for all we know."

"Do you think Jonathan will come?" Byron gazed out the window at the Sandias and ignored her reference to the lawyer.

"Maybe, if he thinks he can grandstand about the environment and someone will listen. For once we're all on the same side—for totally different reasons, of course, but all of us want the land grant to stay in the family."

"We can meet here at the office. Tomorrow afternoon at two?"

"I'll bring samples."

"Of what?"

"Lavender and Lilacs, silly. I'm sure Pru will approve."

Byron didn't respond. His wife and his sister were close. Cherie's business was a mystery to him, but it kept her out of his way. "Remember Julie Conlin? Bev's daughter."

"Sure. Is she visiting?"

"I think it's a little more than that. Connie asked that an office be set up for her. She's going to be working on marketing."

"Marketing, my ass—try snooping."

"Yeah, that's my take. I think Connie wants another set of eyes around here."

"Use the safe for anything you don't want her to see."

"Already done." He hated his sister's condescending airs, always telling him the obvious, but he let it slide. He was tired of talking to her. "Just be here at two." Abruptly, he hung up.

Chapter Seven

Devon Enterprises. Stan Devon, Licensed Private Investigator. The gold leaf lettering on the glass door was the only luxury—only bit of frivolity attached to the ten- by fifteen-foot room. Connie leaned against the back of a metal folding chair. Spartan. No, not even that word really described his office. Transitory. Yes, more like it. Everything portable. Strike the tent and leave whenever. But maybe she was being too harsh. Did she care what he did? No, not if he had been useful.

"The meeting was successful?"

Devon nodded. "Yes."

Connie paused. By whose standards, she wondered. The man who sat across from her wouldn't think a meeting had been successful unless there was some kind of confrontation, some face-to-face interaction. Her mind strayed to the fire dancer.

"Make the check out to Devon Enterprises." He leaned forward, foot tapping against the metal desk leg.

Connie reached in her handbag and brought out her checkbook. The best spent ten thousand of her life? She'd like to think so. Stan Devon seemed discreet. But she knew better—had learned the hard way about the supposed nice people in this world—the ones who had her interests at heart. That's why the non-disclosure clause in his contract brought her here—the bare one-hundred-fifty square foot office under a dance studio next to a costume store on Fourth Street—not the high rent district. On the phone he had seemed … neutral. Yes, that was the best word. A nice balance between interested and disinterested. Someone she could trust? She could only hope so. She trusted the friend who had recommended him.

Meeting him here in his office made her not so certain. Luckily, she hadn't met him first or she might not have hired him. He seemed wired, ready to spring, only his amber, cat-like eyes with pinprick small pupils remained fixed on her. He was short—eye level with her five foot six-inch frame. There wasn't anything extra anywhere on his body—this was a man who still ate banana splits at fifty and no one would guess. There was more to his demeanor, a hardness? No nonsense approach to things? But isn't that what she wanted?

She had retained Stan Devon with a hand-delivered envelope of cash and now the last payment. She had thought of bringing cash but decided a paper trail might not be a bad thing. Just in case. They would need to know she'd sought out a private investigator—that he was paid to find her son. Go beyond sealed records and bring him back to her. Bring her life in so many ways. It would not do to have him just show up claiming what was his … at her death … yet, wasn't he the very one who could give her life? If he would … she had no idea.

She carefully tore along the perforation, separated the original from the copy and slid the check across the desk.

"Everything is there." Stan slapped a manila envelope down in front of her. "Covers birth through the end of high school. You know these cases are my bread and butter now. Everyone searching for roots or what they've discarded. No disrespect intended. We all have reasons for moving on."

Connie didn't comment. She picked up the envelope, a hefty bubble-pack mailer. Yet, so slender to hold a life history, albeit a young history. What had she expected? A box of memorabilia? She worked the two-prong clasp loose and looked inside. A list of addresses, names of guardians, perhaps, or just places where he had lived; then, a few pages of what looked to be a profile, and a high school annual. She pulled everything out.

"Did you meet him?" She needed to ask. It had been a stipulation of his hire—he was only to seek out information—not make contact.

"I honored our contract."

"Good." Everything was to have been discreet. How much did her son know? Very little, she assumed. He had been adopted. Did he even know that? Had to. Indian son to Anglo parents. Had that been the right thing? No, right or wrong hadn't come into play—it had been the only thing.

There had been money on a monthly basis out of her house account. Only a thousand dollars but it continued until this past spring when he turned nineteen. Had the money made his life easier?

"The family? Did you find out anything?"

Stan reached to pick up a folder behind him.

"Interesting. Not the easiest of lives. Father died when he was eight, former military, there was a lawsuit trying to trace the cancer to his work at Los Alamos. Nothing ever came of it—the government settled out of court, but the pension allowed mother and son to live well. Then things turned sour again. Mother was found murdered—a blow to the head presumably occurred during a break-in. The circumstances were murky. Your son was sixteen …"

"Go on."

Stan had stopped and seemed to be choosing his words. "Your son was cleared—"

"Cleared?" Had she heard correctly? Of murder?

"You know, small town, heinous crime—Indian living with a white woman."

"He was her son, for God's sake."

"Prejudice isn't logic. Hear me out. They weren't close. There had been some problems. There were a number of good reasons he was a suspect."

"What kind of problems?" This wasn't what she'd expected—nothing like what she'd expected.

"She'd had him put in detention—the D-home for wayward teens. Actually it wasn't just once. She'd been calling the cops since he turned fifteen."

"Why?"

"Report was difficult to get. An old law enforcement buddy worked the case. I wouldn't have gotten this far if I hadn't had an 'in'."

He paused again. Was she supposed to be impressed?

Ten thousand dollars said she was paying for just that kind of "in."

"The mother was a stickler for rules. A couple times he'd run away or a party got out of hand. Then, seems the kid took her car without permission and she reported it stolen. Guess they'd had a yelling match when a judge released him. Ugly. Lots of witnesses. Cast more than a little suspicion his way when her body was found about a week later."

"It doesn't necessarily sound like unusual teen behavior."

"That's what I thought. But it seems that after he discovered the body, he kept it quiet. Lived with his dead mother a week before going to authorities. When they got into the house, she had been laid out—new dress, hair combed, jewelry—half her head caved in and he just cleaned up and life went on."

"Stop." Her hand had shot out in front of her but stopped midair as if to ward off a blow.

"I think you need to hear this."

She shuddered, then nodded. She did need to hear, but this macabre twist to her idyllic, no, naive picture of his life was almost too much. She'd imagined a case full of trophies—basketball, track—all American, good kid raised in a small town, no gangs, no violence … doting parents.

"The murderer was never caught. The evidence was a little cold after a week but it was determined that, other than suffering the shock of finding his mother and tampering with evidence, he was probably innocent."

"Probably?"

"The kid seemed to blame himself—the fights with his mother—there didn't seem to be any love lost, so to speak, between them. But, finding her murdered, he just snapped. Seemed to think he'd wished it so and it happened, his wishing come true. Lots of pretty good shrinks were brought in—he didn't lack for money; there had been a sizable inheritance. He was sent away for a year."

"Sent away?"

"Hospitalized. Private institution. It was better than criminal charges. Of course, he'd pretty much destroyed evidence. An overzealous DA in the town went for him. Only a very good and very caring shrink with a couple good lawyers kept him out of jail."

"You talked with them?"

"I met his lawyer. The one who handles the trust. He won't be twenty-one until—"

"I know when he was born." A touch of sarcasm.

"Of course, sorry." Stan referred to his notes. "He came back to the local high school for his last year."

"That must have been traumatic."

"Part of therapy. Face the demons, I suppose."

"Was it positive?"

"I don't think so. Left at Christmas, got a GED, tried a semester at Haskell Indian College but then just took off. Frankly, I was surprised when you said he'd made contact."

"Why?"

He paused. Yellow cat-eyes searched her face. "I also talked to the psychiatrist who had supported him. He was against any interference in the kid's life. It was difficult, but I kept your name out of things. The shrink was my contact—the way of reaching your son. I honestly wasn't certain he'd deliver the message."

"What do you think he was afraid of?"

"Don't know. I'm not sure he was telling me everything.

Seemed to think the kid was pretty fragile."

Too fragile to help her? To give her the bone marrow transplant which would save her life?

"He gave me his number. I told him the circumstances and he wanted me to encourage you to call—to be sure and call before you talked with your son. The card's in the envelope."

She reached into her bag for cigarettes and tapped one from a new pack. "May I?"

Stan nodded. Not thrilled but he was not going to deny the gift horse either, she decided. The pause was necessary—to collect her thoughts. Who was it who said quitting this habit involved replacing the ritual as much as the nicotine? The way of ordering your thoughts as you did a mindless repetitious task. The snap of the lighter seemed to echo in the small room.

"Do you think I should call the psychiatrist?"

"I've given that some thought. It may not be what you want to hear. I frankly felt he was disappointed you were trying to get in touch. I believe he'll discourage any further contact." Stan fingered the crease in a trouser leg. "You know, I don't claim to be an expert but I'd suspect a mother's caring—a blood relation thing that can't be denied—might win out. Might be just what the kid needs— some permanent connection."

She nodded. Her thoughts exactly. The fact he'd chosen to communicate with her as the fire dancer, a symbol of his heritage, spoke volumes. Yet, the "permanent" part might not be possible and if he lost another parent ...

She began to leaf through the annual, then put it aside and picked up the page of test scores.

"There's pictures of him." He waved toward the annual.

She wasn't sure she was ready. She ran a finger over the embossing and traced the school insignia. Haskell Panthers. A lopsided, barely discernible cat's head reared out of the black cloth cover.

"I've marked them."

Three yellow sticky notes protruded from the book's edge. On impulse, she flipped the annual open to the first one. R. E. Merritt. The picture was all Adam's apple on long neck, wild black hair spiked up in front, but appeared pulled back at the neck. A braid? She thought so. Dark eyes. High cheekbones. Her smile—just hinted at—pulled up the corners of his mouth. Handsome? Yes. But more striking. In the image of his father. In fact, he was a wonderful blend of the two of them. She felt tears and blinked. Underneath the picture the usual enigmatic caption—"Voted most likely to change." The other two pictures were groups—drama club and culinary arts. Here a tall young man in a chef's white hat leaned over a tray of what looked to be hors d'oeuvres. Not exactly the lawyer or historian or statesman she'd imagined, but under the circumstances …

"Would you say that there's a happy ending in the making?" Stan's question seemed more for conversation than a need-to-know.

Wasn't happy ending an oxymoron? She stubbed her cigarette out in the glass ashtray Stan had pulled out of a bottom drawer. "Time will tell." She put the annual and papers back in the bubble pack. "How does your Saturday afternoon look? I may need you for something else—a delivery around four o'clock."

"Let me check."

The exaggerated turning of pages in his appointment

book was a sham. She guessed he had no other appointments. She took the packet from her purse. The thousand-dollar bill she'd slipped under the rubber band on top caught his attention.

Chapter Eight

Ben sat in the parking lot of the hospital and looked up at the perfect art deco restoration that might now be torn down. No. That was a little drastic. He couldn't imagine the hospital not being there—a change once again in its reason for being, but it would exist. Change and survival—not necessarily compatible terms.

Last year the clinic had cut its evening hours. Beginning in a month, pharmacy services would be scaled back, no longer open on Sundays and holidays. Prescriptions were to be limited to 30-day supplies. Those traveling long distances, especially the elderly and ill, would be greatly inconvenienced. The urgent care/walk-in clinic would be closed on weekends and holidays, and mental health staff would drop to two—a full-time psychiatrist, and a full-time contract psychologist. Ben's two days a week were paid for by a contract shared with the Gallup hospital.

Ben had no doubts that the scale-down was severe and would have drastic repercussions. What could be done about it was completely sobering—very little to nothing. The last statistics Ben saw concerning Indian health over three years ago listed seventy-four doctors for every 100,000 American Indians. The general population had two-hundred forty-two per 100,000. With a national population of 1.51 million Indians and Native Alaskans, health care costs of some four billion were now split between tribes and the federal government. But this was bare bones—still far too little to attract first-rate health caretakers. Doctors, nurses and pharmacists were leaving IHS in droves.

It wasn't that IHS hadn't supported enticements to swell the ranks—he was the product of a scholarship and loan repayment program that would keep him assigned to various reservations for three years. But too little, too late. Testimony before the Senate Indian Affairs Committee suggested Congress consider even greater funding of such programs, but it was only a drop in the bucket. Maybe something was better than nothing, but Ben figured it wouldn't even be noticed in an area like Albuquerque.

Ben got out of his truck and walked to the back door close to his office. He was meeting Emmett or Em today. That is, if he showed. He'd missed two appointments in a row. Odd kid. Ben couldn't put a finger on it, but something else was going on with him—besides the sex-change operation. As if that wasn't enough. Ben didn't think he'd ever seen a more unlikely candidate.

Ben pushed open the door to his waiting room and

there he was. Only this time very obviously a handsome young man—jeans, sweatshirt, hikers. No eyeliner. He'd have to remember to tell Julie it wasn't permanent.

"Em—"

"Emmett."

"Sorry, am I allowed a little confusion? Come in."

"Sure." The grin was boyish, completely disarming as he picked up a book bag and followed Ben into his office.

"You know, you really look great." Ben meant it. Emmett seemed rested. His hair was cut short on the sides, parted on the left, top combed straight up and back, shiny even in the subdued light of the outer office.

"Taking sides?"

"No, I want you to reach an informed decision concerning your sexuality but—"

"I look better as a male."

"I didn't say that."

"Didn't have to."

"I've never been convinced that you were ready."

"Could be true."

"Have a seat." Ben moved a stack of papers from the chair by his desk to the floor.

"I just stopped by to say I was leaving for awhile. Going home."

"Oklahoma, isn't it?"

"Close enough."

"What will you do?"

"School, maybe. Spend more time doing my artwork."

"I wish you luck. I've enjoyed our talks." Even if they didn't seem to go anywhere, Ben thought. But maybe the young man standing before him with purpose and resolve had benefited in some way. "I'd like to know how you're doing. I've been known to accept collect calls." Ben reached in a desk drawer and brought out a card. "I'm adding the number where I can be reached on weekends." Ben jotted down his cell number.

"Thanks, Doc. Don't worry, I'll be in good care." He held out a hand to shake Ben's—the cuticles faintly pink from recent polish—before turning and taking those characteristic over-long strides out the door and around the corner.

Ben pulled out his chair and sat down, but suddenly he didn't feel like doing anything—certainly not the pile of paperwork beside him on the floor. There was something vaguely disconcerting about Em's departure. Too glib. But he had stopped by to say good-bye. Was he simply leaving to seek another opinion? What was that quip about being in good care? Were Ben's feelings ones of wounded pride? Some overblown paranoia? He'd just gotten started with Em. A brief five weeks, a half dozen appointments counting this one; yet, he would miss him. It had promised to be an interesting case.

Chapter Nine

What do you mean he just left? Walked away? Is that his decision to make?" Julie was sitting crosswise on the truck's front seat and, as usual, fired off twenty questions before he had time to answer one. Maybe the mouthful of Lotaburger would slow her down. Lunch was burgers at Albuquerque's finest and then it was back to work for both of them.

"I don't feel good about it, but there's no way or reason to hold him." He shook his head as Julie held out the sack of French fries.

"I just don't believe he could change his mind so quickly. He seemed pretty determined to do this sex change thing when I saw him. I mean he was really into makeup and pantyhose."

"I *know*." Julie ate fries three at a time slathered in ketchup.

"He looked good as a female. Seemed like he'd been practicing for awhile. But you didn't see him today. Totally natural. Just another guy."

"A lack of nail polish does that."

Ben laughed. "More than that. There seemed to be a resolve. I wish I knew who talked him out of the operation. I worry that I witnessed some schizophrenic—"

"You worry too much. I'd think you'd feel relieved. His life wouldn't have been easy."

"A hundred years ago it would have been easier. He would have just been labeled a 'contrary' and life would have gone on."

"Another one of those concepts that the Anglo world could have benefited from?"

"Maybe. The Plains Indians had a separate camp for those who were different. Someone wanting to dress as the opposite sex or who had opposite interests lived away from the main group and was ordered to do everything backward. They rode horses backward—"

"You're kidding."

"Nope. Clothing was worn backward. But there didn't seem to be a stigma attached. It was just accepted—those members of the tribe were different."

"What did the pueblos do with their contraries?"

"One pueblo called them *berdaches*. They simply were thought to follow a different life-calling."

"Sounds too civilized. You mean someone showing obvious homosexual tendencies isn't ostracized? Even today?"

"Not really. They're accepted as different and, in a way,

honored for being different. Parents or grandparents talk about sons who always take the female role in play, but it's never in a derogatory way. There seems to be some teasing but it's not an offensive thing."

"So, a hundred years ago, what did these *berdaches* do?"

"Cooking, weaving, laundry—they took the female role early in life. Even in clothing, as a child a *berdache* might adopt some female slip or short skirt or a *bidonne*, the blouse that bares one shoulder."

"There are documented cases?"

"Many. The Zunis had a young man named We'wha, who became rather famous in the late 1800s."

"What do you mean by famous?" The fries were forgotten and getting cold on the dash.

"Well thought of, devoted to his family," Ben added. "If I remember the story, he was raised by an aunt after he lost his own parents to smallpox."

"That must have been difficult."

"Maternal aunts are often thought of as little mothers and I think it was a maternal aunt who took him in. That meant he could remain a member of his mother's badger clan so the transition wouldn't have been too drastic. Family ties would have stayed intact."

"I still can't believe that there wouldn't have been a problem, I mean a little boy who dressed like a girl."

"You're judging by present-day standards. Most Indian children slept with other adults in one big room—whether it was a teepee or an adobe house. Sex was never a secret. It was even discussed freely. There were just a lot fewer taboos all the way around."

"Beats how I got my questions answered."

"Do I dare ask?" Ben teased.

"I think most children want to believe in Immaculate Conception at a certain age. My mother wasn't into explanations or picture books. It's a shame our house had more than one room."

"I think it was a blessing." Ben ducked a blow to his shoulder.

"Hey, is that some kind of comment on my parents' sex life?"

"I'm not going to say, but things might have been different if you had been raised by Connie."

"I'm sure of it. She just exudes sexuality. Odd she never had children."

"She married into a ready-made family."

"All three within five to ten years of her own age. I get the idea there's still no love lost. Byron is supportive of her only because she has the money."

"What's it going to be like working there?"

"Guess I'll know more this afternoon. There's a hearing in Bernalillo. Two o'clock at the County Courthouse. Connie, et al., stand to lose a lot if the Sandia Pueblo wins its claim."

"There's a chance the housing project will have to be scrapped?"

"More than a chance."

+ + +

"Wayne." Julie had just pushed open the heavy carved wooden door to the private conference room on the courthouse's second floor, and there he stood. Five years was a long time since she'd thrown the half-carat diamond at him and walked out, but he'd put the time to good use.

His curly, sandy hair was neatly trimmed; he wore copper wire-frame glasses, a lightweight wool black sweater over chinos and five hundred dollar loafers—she'd bet on that. In fact, everything about him shouted success.

"That's Esquire to you," he said laughing. "I thought you knew I was the corporate counsel."

"No." She hadn't been in the office long enough to know.

"Who'd you think knew you well enough to fill the candy dish with Jolly Rancher watermelon candies?"

"Funny what we remember."

"Good things, Julie. I've missed you." He squeezed her hand and leaned in to kiss her on the cheek. "I've dreamed of us being together again."

Three people entering the room saved her from having to respond. Stammer something politically correct under the circumstances but which would preserve their working relationship because, like it or not, it appeared he was part of the team. A man in a cowboy hat threw an arm around Wayne's shoulder and led him to a table in the front. Wayne looked back and winked, smiling as broadly as if he'd just won the lottery. Audacity? Yeah. She got the distinct impression he expected her to fall into his arms.

Julie took a seat near the back. She needed distance. What an odd twist of events. In five years, Wayne had not tried once to get in touch. So why the chummy act now? Funny Connie hadn't mentioned his working for her. Julie and Wayne had visited the CdeBacas more than once. It was no secret that Wayne was Bev Conlin's favorite. Had Julie been set up? Some plan hatched up by two good friends to get them back together? No, she couldn't think that. It truly didn't make sense. Wayne had more than likely approached Skip with law degree in hand and asked for work. It simply must have slipped Connie's mind or she would have mentioned it. And now that Julie was engaged, did it matter?

People were entering the room in a steady stream. County officials, representatives from several federal agencies, and a large coalition of neighboring landowners were expected to attend. A contingent of ten governing members from the pueblo walked past single-file and took seats in the front row. Julie recognized the pueblo's young governor, Stewart Paisano. He looked grim. No, that was too harsh, he just looked determined—doggedly determined. The case had been in and out of the courts for years. It was time for closure.

Connie swept past her, head bent in conversation with Byron on her right side and Cherie hugging her left. Connie's simple white blouse, tucked into a denim skirt drawn together by a wide concho belt, the silver discs catching the lights, drew people to her stark beauty. Julie watched as heads turned and many openly stared. Julie marveled at the perfect bun of dark hair barely flecked with gray. Time had been kind—much kinder than it had been to her mother. She would bet Connie hadn't had a thing lifted or tucked.

Wayne rose to greet them and sat just behind the trio, below the podium that loomed between two flags. A commotion at the back diverted attention and Julie couldn't help but stare as Jonathan loped down the aisle to join the group in front—long-legged stride, head full of bushy hair stuck forward as if to balance his gangly frame. Seeing them together, Julie was again struck by how he seemed a misfit, an outsider among beautiful people. She watched as

Wayne rose to shake his hand only to have it pushed aside. Family dynamics were fun to watch. She just wished she wasn't so close to this demonstration.

Someone started to lower a screen using a remote, but Governor Paisano waved it away. A news crew from an Albuquerque station had set up in the back of the room. The case had received a lot of attention. Some felt a win by the Indians would set precedence—other tribes would try to regain land lost to them.

After a few introductions and a statement of the meeting's intent, Governor Paisano got up to speak.

"I was twelve or maybe thirteen when I knew that the mountain had crept into my body. The mountain fed my spirit and awakened my soul. Even as a young man it was important to my very being." There were appreciative murmurs from the audience. "I was on the mountain with my father. We were hunting. I think it was February because it was bitter cold, but I remember the peacefulness, the quiet. I stood and listened to the birds and the wind and let the scent of cedar, piñon, wild sage and chamisa wash over me. You can hear things there that you can't hear anywhere else. It gives you a sense of peace and of hope. It brought me back to reality, to who I was, who we are as a people and how we've been able to exist for all this time."

He paused and poured a glass of water from a pitcher balanced on the edge of the podium. "Long before there was Sandia Pueblo, there was Sandia Mountain. In our language, T'uf Shur Bien, Green Reed Mountain, in my native Tiwa language. Green Reed Mountain is the altar of my people's faith."

Someone near the front had uttered an "Aye, Aye" and the governor nodded in the man's direction. "Every morning we pray to the mountain. It's where the sun rises. In our culture when the sun rises, Mother Earth is being replenished with sunlight. 'Sunlight' is a key word in our language. So is 'mountain' and 'water.' I would compare these to the host and the wine."

Wonderful analogy, Julie mused, so eloquent, and the governor was probably no more than two years her senior.

"I hope you can understand that to continue to see development up there, the overuse of our sacred altar is disheartening to us. We compare it to the desecration of a church. We have been in litigation since 1978. It is our contention that the U.S. Department of the Interior botched an 1859 survey, thereby robbing us of 9,890 acres given to us in the 1748 Spanish land grant. We are only fighting to regain what is rightfully ours—ours under law."

Once again, he paused for effect, sipping water and gazing at the audience. "We have nothing to lose. We will protect this mountain at any cost. And that cost can be met. We are no longer the poverty-ridden people shackled for generations by a lack of capital. Tribal gambling establishments have allowed us to fight on a level playing field. I have the council's direct order to protect our interests. And let me reiterate—at any cost."

The governor sat down amid wild applause. It was some minutes before the next speaker was able to get anyone's attention. When Wayne turned to survey the audience, Julie thought he looked tired, a twitch under his left eye belied tension. Connie didn't move but stared straight ahead, back rigid. Cherie and Byron conversed, heads bent over some document on the table in front of them. Jonathan turned to glare at the audience, defiant, a chip-on-the-shoulder dare for someone to challenge him. There was a tremendous amount of money and pride and hope on the line. Julie felt herself drawn into the argument—no, battle. Anglo versus Indian and if the governor could be believed, money was no object. In a few short years the tiny pueblo had amassed the fortune necessary to take on Goliath.

She assumed Connie's team would be up next, have some sort of rebuttal, and she wasn't surprised when Wayne stood and picked up a stack of papers from the table. But Connie detained him with a hand on his arm and simply shook her head. Julie could tell Wayne was protesting, but once again, Connie shook her head. And by the abrupt way Byron pushed back from the table, her decision wasn't met with support.

Wayne walked to the podium, hesitated, looked at Connie and then said, "Ms. CdeBaca requests that we forfeit our turn to refute the argument set forth by the honorable governor of the Sandia Pueblo."

"You goddamn lying Indian bitch! You have no right to decide what happens to my father's land." The room quieted as if all the air had been suddenly sucked out of it. Jonathan leaned across his two siblings, hands flat on the table. "You've waited all our lives to screw us—waited until Dad died to throw everything away. Those ten thousand acres are ours. Ours!"

Byron grabbed his arm and Wayne hastened to restrain him from the opposite side but Jonathan twisted away and, knocking his chair aside, strode up the aisle and out the back exit.

Julie knew the cameras had caught it all. The audience now was alive with murmured speculation. She marveled at Connie's composure. Connie faced the podium, her head slightly inclined to her right, as Wayne seemed to be pleading. She again shook her head. Wayne stood and, looking at Byron, shrugged his shoulders. Whatever the topic of discussion, and Julie assumed it was not refuting the governor's claim, Connie seemed to be adamant. A rapping on the podium by the next speaker brought everyone's attention back to the front.

Representing New Mexico, Senator Jeff Bingaman, the next person to speak, set up a slide presentation. Senator Bingaman was sponsoring a bill in the U.S. Congress that might end the decades-old battle. He approached the podium, cleared his throat, and begged the audience's indulgence as he reiterated the history of the land. He added that he thought an overview would be helpful in realizing the scope of the concerns on both sides. Someone in the back of the room dimmed the overhead lights.

"The history had its beginnings in 1748 when the Spanish lieutenant governor of New Mexico set the eastern boundary. The pueblo said its land extended to the crest. To muddy the waters, the same grant recognized the Roberto CdeBaca claim to some 10,000 acres and said the family's land extended to the top of the mountain. The lieutenant governor ruled that the family's claim superseded the pueblo's interest. In 1848, Mexico and the United States signed the Treaty of Guadalupe Hidalgo to end the Mexican War. Under this treaty the U.S. agreed to honor Spanish land grants, but they did not specify which claim—the CdeBaca family or the Sandia Pueblo.

In 1859 the errant surveyor, Reuben E. Clements, set the pueblo's eastern boundary along the Sandia foothills despite a translation of the Spanish grant that states it is at the main ridge of the mountains, and he gave the crest to the CdeBacas. It is thought that the very powerful

CdeBaca family coerced the surveyor to limit the pueblo's land and state once and for all that the boundary ended at the foothills. It took a hundred years for the pueblo to realize what had happened."

Governor Paisano interrupted to point out the difficulties his people had with the language. A treaty written in English was simply not understood.

"That's a valid point, thank you, Governor." Senator Bingaman took a moment to look at his notes before continuing. "Not realizing the error, Clements' survey was used as a basis for a patent issued by the U.S. Congress. In addition, the CdeBaca family had, by then, built a hunting lodge and various other buildings on the land. It was 1986 before the pueblo asked the Secretary of the Interior to correct the government's land patent and to evict the CdeBacas. This request was denied in 1988. In 1994 the pueblo sued to have the solicitor's opinion reviewed on the question of whether it was arbitrary and capricious." The Senator paused to take a sip of water and reverse the order of two slides.

"In 1998, U.S. District Judge Harold Greene ruled that the U.S. Interior Department erred in denying Sandia Pueblo its claim. He ordered a resurvey of the boundaries. Later that year the federal government gave notice that it was reserving the right to appeal Greene's ruling. The private landowner, New Mexico Senator Skip CdeBaca, also indicated plans to appeal. Poor health and his death left his widow, two sons and a daughter to protest. The multi-million dollar development with fifty exclusive homes hangs in the balance.

"After the Senator's death, public interest seemed to lean toward the pueblo. The Bernalillo Town Council unanimously supported the pueblo's claim and a public relations firm working for the pueblo launched a phone campaign to raise public interest and gain support. In the meantime, several compromise bills were introduced but none met with the pueblo's approval—including the T'uf Shur Bien Preservation Trust Act, which would have removed ownership from the picture entirely and made the area a game preserve if passed by the U.S. Energy and Natural Resources Committee. It failed because of vigorous lobbying by pueblo representatives and solid representation by the CdeBacas.

"In the last two years the pueblo has been busy buying up any individual parcels of land—some remnants of land grants—that border the ten contested acres. Development of the mountain has been quickly curtailed." The Senator took another sip of water. "I'll entertain any questions anyone might have."

Questions seemed to center around rights—the 'what ifs'—and the Senator led a brief, but spirited discussion. Pueblo representatives and government spokesmen then stood and also opened discussion to the floor and fielded several questions concerning their rights. The meeting concluded after hearing objections to the CdeBaca building plans and listening to a number of compromises. Conspicuously absent was any comment by the CdeBaca family. Julie felt certain that hadn't been planned. This was to have been their forum, and Connie had forfeited the opportunity.

As the crowd dispersed, Connie motioned for Julie to join her as she walked out.

"Let's go visit the mountain," Connie whispered. "I have the Range Rover parked in back."

"I'd love to see it. It's been years since I've been to the crest."

+ + +

"So what did you think?" Connie had given Julie the keys and was leaning back against the soft leather passenger-side seat.

"There's a lot of history."

"Understatement."

"I can certainly see both sides." How could she say she felt the Indians had been shafted? Probably not a popular opinion to share with her boss. Safer, perhaps, to change the subject. "Why did you keep Wayne a secret?" There—probably best to just ask before she came up with too many wrong answers, Julie thought.

"I was afraid you wouldn't come. You know, your mother could have come with you. But she knew Wayne was with the company—I think they've kept in touch. Didn't you know that?"

Julie shook her head

"Typical Bev to try to maneuver—"

"Mastermind."

"Julie, Bev has good intentions."

"She's not your mother."

Connie laughed. "I know that makes all the difference. Personally, I believe you've made the right choice. Ben is perfect for you. Bev will come around. I'll be putting in a good word for him."

Julie didn't say anything. She wasn't sure a 'good word' would change things. But she let it drop and concentrated on driving, steering the bulky Rover into turn after turn as they wound higher up the mountain. The late afternoon shadows lengthened across the road and the parking lot was almost deserted by the time they reached the top.

"Park here and let's walk for a bit. I always keep a couple warm jackets in the back. I want to see the sunset from on top."

The temperature had dipped to the low 30s as the sun began to sink in the west. Julie grabbed two down jackets and slipped one on. The air was cool and the whispering of the pines hinted of a light breeze some thirty feet overhead. They took a path away from the ski lifts, curio shops and tram restaurant to walk along the edge and leave the area comprising the three private commercial holdings, the only businesses on the mountain. In warmer weather hang gliders would launch themselves from this height to soar above the trees and look down on the city nestled at the mountain's base.

Lights twinkled far below and the blood-red sun slipped lower to light the underside of hovering clouds a marmalade orange. Sunsets in New Mexico. Julie had never seen any to best them. They both stood silently as the light changed to pastels and a layer of peach hues banked the horizon.

"I'm backing out."

"Of?" Julie watched the soft afternoon light rob Connie's face of any wrinkle or crease. Funny, but she knew she'd always remember this moment, remember Connie in this light. Beautiful, the black fox fur trim around the parka hood framing her face. Her dark luminous eyes seemed fathomless.

"I knew what Stewart was saying this afternoon. I felt it. I know what it's like to be owned by something. This mountain is a part of him—a part of his people. All of the mountain is theirs. It was meant to be. I know that now."

"But the project?"

"In comparison, it means nothing. My ego-driven need for a monument cannot be compared to a gift from God."

"I totally agree with your decision, but I don't think it will be popular."

Connie smiled. "I've given up trying to please Skip's children. They're adults now. They have enough from their father to sustain them. But I've been given a chance to do something lasting—something that has meaning to so many."

"But your home?"

"A museum. When I built it, I thought of it as that. It's something the pueblo could use."

"I think your intent is admirable. I just don't envy you the wrath of your family."

"Funny you should call them my family. I've never thought of them as other than barely disguised enemies— the more vicious since their father died. Wolves circling the prey, so to speak."

"Your life always looked so perfect." Julie thought Connie suddenly looked tired. She put her arm around her friend's shoulder for a moment then let it drop. "What will you do now?"

Connie seemed to wait a long time before answering. "Go back to my people. It's time I move on—leave what has been my life for so long."

"But what will you do?"

"Begin the endings."

Julie waited for an explanation but none seemed forthcoming.

Chapter Ten

Julie was right about Connie's decision being unpopular. The hastily called meeting Saturday morning at the office was more a shouting match than anything sane and productive. Wayne was reduced to something just this side of hand wringing and finally sat down and became a spectator. Jonathan was the first to bang out the front door, waving a fist in the air and threatening a lawsuit that would put them all in their graves. Not a happy thought. Julie watched Connie brush his comments aside and turn her attention to Wayne.

"We need to come up with a formal offer. An offer in that I have a few requests which, under the circumstances, I think the pueblo will honor. I don't expect them to turn down my gift. If I'm not contesting the land grant survey, the government will not stand in the way of the pueblo having full authority over the ten thousand acres."

"What stipulations are attached?" Wayne seemed defeated or maybe just bitterly disappointed. Julie couldn't tell which. Connie's decision certainly affected his livelihood.

"I want my residence to become a museum of Southwestern art. I will leave my collection of pueblo pottery—"

"You'll hear from our lawyers." Byron pushed back from the table. "Cherie, I don't think there's any reason for us to be here. This isn't going to happen. You can't screw us out of our inheritance."

"Can she do this?" Cherie seemed to be the one in shock. The question was directed at Wayne.

"Your stepmother has controlling interest through your father's will."

"I'd like you to understand and have compassion for people wronged. Wronged for centuries." Connie looked tired but resigned.

Julie guessed she'd been considering this move for a long time.

"Don't give me this blood-is-thicker-than-water crap. The pueblos aren't even your people or however you'd describe it. Or are all Indians the same? Some red man's kindred spirit that transcends tribe?" Byron's laugh was derisive.

"I'll have Wayne share our rough draft with you."

"That would be thoughtful." Cherie seemed to have regained composure and a measure of sarcasm. She followed Byron out the door.

Connie waited until there were just the three of them.

"I'd like—" Connie began.

"I'd like to change your mind," Wayne interrupted. "Don't make a gift of the entire tract. Divide it. Give them half but not all. Don't throw away all this." His gesture included the office but, more exactly, the pictures lining the walls. Pictures of the mesa, the lodge, the homes under construction.

"I think it has to be all or nothing. Sometimes in life it's important to simply do what is right—not what's easy but what will be best for the greatest number of people. I'm tired of feeding the egos and lining the pockets of three people who don't understand this land, don't understand the ceremony, its link to the past, and how it can guarantee the future. Guarantee the herbs, the medicines that have healed these people for centuries will remain in their possession; guarantee their religion, the place of their beginnings, will not be commercialized and ruined. What price can you put on that?"

"I feel like there's nothing I can say to dissuade you."

Connie shook her head. "No, nothing. I'm just disappointed in myself that I didn't do it sooner. I've always felt the land wasn't meant to be ours—that the CdeBacas used their money to cheat the pueblo."

"Strong wording."

"You know this family. My words are not strong enough for some things that have happened."

"I've heard rumors. But any family with money and power incurs the jealousy of others. I've never thought it was anything more. There'll be paperwork—a change in your will." Wayne was making notes on a legal pad.

"Nothing that can't wait a day or two. Let's plan on keeping this office open for six months. Does that sound reasonable to complete everything? Meet our obligations to those who had planned on building?"

"Six months should do it. Is that my severance?"

"Wayne, I think you've done an admirable job. I'll encourage Byron to keep you on as counsel for the construction business."

"I've been thinking of going back to school for a year. I've always wanted to specialize in contract law. Maybe now's the time."

Julie thought he didn't sound very convincing.

"Now if the two of you could leave me alone … I hate to shoo you out, but I'd like to be alone for awhile. Go through some papers or maybe just sit here and think." Connie smiled wanly, then pushed back from the table and stood.

"I understand. I'll drag your almost-niece off for some brunch." Wayne gave Connie a peck on the cheek.

Julie couldn't help but feel forced into a situation she'd been dreading—alone with Wayne— but maybe better to just get it over with.

"Should I come back for you later?" She wasn't meeting Ben until after lunch.

"No. I have some shopping to do. Let's plan on dinner at seven. Wayne, if you'd like to join us?"

Julie turned back from the front door and almost shouted, "Ben will be there." But, then why not include the company lawyer at dinner? Maybe it was time for the two to meet. There was certainly no reason Wayne should not come. Or was there? Was she ready for her past and present love lives to collide? She continued across the parking lot, opened the car door and got in.

She rolled down the car window and Wayne leaned in. "Hungry?"

"A little. Is there something close that's good?" Julie was suddenly ravenous.

"Flying Star, a local favorite but it might be crowded."

"Sounds great." A noisy, crowded restaurant would keep things from getting personal.

"Follow me. It's less than a mile."

Julie watched as Wayne got into a black Porsche Boxster. Nice car. He certainly appeared to be the picture of success.

+ + +

"So, tell me what you've been doing." Wayne chose a table in the corner against the restaurant's plate glass south wall. This was about as private as it got and Julie began to relax. There really wasn't any reason they couldn't be friends. They had said some things in the heat of anger, but they had been young then—five years younger than now.

"I've stayed in broadcasting. My most infamous stint to date was a six month contract with *Good Morning America.*"

"I caught the series on southwest fetishes. Good stuff. But I'm not interested in who you're working for, I want you to tell me about Ben."

Julie tried to smile, give some nonchalant look that said 'Oh, that.' Suddenly she was doubly thankful the restaurant was crowded.

"I'm not sure there's much to tell. We met five years ago—you remember that. And even though we were in Chicago at the same time, we drifted apart. We met again last year when I was researching the fetish series."

"And you're convinced this is it? Until death do you part?"

Julie suddenly wished he hadn't chosen those words. An involuntary shiver skittered between her shoulder blades.

"Yes." She tried to smile confidently but felt the smile fade prematurely.

"I just can't believe you. He's an Indian, for God's sake."

"Are you trying to sound like my mother or is bigotry just a normal part of your makeup?" Stupid, she needed to watch it. The clenched jaw hinted of real anger.

"Julie." He reached over and took her hand. Monumental fortitude kept her from jerking it away. "We were friends, lovers, engaged to be married—that's a lot of history. I don't want to throw it away. I believe we can be friends again. Start over."

"Friends, not lovers." She watched him look away, his jaw set.

He turned back. "Do me this favor. Don't rule out our getting back together. Please? You have no idea how I've kicked myself for letting you go. You broke my heart, babe."

"Wayne, you never tried to reach me. In five years I never heard from you. You'll excuse me but I find this hard to believe. We were together two years. We grew up and out of our relationship. I've moved on with my life."

"I talked to Bev."

"Good for you." Now he had struck a nerve. Calling her mother was altogether dirty pool. "I hope you had a good conversation."

"She agrees with me."

"In what?"

"That you don't know what you're doing. You're dazzled by this guy and you're throwing your career away.

You could have New York, Los Angeles—any station or news program you want. You won't have those kinds of chances being a squaw woman."

"Clean it up, Wayne. I'm not going to sit here listening to derogatory remarks about my life."

"So what makes this guy so great? Is he good in bed?"

"Out of line, and I'm out of here." Julie swung her bag over her shoulder and pushed back from the table.

"Wait. I'll be nice. I just promised Bev I'd make you change your mind."

"Fat chance. I know who I am and what I want out of life. That's probably more than you can say." Julie ignored the curious stares as she walked out the front door.

He was out of line. And she wouldn't be pushed—manipulated by Wayne here and her mother in absentia. She paused just long enough to slip her jacket on and press the Beemer's automatic door opener. Ben was getting into town in four hours. If she hurried, she'd have time to go up to Connie's, change clothes, run a few errands and be ready for dinner that night.

Chapter Eleven

Connie had watched the two of them walk across the parking lot. Wayne obviously giving directions as he leaned in the window of the BMW before going to his car. She'd pushed them together. She was acting like Bev, but she didn't have a choice.

He was coming. Here. Any minute. She'd left a note by the stack of wood behind the wall. It was gone the next day. Yes, someone else could have taken it, but she felt it was the Fire Dancer. She knew he came to the house—stayed a discreet distance away but watched over her. It never felt like spying or some type of voyeurism; there was too much empathy. And longing, at least on her part, to just hold him, touch him, try to bridge those twenty years. Say all the things she wanted to say and that needed to be said. That she'd spent a lifetime rehearsing.

She closed all the mini blinds across the front and sides of the entrance and then continued closing blinds throughout the office. She had directed him to use the side door shielded from the parking lot and neighboring high-rise apartments. This entrance had only an open field in back of it. They must be discreet.

It wasn't time to announce to the world that she had a son.

She checked her makeup. Her hair. This was just plain nervousness; she looked great in her leather jacket and slacks in luggage tan topped off with a black turtleneck sweater and her trademark silver jewelry. She caught her reflection in the floor-to-ceiling glass. Slim and trim and full of life—she wished. There were more signs now that death was not going to be patient much longer. She tired easily and even one flight of stairs left her breathless. She couldn't succumb to an oxygen tank and tube in her nose. Not yet. Maybe not ever.

The liquor cabinet in the conference room was unlocked and stocked with tequila. A double shot of Herradura over ice might be just the thing. She stirred it then sucked the amber liquid off her index finger. Just what she needed. She filled an ice bucket, grabbed the bottle and walked to her office. Most of the room was a sitting area, comfortable leather couches arranged around a fireplace. The desk in the corner looked like an afterthought.

She heard the knock and sucked in her breath. She had waited so long, why the hesitation now? What would he say? Would he like her? Would she like him? She crossed the hall and bent the blinds to look through the glass insert in the door. Her eyes looked back at her. Her eyes in a lean, finely chiseled face, black hair brushed back, an earring, gray turtleneck, black leather jacket over blue jeans. The pictures in the school annual did not do him justice, but that had been two years ago. She opened the door.

"Come in." She stood aside as his six-foot-plus frame passed her, then he turned and stood looking at her. She touched his arm, "I've waited for this moment for almost twenty years." She marveled how in one instant she was transported twenty years back, to Spain, to the arms of a man who could make her heart stop.

He moved his arm back. "You threw me away. You never wanted me and now you do. How can I believe anything you say?"

It wasn't the opening line she'd imagined. It took a moment to get her bearings. "Don't judge until you've heard what I have to say. Just do me that favor."

Was that a nod? Hard to tell. But he followed her into the office. She indicated a couch and he slouched down on the cushions, dark eyes unblinking, watching her—waiting for her to begin the conversation?

She thought so.

A deep breath, exhale, then, "Tell me about yourself."

"Your turn first. Tell me about my father." Lidded black eyes bore into her.

"What do you want to know?" Stalling? Yes. What should she tell him? How many times had she played this conversation over in her mind? But it had been a fairytale— all gushing thank-yous for finding me, how could we ever have been apart?—maybe we weren't, weren't you always in my thoughts? Aren't you a part of my soul? Stupid. She had been so stupid. Not one tinge of the reality she was facing now.

"There's a lot to tell. I don't know where to start."

"Why don't you start by telling me if you had him killed?"

"What?" Her hand flew to her throat; her pulse quickened. "What are you talking about?"

"He mysteriously disappeared a few months before I was born. No one ever heard from him again and no body was ever found. You had the money and you had reason to get rid of him. I don't think the Senator would have been too pleased with me."

She pushed herself up out of the chair, stood and then reached for the pack of cigarettes on the coffee table. She lit one, drew in deeply, and didn't ask his permission to smoke.

"How do you know these things?"

"That dick you hired. He said he'd give me a little extra information on a mother and a father—more than you'd paid him for. He'd done his research. Figured out that summer in Spain probably got you in trouble. You'd taken five of this guy's classes. Another instructor who had been on the trip confirmed it—said the two of you were inseparable. Said he'd always suspected something but with you being the Senator's wife, he'd just overlooked it. Figured it was probably his imagination."

"You met with the PI?"

"Yeah. I don't think he was supposed to meet me … had told you he wouldn't. But he was a dick—no pun intended."

She stubbed the cigarette out in a dish that usually held candy. Her mind was racing. Should she tell the truth? Didn't he deserve, at least, the truth? She sat back down and met her son's stare.

"Your father was the only man I ever loved."

"I bet you say that to all your victims."

"You need to listen, not be snide." She could stop now, turn, walk away. It would probably be less hurtful—for both of them. She had never imagined this. She had always thought that intuitively he would have known her pain, her sacrifice. And he would have understood—he never would have blamed her. Had she really expected some Hollywood version of *This is Your Life* with a trumped-up happy ending? Well, there wasn't going to be a happy ending. There hadn't been a happy beginning.

"Sorry."

"I met your father twenty years ago last summer. The 'dick' was right. The University was offering a summer course called 'The Poets of Spain.' I didn't need college credits, but I did need to get away. I was forty and spiritually dying in a marriage that had never been good—"

"Why didn't you just leave him?"

A snort of a laugh. "Leave Skip? It wasn't that easy. I don't think I could have. First of all, he wouldn't have allowed it. He owned things; everything was a possession. And I'm not sure I could have left all this. This opulence that gave me strength—guaranteed I would survive. Defined who I was. You have no idea what it's like growing up on a reservation so poor you don't know where your next meal will come from or even if there will be a next meal. Not having clothes that weren't donations from the community church women. Cutting the toes out of sneakers when they got too tight—"

"So, you did everything for money?"

"Is that what I said? I did everything for security, protection from ever wanting for food and clothing again. The fear of poverty is a powerful motivator. Once experienced, it never leaves you."

"But killing my father? You could have just left him."

"That was the cost of being owned. Once Skip found out, he had to eliminate the competition. But why don't I start at the beginning?"

"Okay."

Connie paused and studied his face. "You know, you look like your father. He was Mescalero on his mother's side. Your grandfather was Hispanic."

"I have your eyes."

"Yes. I noticed that—it's like looking in the mirror." But do you write poetry? Do you play the guitar so that every note goes to the center of a woman's being? These were the questions she wanted to ask, but couldn't. There would be much left unvoiced. But maybe if she were granted time, they could learn about one another. "Do you know anything about your father?"

"Very little."

"He was a poet and, as you know, a professor at UNM. He taught poetry as well as creative writing and a history of the masters. The poets of Spain were his specialty." She paused and smiled, "He was so handsome he made my heart stop."

"So, it was love at first sight?"

She laughed. "I suppose you could say that. Do you believe love can happen that way?"

"I wouldn't know."

Of course not. She was dealing with a baby, really. He had been sheltered in a small Midwest town and maybe a late bloomer if there were no girlfriends.

"Your father and I were so alike. I could finish his sentences. We were inseparable that summer."

"It would seem."

Connie caught the note of anger. How had she ever thought she could overcome it, the anger? Waltz back into her child's life and expect to be welcomed or, at least, pardoned? She took a breath and continued.

"The summer was glorious, idyllic—three months to know what we'd found in each other. To know something so special didn't come around but once. We traveled on weekends, sometimes alone, sometimes with a group. We slept in a cabana at the edge of water and let the sea lull us to sleep and wake us with its fury during a storm. Every day we walked the streets of towns steeped in history; we walked the beaches and we slept in each other's arms every night. He was my lover, my muse, my life." She reached for the cigarettes, pulled one from the pack but didn't light it.

"I was pregnant by the end of the summer. When we got back, reality set in. I was a forty year old woman, pregnant, in love with a thirty year old man and married to a sixty year old who happened to be a state senator. Power-wielding, treacherous—a man who could snap his fingers and people jumped to do his bidding. Skip hated dirt. He was above it. I should amend that and say he paid people to keep him above it. He'd ruled his children with an iron fist and dared me to step over the line. If he had found out about the pregnancy—"

"He didn't know?"

"No. After the death of your father, I was distraught. A psychiatrist prescribed rest. I went back to Europe for a few months. Skip thought I was having a nervous breakdown. There was gossip but more to do with this." Connie picked up the glass of Herradura from the end table. "Rumors were that I was somewhere drying out."

"That was the official story?"

"No, Skip put out a statement saying I'd had a cancer scare and was at a treatment center in Mexico. Much more acceptable than a mental breakdown."

"And this Skip didn't try to visit you?"

"The psychiatrist who treated me knew I was pregnant. He insisted on six months of complete solitude and care for depression. Shared with Skip that I might harm myself. Under the circumstances, Skip went along."

"Who else knows about me?"

"No one, that I knew of, until the private investigator—"

"You're dying, aren't you?"

"Yes."

"That's why you sent that dick to find me. You need me to save your life."

"Will you?" Too abrupt. She watched him quickly glance away. But maybe this was better. Everything out in the open. She carefully set her glass on the end table and sank back into the rich-smelling leather of the armchair.

"I don't know."

She waited. Wasn't this better than an unequivocal, no? Was she grasping at straws?

"Why don't you know?"

"I learned to hate you. You, the faceless image from my childhood full of questions. I hated you for the selfishness. Hated you for putting me in the position you did—throwing me away. Separating me from my heritage. Was your security worth it?"

"No. But saving your life was."

"How was I in danger?"

"Skip and I had tried for years to have a child. For me to be pregnant by someone else would not have been tolerated. I could never have survived his anger. I believe I would have had a discreet accident—one or both of us would have died."

"But my father—"

"Jose Rodriguez Mondragon. To me, just Joe, my darling Joe."

"I never knew his name."

"I wanted so much to give you his name."

"You don't like R.E. Merritt?" Sarcasm again. She couldn't blame him.

"I only knew your last name. Colonel Merritt was the one I dealt with. He was stationed in Spain. He was an acquaintance of a friend and came to see me before you were born. He seemed a kind man. He and his wife had lost a baby and couldn't have others. They were secure; there would never be a lack of money. I never met your mother, but I saw pictures of her." She hesitated but decided not to say more. If there was something he wanted to tell her, he would in his own time. "I believe the R stands for Robert, but I've forgotten your middle name."

"Emmett. For my white pseudo-grandfather."

"What do people call you?"

"Robby."

"I could say that I'm sorry, Robby."

"And I could laugh at you. How do I know what is behind your trying to find me—besides I might be able to save your life. What have you ever really cared about?"

"Your father ... and you."

"So you threw me away and killed him. Or set him up to be killed. The dick thought it was the latter, but he was only guessing. You were sent away while it was covered up and in the meantime you just happened to find the perfect family match for your unborn child. Only everyone didn't live happily ever after."

"Least of all me." Connie leaned over and picked up the cigarette on the coffee table—this time she lit it. "Not a day has gone by for twenty years that I didn't think of you and your father."

"You expect me to believe that?"

"Believe what you want. But you need to know the rest of the story. I was naïve enough to think that I would get off with a reprimand, a slap on the wrist for being naughty if Skip ever found out what happened that summer. Then we'd forget the whole thing—as if it had never happened. The silly weakness of an aging woman. But as you know, I was pregnant. I would have had to hide it. I could not have terminated my pregnancy. It was never an option. Joe wanted us to be together. He wanted to go back to Spain. He could write and find teaching jobs. Parentheses reads, we would be poor. In love, but living hand to mouth. My thirty year old lover was an idealist. Love would conquer all. I knew better. The practical side of me knew it would have been very, very difficult. I believe it would have eventually cost us our love. Yet, I couldn't break it off, deal with my pregnancy, go back to my life. I loved your father beyond reason.

"It was my fault the affair was discovered. I wasn't being careful. Skip had me followed and then sent his bodyguard to kill—maybe both of us, but then decided to settle for setting me up. His man found us in bed and forced me to hold the gun—pressed the trigger with my finger. Then kept the gun with my prints as blackmail."

"Is that the truth?"

"On my grandmother's grave. But there's one other thing."

"What?"

"The bodyguard is back. Skip had been paying him to stay away, but he's decided he needs more money. He's threatened me," a deep breath then, "and you."

"Me? How do you mean?"

"He wants a lump sum and if he doesn't get it, he's threatened to harm you." She simply could not bring herself to say 'kill.'

"How does he know I'm here?"

"He only knows you as the Fire Dancer. I don't believe he knows you're my son. Just be careful. I'm going to pay him but know that he's dangerous."

He was silent staring at the rug. When he finally looked up, his eyes locked with hers.

"What do you want besides the bone marrow to save your life?"

"More? I don't want more."

"Well, I do. I want the mother I never had. I want to get in touch with being a Mescalero. I want to honor who I am and where I came from. I want to honor my father's memory."

"You'll have that. We can do those things together—"

"Wait. I haven't said I'd save your life."

"And you haven't said you wouldn't, either." She sat up straighter and leaned forward. She continued to look in his eyes, but her gaze softened. How very much like his father and how very much like her. In looks, in actions. "You don't have to give me an answer now. But soon."

He just nodded. "I could never call you mother."

"No one is asking you to. Just call me Connie."

"You don't know anything about me."

"I know enough to say that I'm proud that you're my son."

"No. Don't say that." He suddenly stood, first with his back to her then whirling to face her. "There are things. Things I've done." He towered over her. "Things I can't share—even with you."

Just for a second she felt uneasy, fearful even. Why this threatening stance? "That's all right. I don't expect you to tell me everything. You don't know me. We need to get acquainted."

"I'm not sure."

"Not sure?"

"Whether it's what I want. I need time."

"The one thing I don't have to give. I don't want you to feel pressure, but I don't know how to keep you from it."

"Then let's leave it at that. Let me think. I'll get back." He walked to the door and she didn't follow. He turned slightly and acknowledged her with a nod and then he was gone.

She lit another cigarette, finished the Herradura and reached for the bottle. The light shone in now at a lower angle. She wished she had the time to replay their visit. She felt a sort of relief. A relief born of truth—and she had been that—truthful, maybe to a fault. How could you learn to love someone, maybe even accept someone, who had put another person's life in danger? Gotten that other person killed ... especially when the person was your father?

Answers. The questions were plain, but the answers were a muddle. Could she blame him for being hesitant? Keeping her at arm's length? Not committing? No. So much had been done. And would she be able to understand, to accept his secrets? Those things he couldn't share? She didn't know. Why, why couldn't their lives have been easy? A mother, a child, a loving father ...

Chapter Twelve

Julie turned on the county road that led to Connie's, past the new housing area and eventually to the lodge. The first police car to overtake her and go screaming by, sirens at full volume, was a little unnerving but the second and the third followed by an ambulance made her accelerate. Connie? Had there been an accident? Connie was probably thirty or forty minutes ahead of her if she'd come straight home. Try to think. Did Connie say anything about errands? Was she even headed home?

Rounding the first turn, Julie could see the Range Rover at the end of the drive and Connie standing beside it, waving frantically. Julie pulled up and braked.

"Let's take the Rover—you drive." Connie got into the passenger side of the Rover. Julie pulled the BMW into the drive, parked, and ran back.

"What's going on?" She backed onto the county road and accelerated.

"Just follow the cops. Some hikers up by the lodge came down to the house to call it in. There's been a terrible accident."

Julie deftly nudged the Rover up to sixty.

"Did someone go off the road?" Julie was trying to remember the terrain. There were a couple tight turns with steep embankments but the graveled road couldn't really be considered dangerous. Of course, speed, drinking—even though it was barely three o'clock—could kill. Maybe kids. If she believed the newspapers, they could roll anything, even a box without wheels.

"I don't think it was a car accident."

Julie looked sideways at Connie. She was absolutely white—blanched of all color.

"Do you feel all right?"

"I'll be fine. This is just a shock." Connie attempted a smile.

Connie obviously knew more than she was saying. But why be secretive? Julie decided not to pry. She'd know soon enough.

Turning the last corner, Julie slammed on the brakes in front of a police barricade.

"This road is closed. I have to ask you to turn around." The policeman who approached the Rover was curt.

Ignoring him, Connie slipped out of the car. "I'm Connie CdeBaca. I own this property. I need to know what's happened."

"Do you have family, Ms. CdeBaca? Someone you're expecting at home now?"

"No, why?"

"Ma'am, with all due respect there's been a loss of life here. We will have the area sealed for the rest of the day. Are there any other houses off this road? Others who might be using the road?"

"No. There's a lodge and a gamekeeper who has been staying there. Hikers called in the accident from my home. There could conceivably be others hiking in the area."

"I see. If you'll excuse me for just a minute." He turned and walked to a group of uniformed officers and one man in jeans and sweatshirt. The cop seemed to be explaining who they were with nods in their direction.

Julie slipped the Rover into park and got out to join Connie. Whatever seemed to be the problem wasn't too far from the road. But loss of life? How did it happen? There wasn't another car in sight. And this wasn't a place to go off the road for any reason; the road widened and curved at this point to accommodate delivery to the mailbox she'd seen last week. This was the exact point where she'd dropped Connie off to go check the propane tank. Only today there wasn't any mailbox. Julie was about to comment when the man in sweatshirt and jeans broke away from the group and walked toward them.

"Ms. CdeBaca? I'm Mark Samuels, Lieutenant Samuels, APD. Let me tell you what I know and then I'd like to ask you some questions." He smiled. The man was good, Julie thought, good at his job and putting people at ease. "Let's step over here." He ushered them toward the nearest cruiser—its lights still flashing. "We might be more comfortable inside." He opened the back car door and turned to Julie, "I don't think I caught your name?"

"Julie Conlin. I'm an administrative assistant to Ms. CdeBaca and longtime family friend."

"I see." He gave Julie a long look and closed the car's door after she'd slid in beside Connie.

"Well, this is much more cozy." He turned to look at them from the front seat, a clipboard in his hand. "Was there anyone living at the lodge? Anyone who used this mailbox?"

"I believe the caretaker had returned."

"But you don't really know?"

"Um, he was living here. He had been gone for a number of years and I believe just returned recently. I saw him when I was up here last week to check the propane tank."

"What is this man's name?"

"Excuse me, but shouldn't we know what this is all about?" Julie was finding it difficult to sit through a game of twenty questions. What had happened? And what did it have to do with Connie?

Samuels looked at Julie again with that overly long stare. "You seem in a hurry, Miss—"

"Conlin."

"Conlin, of course. Do you have another appointment?"

"No. Nothing pressing." And now she was really curious. Just what had happened?

"Have the two of you been together all morning?"

This time Connie took offense. "What are we supposed to surmise by that question? Is this an interrogation? Are we being detained?"

"No, no, nothing like that. But I do need the name of the groundskeeper."

"Art McNamara—Mac."

"How long has he been in your service?"

"He was never in my service. He was my husband's

driver, bodyguard, gofer—and he was allowed to live here at the lodge as part of his salary. He left many years ago. I was frankly surprised to see him back."

"How many years ago did he leave?"

"Probably twenty."

"That's a long time." The man said it more to himself than as a statement meant for them to comment on. "Why do you think he came back?"

"I have no idea." Said much too quickly. Julie knew in that instant that Connie did know. Hadn't Julie seen a man vault over the porch railing when she turned down the lane to pick Connie up that day? Did Connie even check the propane tank? Or was it just some kind of ruse to meet with this man alone, yet have the protection of numbers?

"Was he allowed to stay here? I mean now."

"It had been his home before. I need to raze this building but have left it alone over the years. Time was we would have retreats out here—seminars on team building, heightened consciousness, that sort of thing. We haven't sponsored anything since my husband died."

"So, it was okay that this Mr. McNamara,"—a quick check of the name on his pad,—"was living here?"

Tenacious, Julie thought. Wouldn't work to try to verbally out maneuver him.

"I had not given my consent. I didn't even know he was here until this week."

"So the building has been empty the last two to three years?"

"Yes. Possibly vagrants or hikers for an overnight, but no permanent tenants."

"Did you tell Mr. McNamara to leave?"

"What?"

"When you met with Mr. McNamara this week, did you tell him to leave?"

"No."

"So, he had your approval to stay?"

"We didn't talk about his staying or leaving. It was my impression, though, that his being here was very temporary, that he'd be moving soon."

"But he didn't say when?"

"No."

"Were the two of you on good terms?"

"I knew him only as the hired help of my husband. Nothing more, nothing less."

"Do you know if he had any enemies?"

"I've told you. I hadn't seen the man in twenty years."

"Did he leave your service on good terms?"

"My husband's service. And as far as I know, yes. I would have heard if there had been a problem."

"Describe him to me."

"Art?"

"Yes."

Where was he going? Had this Art McNamara had an accident? It seemed to Julie that Connie didn't really want to discuss her husband's bodyguard, although she continued to answer the lieutenant's questions.

"Well, last week it struck me that he'd been working out. He seemed well muscled as if he'd put in lots of hours in the gym. He's tall and the muscle looked good on him. Made him look healthy, actually younger. He's probably forty-five by now but you'd never know."

"And you think he'd just live up here? The lodge, as you say, is in disrepair."

"He's an outdoors person—living in a place without

amenities would not be a problem for him."

"I see." Lieutenant Samuels spent an elaborate amount of time finishing a block of notes before looking up. "Would you feel comfortable identifying the body?"

"Whose body?" The two women asked almost in unison.

"That's for us to figure out, isn't it?" That fleeting, rueful smile again. Probably qualified as a boyish grin some twenty years earlier, Julie thought. Now, it just made him appear insincere.

Lieutenant Samuels slipped out of the front seat and held the back car door open. "I want you to be as comfortable as possible with this. It would greatly help us if we had an ID."

"What happened?" Julie figured they had a right to know.

"As near as we can figure—and we'll know more when the explosives expert gets here—there was some kind of letter bomb."

"Bomb? You can't be serious." Connie's voice held a touch of exasperation. "This is private land. Who would come up here—"

"As I asked before, do you know if this man had enemies?"

"As I told you before, I haven't seen Art McNamara in twenty years."

"Until last week. I made a note of that."

What was the man thinking? It was almost as if he was accusing Connie of something. But what? Julie had no clue.

"If you're up to it, I'd like you to step over here. You too, Miss Conlin, if you'd like. I must warn you that this may be a little challenging. The guy didn't have a chance. Our bet is he leaned down to open the mailbox and kaboom—he was outta here." He lowered his voice. Was there a hint of concern? "You don't have to do this if you'd rather wait in the car."

Not on your life, Julie thought. I'm here, even if curiosity may kill me.

"I'm fine. Connie?"

"Yes, I'll be all right. Let's just get it over with."

"Good, then follow me." Lieutenant Samuels led the way between two other police cars. The area was marked off—about twenty-five square feet. In the center was a tarp-covered mound, presumably the body, Julie thought. The mailbox, one of those rural metal type with a pull-down door, securely anchored on top of a pyramid of cemented rock, was barely recognizable. It was completely mangled and looking as though it had been tossed aside. But the confetti was a puzzle. Bits of paper, newspaper from the look of it, were everywhere.

"What's this?" Julie asked. She pointed at a handful of the stuff with the toe of her boot.

"Could have been the stuffing around the bomb. Could have been the contents of the package itself—meant to be read by the recipient. Or, if you'll look over here—" He walked a few steps and leaned into the cordoned off area. "This looks like newspaper cut to a certain shape."

"Money?" Julie offered.

"That's my guess. Looks like our friend here was expecting a package and instead of holding what he assumed, it was filled with stacks of paper. See, there and there? Those appear to be remnants of real bills—a couple single one hundred dollar bills. Were they showing on top?

Just a little bait for him to reach in and draw out the death weapon?"

"My God, this is—"

"Homicide." The cop supplied the word Julie couldn't quite bring herself to say.

Julie looked away and caught a glimpse of Connie. She was staring at the ground and looking as if she would faint.

"Do you need to sit down?" Julie hurried to her side.

"No. It's just a shock. Someone I know. So close to my home."

Connie's hand was ice cold as she put it on Julie's arm.

"Ladies, if you'll follow me. Please do not disturb anything and stay on the plastic sheeting."

A strip of plastic made a bright blue path to the covered mound inside the roped-off area. The lieutenant held down the police ribbon for them to step over.

"He took the brunt of the explosion straight on. Killed instantly is my guess. There's not that much to see. Pretty much obliterated the poor guy. I would like you to look at this."

"Please, could I change my mind? I'm just not feeling very well." Connie now clung to Julie's arm. She looked like she'd be sick any minute.

"No pressure. Not everyone can do this. We'll try to find next-of-kin. Maybe you could take a look here though." Leaning over he pulled a scrap of material from under an edge of the tarp. "Not much left but here's a remnant of the shirt he was wearing."

"Black Watch," Connie offered.

"Pardon?"

"It's a pattern—dark green, blue and black—represents clan membership. He was wearing the same shirt when we met last week."

"And this. How about this? We took it off the victim's ring finger." He held out a plastic bag containing a man's ring, heavy gold with an insignia, a date and what looked to be a deer with antlers on each side in bas relief.

"Yes. The ring is Art's. My husband had them made one hunting season when a group came up to bow-hunt. Art took top honors."

"Thank you, Ms. CdeBaca, we'll take over from here and get Mr. McNamara to the Office of the Medical Investigator."

Connie nodded then slumped against Julie, a hand covering her eyes. "Please drive me back to the house." Her voice was barely a whisper.

"I'm assuming we're free to go?" Julie asked.

"Yes. I know where to find you. By the way, did I ask if the two of you have been together all morning?"

"Yes, we have been." Julie wasn't going to tell him any differently.

+ + +

The ride to the house took place in almost total silence. Connie drove—she needed something to pull her back from the shock. She knew Julie was suspicious—thought she knew more than she had told the Lieutenant.

But what could she say to Julie? The package was supposed to hold fifty-thousand dollars, the first of three installments, and be delivered by a screw-job of a private eye who lied and couldn't resist temptation. But wasn't he bonded? That was a laugh. How could she report it? What would she say? It was a payoff to the man who knew what happened twenty years ago? Something so heinous it was worth one-hundred-fifty-thousand, even at this late date, to try and silence the observer? Well, officers, there was this murder. Maybe not an important murder, just the father of my unborn child. My lover, my soul. And the gun—of course, it wasn't supposed to be loaded. Isn't that what they all say?

No, Stan knew she wouldn't come forward. She'd lie to cover up her part but never name him and certainly never divulge what the money was for. No, it was probably the safest fifty grand he'd ever pilfered. And wasn't he counting on her death? What would anyone do to a dying woman?

But murder? Even Art McNamara somehow deserved better. More of a fighting chance. And *she* deserved better. Connie Bigrope CdeBaca didn't throw away money and didn't bankroll losers and murderers. Maybe if she talked to Stan Devon. Confronted him in broad daylight. It might only make her feel better, but she had to try. How dare he implicate her? How dare he steal from her! Kill on her own land—nearly at her back door.

Even so, a small part of her felt relieved. There was no one to threaten her now. Or threaten Robby. Perhaps, she should just be thankful and let it go. By the time they reached her driveway, she'd made up her mind.

"I need to run a couple errands. I'll drop you here at your car and be back in an hour."

"Are you sure you're up to it? That was quite a shock. I'll go with you if you'd like."

"No, I'm sure. You need to get ready to see Ben. I'll be fine." Connie didn't think Julie looked convinced, but she stopped the Rover next to the BMW.

"Seriously Connie, I'd really be glad to go with you."

"Thanks, but this shouldn't take long. I'm looking forward to seeing Ben tonight."

Connie waved and watched Julie turn and get in her car. No one could be with her when she confronted Stan.

Traffic was heavy in the Valley even for a Saturday. She took Montaño across town, toward the river, turning left onto Fourth. The parking lot of the two-story building was empty other than four spaces underneath the second floor dance studio. She pulled the Rover in next to an SUV full of children in tutus and tights. Ballet lessons. A pang of regret that she had never been the one to chauffer a carload of children. And more than a stab of pain when she remembered the conversation earlier with Robby. How could she have been so wrong? How could she have assumed he would understand what she had been forced to do? He was young and male and coming to his heritage second hand.

Rounding the corner of the downstairs suite of offices, she stopped. All the blinds were pulled. Strange. He had kept office hours on weekends in the past. She tried the door and was surprised when it swung open—but not for long.

The room had been stripped. The desk was pushed against the wall. File cabinets, shelving, computer, fax machine, phones—all gone. She'd given him three days to plan this. But the moment he realized the package held fifty thousand dollars, his decision was made. Nice tidy sum for little or no work. Must have waited a lifetime for this kind of one-job payoff. But did he have to kill Art McNamara? Maybe that was his gift to her. Not that she would miss Art. But still, taking a life. Life was all too precious.

A box of wastepaper sat in the middle of the floor. A

wall safe was standing open. A quick look inside revealed it was just as empty as the room. Just to be sure she ran her hand around the inside and felt the recessed bottom. She pushed her hand shoulder-deep to the very back. And was rewarded.

A small black book had been overlooked. She quickly placed it in her pocket and, just to be sure, did another once-over of the safe.

"Mind telling me what's going on here?"

Connie jumped and whirled around to confront a man who must surely be the janitor.

"I was looking for Mr. Devon. But it appears that he's gone."

"Yep, it appears that way. Mr. Padilla is going to be one pissed-off landlord."

"Looks like Mr. Devon left suddenly."

"He was here at noon. I stopped by to fix an electrical outlet. Musta gotten out of here real fast. I told Mr. Padilla when he rented to this guy he was going to be trouble."

"Why do you say that?"

"Just a hunch. And the people who came in and out of here. Not the type you'd want to meet in a dark alley. You know what I mean? And he never kept regular hours. He'd be gone for weeks and the phone would just ring and ring. Too cheap to even get an answering machine."

Connie nodded. Stan's whole operation was cheap. A real one-man show. And why, *why* had she trusted him? Because he had been referred—a discreet referral by a friend. And hadn't she gotten what she wanted? He had made contact with Robby. Even though he'd lied about actually talking with him. He had given her the material she'd requested.

"I'd better go call Mr. Padilla."

"That's a good idea."

"And who can I tell him you are?"

"Bev Conlin." The first name that came to her mind.

"Well, Ms. Conlin, in my books you're far better off finding this empty room than making connections with Mr. Devon."

"I'm sure you're right."

Connie hurried out to the Rover.

Did it matter she was out fifty thousand dollars? Maybe under the circumstances, no. She'd just saved another hundred thousand, but it was the principle of the thing. The lying, the murder. What would happen when the police came to talk with her? And they would. She thought the scraps of wrapping she saw this afternoon looked like the wrapping she had used. The wrapping with her prints all over it. One summer job at the BIA had put her prints in the system. Would it even take them until Monday morning to show up on her doorstep? Stan had been clever. Maybe he'd committed the perfect crime. If there was such a thing.

She reached in her pocket for the black address book or whatever it was. Barely three inches by four, and about a half inch thick. Important enough to be kept in a safe. She jumped at the tap on the car window. The janitor. She quickly stuffed the book into her purse and pressed the button to lower her side window.

"Yes?"

"Just checking, ma'am. Mr. Padilla will be here in a few minutes. He said he'd like to talk with you."

"Oh, I'm so sorry. I have a dinner party. I was just checking my list. Do you have a card? I would be glad to call him."

"Well, no, but it's Padilla Enterprises in the phonebook."

"I'll call tomorrow. Thanks again."

With this, the window whirred shut and she turned the key in the ignition. Close. She needed to be careful. Not call attention to herself. But if there was a silver lining to all this? Robby was safe. Art McNamara wouldn't be out to kill her fire dancer. Hadn't Stan really given her a gift worth far more than the fifty grand he'd pocketed?

Chapter Thirteen

"Come in, Ben. You are handsome as always." Connie offered her cheek then, closing the heavy carved door behind him, linked arms and led him toward the living room. "I'm so glad you could come. I was beginning to think Gallup Health Services was holding you hostage."

"They've just been understaffed."

"Isn't that everywhere? There's a shocking need for help both on the reservations and throughout Indian Health Services."

"The passing of the bill to let tribes handle their own health needs has brought with it a new set of problems."

"I wondered if it would work. Maybe it's too soon to pass judgment. Well, here we are. Wayne, have you met Ben?"

Ben tried to give Julie a reassuring look over Connie's

head as Wayne stepped forward but felt it fall flat. The handshake was firm enough. There was no love lost between them, yet the man was a professional. He wasn't about to make a scene in front of his boss and old girlfriend. Or at least Ben hoped he wasn't.

"What can I get you?" Wayne walked to the bar.

"Nothing for me. Julie?"

"Wine. Red if you have it."

"How about my favorite Merlot?"

"Great." Julie sounded wooden.

"And I know what the lady of the house is drinking. Let me fix you one of my specialties—a margarita like you've never tasted before."

Connie laughed and shrugged, "My weakness. What can I say? Julie, I must show you the Indian corn maiden by Maxine Toya."

Ben watched the two women leave the room. One darkly beautiful and sensuous in wine velvet cropped pants and big shirt, almost barefoot other than the wisps of leather straps that bound her feet to a sliver of wine-colored sole. The other woman vibrant with copper-gold hair and brown eyes. Her skin-tight jeans accentuated every hollow and curve that he loved. Too freckled to be a classic beauty but with a body that would turn every head in the room. Including the bartender's, Ben decided as he turned back to watch Wayne.

He found himself studying the fair-haired man busy behind the bar. Handsome? Yes. With rugged, model good looks. He half expected Wayne to strip down and pirouette in jockey briefs. There was the hint of a good body beneath the casual bulky sweater and jeans. And his smile? A real dazzler. Not believable but only because he seemed so in control of it. No spontaneous grin, more of a studied 'turn it on or off at will' sort of thing. Instinctively, Ben didn't like this man then admonished himself for premature, judgmental thoughts. Just because five years ago Wayne was engaged to Julie? No, it wasn't that simple. And maybe he was influenced by Julie. He'd make himself be fair.

"Interesting that you don't drink. How 'bout a soft drink?"

"I'm fine, thanks."

"Is that an Indian thing?"

"I'm not following."

"Not drinking. It's pretty well known that you guys can't hold your liquor."

Ben found himself counting to five, then, "What is it they say? The Indian gave the white man tobacco and he couldn't handle it and the white man gave the Indian booze and he couldn't handle that. Doesn't every race have its Achilles?"

"Interesting. But then you're not a full breed, am I right? Isn't there some question about your father? As to who he is? Other than he seems to have been white."

"Are you going somewhere with this?"

"Hey, man, no offense. Just curious." Wayne flashed his fake smile and returned to making himself a Tanqueray martini. Ben sensed it wasn't his first of the evening.

"Actually, I have to drive back to Gallup tonight."

"No. Why?" Julie was walking back into the room and paused in the doorway. "I can't believe that you have to get back tonight. Tomorrow's Sunday." She walked up to him and slipped an arm around his waist.

"I promised to help with evaluations of some of the elderly whose family can only bring them in on weekends.

Hey, I'll be back Monday."

"I hate to break this up, but Julie here's your Merlot, and Connie, your marg. I don't know about anyone else, but I'm starved."

Ben and Julie hung back as Wayne walked past them to join Connie in the foyer.

"How are you doing?" Julie whispered motioning toward Wayne.

"Okay."

"That good?"

"Don't think we'll ever be buds."

"Understatement."

Ben grinned, "Hey, I think the prize is worth fighting for." He kissed the top of Julie's head. "Now let's go find some food."

"I think we're too intimate a group to eat in the formal dining room so I asked Rosa to set up a buffet in the sitting room off the library." Connie had taken Wayne's arm. "Follow us."

The room wasn't small. A fireplace dominated the south wall. Indian artifacts were everywhere, mostly pottery but a glassed case of beadwork looked collector-worthy, Ben thought. The buffet was on a rollaway steam table and judging by his nose's reaction, they were in for a treat. Rosa was tending a sizzling skillet of fajitas surrounded by pots of beans and rice with all the condiments.

"Any idea what happened today up at the lodge?" Julie had filled Ben in and he was more than vaguely worried about the two women being alone most of the week. This house was isolated.

"None. The man killed was someone from the past. I have no idea why he returned."

Interesting, Ben thought as he watched Connie's eyes shift quickly from his to the food table. She does know. I'd bet on the fact that she knows.

"What's more interesting is the poor guy was duped and killed. Looks like he was expecting some kind of payoff and when he reached for the package—with a couple hundred-dollar bills in plain sight, the bomb went off," Julie added.

"Bomb? Someone died? Somebody want to fill me in?" Wayne was looking from one to the other.

Connie spoke up. "Did you ever know Art McNamara? Skip hired him as all-around handyman. He did everything, and a part of his salary was living scot-free up at the lodge. Skip must have kept him on five years or more and then Art left to find his fame and fortune somewhere else. It's been twenty years since I've seen him. It was a shock to find he'd come back."

"Came back to be killed?" Wayne asked.

"It would seem so. It all seems too bizarre."

"Sounds like someone followed him here. Do you know where he was living before?"

"I have no idea."

"Did you like the man?" Ben asked.

"Like?" Connie seemed to be searching for words. "I really didn't know him. It wasn't a matter of liking or not liking."

I've struck a chord, Ben thought. Connie's testy answer belied a lot more involvement than she wanted everyone to think. He caught Julie's eye above Connie's head. She had noticed it too. Something wasn't quite right. For one thing, Connie didn't seem frightened. The fact that a man had been blown to bits a scant two miles from her front door seemed to mean nothing. But in deference to his hostess, he'd let the subject drop.

Conversation was kept to small talk while they ate and it wasn't until the flan was served and Ben had stoked the fire, piling on two more logs of piñon, that Wayne broached the subject of Connie's decision to give up the land grant.

"I still can't believe you're doing this." Wayne sipped what Ben thought was at least his fourth martini. "You know, I can't keep Byron and Cherie from suing. In fact, I expect Jonathan to lead the pack."

"That would be my guess." Connie sighed and leaned against the back of a tan leather couch. Ben thought she looked tired with a hint of dark circles under her eyes that defied makeup. More than once during the evening he'd noticed a tremor that she sought to conceal by holding her drink with two hands. She seemed worried, almost preoccupied with something and it was more than her decision to give up the land grant. A couple sleepless nights and dreading the legal battle that was inevitable— that would tax anyone, but couple that with a murder— could this Art McNamara have something to do with the land? With giving it back?

"If you could have been on the mountain with us yesterday afternoon, you'd understand why Connie's decision is the right one." Julie smiled at Connie. "I'm not sure I really understood until then."

"I don't think secondhand sentimentality should overrule sound judgment. Forgive me, Julie, but I just don't think you understand the ramifications—"

"I understand that you might be more interested in protecting your job than being fair." Julie met his stare.

"That's underhanded. I look around and see the beauty

Connie has created. Created for her family—Skip's children and grandchildren. This is a legacy." Wayne gestured to include their surroundings, sloshing some of his martini onto his jeans. "I feel I have a duty to represent those who aren't here—those who had no idea what you were thinking of doing."

"I know how you feel Wayne. I'd like to hear from Ben." Connie put her drink down on a side table and leaned forward. "Can you understand why I'm doing this?"

"You have the ability to right a century-old wrong. You're not just thinking of a handful of people but of a tribe who stands to be reunited with their birthright. You are giving back the center of their religion, their access to herbs that have healed their people for centuries. I cannot praise your decision enough. It's a gift which cannot be measured in money."

"Thank you." Connie smiled. "I knew you would understand."

"Jesus. You're letting some Mormon-raised half-breed, some pretend Indian give advice? The Indians could have everything you mentioned, *and* we could still build an exclusive community."

"I've come to think the two are incompatible. And I think you owe Ben an apology."

"I don't owe him a goddamned thing. He's a user. He's used the system to get his education—eight years free, just a little tab for the taxpayer. I have student loans to pay back but not Mr. Half-breed who, I bet, can wax eloquent on just about any Indian topic we throw his way. Yet, he was raised in Utah by some middle-America, middle-class all white couple and to keep his luck going plans to marry into all white—"

"Shut up, Wayne. You're drunk. Don't mix your anger at me with an attack on Ben. I left you. I gave your ring back before I met Ben."

"This has nothing to do with you. If you can't see how you're attached to a user, then I can't change your mind. But the next time he puts that half-red dick in you—"

Ben stood, "Enough. If you have a beef with me, let's step outside."

Wayne pushed up out of an overstuffed chair. "I think we can settle this right now." His swing just grazed Ben's temple as he ducked, but Wayne caught Ben's perfectly thrown right that landed squarely on his chin. Ben caught him as he crumpled to the floor.

"Sorry, that was more reflex than intention. I wasn't planning on losing my temper and certainly had no plans to deck him." Ben eased Wayne to the couch.

"Served him right. It was stupid of me to invite the two of you and think Wayne was adult enough to act like one."

"You couldn't have known. I haven't seen Wayne for five years. I've been surprised that he's still interested."

"More like sore loser. He seems more than a little controlling," Connie said. "I won't let him leave here tonight. He's coming around but he's bound to have a pretty sore jaw. Can you put him in the guest room off the foyer? I'll get him a bag of ice. Then let's have a nightcap and call it a day."

+ + +

"Tired?" Ben was stacking piñon logs in the horno fireplace across from their bed.

"A little. I'm glad you're not driving back until the morning."

"You think I'm fool enough to leave you here with a half-crazed jilted fiancé who just may sleep it off and come looking for his former love?"

"I have to admit I feel better having you here." Julie crossed her legs yoga-style in the middle of the Taos cottonwood-post bed.

"I love you, Julie. That was a stupid thing I did tonight." Ben stood, tossed a match into the crushed newspaper nestled beneath the logs, and watched the fire roar up the flue. "But he was out of line. What do you think? Should I send our hostess roses?"

"That would be nice, but I don't think you have to do anything. Connie's pretty understanding."

"Did you notice how tired she looked?" Ben crossed to the bed, sat on the edge and flopped back. Most of his six foot two inch frame was on the bed and he scooted over until his head rested in her lap.

"She worries me. Too many things going on. I know this is crazy, but I swear she knows more about that letter bomb than she's letting on." Julie absently stroked Ben's hair.

"The guy who was killed was an old bodyguard of Skip's?"

"Right. But last week when I dropped her off at the road to hike in and check the lodge's propane tanks? I think she spent a lot more time talking to this Art McNamara than she wants us to know. When I turned into the long drive that leads to the lodge, I saw them. And the conversation wasn't pleasant; I'd bet on that. At one point Connie sort of slumped against the banister. And then this guy just takes off running when I pull up. Something's strange. And now he's dead."

"Of course, it sounds like the guy could have made some enemies in his line of work."

"But the fake money. Obviously, a payoff."

"And a double-cross." Ben sat up and pulled Julie against him.

"I hope Connie's not mixed up in all this somehow … Hey—that tickles."

"I need to get out of here by five-thirty and I'm thinking of doing a little more than just tickling you."

"I'd be disappointed if you weren't."

Chapter Fourteen

"Damn." Connie paced, lit a cigarette, puffed once, twice, put it out, emptied the ashtray in the fireplace, lit another. "Damn, damn, damn." Thank God she'd found Stan's little black book which contained her initials, phone number and the numbers she assumed belonged to the psychiatrist who had treated Robby. Even a notation to call the shrink. But there were other numbers—probably all people who would not want it known they had used Mr. Devon for some dirty work. If Stan was smart, the black book was the only place her name was recorded. She wished she knew for certain. But at least she had it. And she had time to prepare her story. When the cops came, she knew what she would say.

First, she needed to do a few things. Things she'd put off. Put off because she'd been counting on not having to do them. But it was time to empty the safe, put her papers in envelopes and write notes to the addressees. For the first time since learning of her illness, she was admitting defeat. There would be no life-saving treatment. No son was going to step forward and offer to save her life. She knew that now. And strangely, she was beyond tears.

She carried the box of contents from her safe through the rows of dresses and stacks of sweaters in her dressing room and dumped everything on her bed; then, pushing things into a pile, climbed into bed to begin the sorting. She was out of breath. The least exertion left her gasping. She knew her lungs were filling with fluid. Slowly. The insidious illness was claiming her body in small increments, but steadily, and not letting go of its small victories. Today her lungs ached and breathing was becoming difficult. Tomorrow it would be swollen ankles, fluid retention that would puff her up like a balloon. But enough of that. She had work to do.

She had changed her mind. She didn't want anyone knowing how she'd found Robby. If he wanted to talk about it, fine. She didn't. She didn't want any more links to one Stan Devon. Not under the circumstances. She did not need to be tied to Art's murder. She thought she could lie her way out of the package of money even though she knew they'd find her prints. Her prints and no one else's. Stan was smart enough to see to that.

She pulled the large envelope from the stack. Robby's yearbook, the pages describing his adoptive family, Stan's conclusions. Everything needed to be destroyed including the little black book she'd found in his safe. She couldn't change her son's background, but she could make it harder for someone to find out. She was sure Byron or Jonathan or Cherie would do just that. Dig everything up, try to discredit him. But the money was Robby's. Her will was ironclad—not open to interpretation. One half of Skip's estate—her half—would go to Robbie. They would contest it but to no avail. Robbie would get millions.

Should she mention his father? She'd told Robbie the story—the truth. Yes, there needed to be a record. She had his birth certificate—the papers from the hospital in Spain. She'd write an explanation, get everything out of the safe and put into envelopes. She almost chuckled out loud imagining the shock, the outrage. If she were the vindictive type, what a nice little payback for the pain their father had caused, the pain *they* had caused. She was tolerated, barely. She'd always felt the outsider. Skip's squaw. Well, it was nice to get the last laugh.

She slid feet first from the high four-poster, turned back and gathered up the yearbook and envelope. The fire in the banco-height fireplace was just taking off. She paused. What mother would burn her child's yearbook? Especially when she had nothing that was his. Then she smiled. These weren't exactly "usual" circumstances. She had the memories of the fire dancer. Maybe that's what kept her going. In the face of his rejection, she knew he showed his caring for her in the traditional way. Deep within, he connected with her and made the offer to heal her—in his way—and hers. He truly was her son.

Ah, but this wasn't getting her anywhere. She quickly bent down and stuffed the envelope between the logs, the yearbook on top. Digging into the pocket of her robe, the little black book was next. She watched for a minute then walked back to the bed and climbed on top of the covers. Fluffing the pillows, she pulled the stack of papers toward her.

The first envelope contained her will. Not one drawn up by Wayne but one done last month by a firm in Denver. The will which left so much to Robbie. She leaned back and reached for a cigarette, flipping open the lid of the lighter and holding the flame to its tip. The first spasm of coughing left her clutching the quilt with both hands. The first drag was always the worst—maybe she wouldn't be able to continue her habit much longer. She sank back against the pillows and closed her eyes. Better. She stubbed the cigarette out in the ashtray.

Would she let the will stand? Yes. She wasn't angry about his reaction. His rejection of her. She could understand. She wouldn't be punitive. She'd add a handwritten page to cover some things she'd forgotten, and she'd add a page of explanation about Robby. Not necessarily all the particulars but enough—times and places and the names of the Merritts. She leaned over to retrieve a pen from the nightstand.

She'd been toying with telling Julie about her illness, and set her up as executor along with Ben. There weren't many people she could trust, but Julie and Ben were the right choices. It was time. She'd tell her in the morning.

The knock interrupted her reverie, soft, tentative, as if the person didn't want to intrude. The door at the far end of her sitting area opened out to Koi ponds and a rock garden with private prayer areas. Her own space unlike almost any other surrounding the house, this was private. But how fitting that he would come to her to share his decision. Face-to-face. She admired that. He was as forthright as his father. She couldn't keep the smile from spreading across her face. Her son. Her hope. She slipped from the bed, lifted up the edge of the gold brocade comforter and stuffed the packet of papers underneath. There, safe for now. She padded quickly across the tiles to open the door.

Chapter Fifteen

Ben was on the road by five-thirty, but Julie didn't go back to sleep. The wind had come up around daybreak, pushing a cholla cactus against the window, batting it back and forth to screech its disapproval against the glass. She double-checked the side door, stoked the fire and headed to the shower. But the screaming stopped her.

Connie? Was there a problem with Wayne? She presumed that he was still in the house. She pulled on a sweatshirt and jeans and ran barefoot into the hall. The screaming was coming from the west wing. Connie's bedroom. Julie ran across the kitchen, the dining room, a sitting room, the atrium. The house was cavernous. The light of a pale gray dawn stretched the shadows of furniture into grotesque humped pachyderms. Suddenly the screaming stopped and only the muffled slap of her bare feet against Italian marble broke the silence.

Rounding the corner, she almost fell over Rosa keening on her knees, rocking silently so out of breath there was no longer sound, merely tears.

"Missy," she whispered. "Missy gone." She crossed herself.

Julie didn't wait to hear more but ran toward Connie's bedroom. The door was open.

"Connie? Connie?"

The form on the bed didn't move. The room was lighted by a roaring fire and it was hot. Far too hot for Connie to be under the huge satin-covered comforter. Julie shivered but not from cold. The fire was casting dancing shadows up the wall. Eerie. She called out louder, "Connie?" No answer. Now the eeriness turned to dread.

How could Connie move, weighted down under such a mountain of satin? And all that net. Julie moved to the bedside and gaped. Connie was not under a satin comforter but pinioned by the billowing skirt of a wedding gown. Her hair was beautifully braided and shimmered in the light from the fire. Pearl studs outlined each twist as it wound to her waist. Her veil floated around her head, covered her face, and reached past her shoulders. The generous circle of stiff net was gathered and tucked into the narrow band of a crown that perched on top of her head. Encrusted with diamonds and pearls, the headpiece caught the firelight and sparked with color.

The ankle length gown showed off her shoes—even in repose. They were something Italian, two straps that wound their way across the instep to end in bows at the ankle. Very expensive pale cream satin to match the gown. But it was the buttons that made Julie stare. At least a hundred tiny pearls—real ones, Julie thought—lined up like sentinels down the entire length of the dress from high collar to the hem, each nestled in its loop fastener.

Another thing gnawed at her consciousness—Connie looked beautiful, vibrant, but somehow at peace. She seldom wore makeup, but what she had on was perfect in its understatement. Julie shook herself out of this reverie, stepped up to the bed, and felt for a pulse. None. Connie felt warm and not just from the fire. She hadn't been dead long. Julie reached for the bedside phone. She needed to call someone. Police. Ambulance.

"Miss Connie was very sick."

"Sick?" Julie turned to look at Rosa who was now standing behind her. "She couldn't have been."

"I think she wanted to be with the angels."

"Suicide?"

Rosa nodded solemnly. "I think she knew it was time."

"No. I can't believe that. How do you know?"

"A nice lady doctor calls almost everyday. She says I am to see that Missy Connie take her pills and don't get too tired. She tells me that Missy Connie will need me. I must make time to be here."

"Who is this doctor?"

"Doctor Bancroft. Her number is by the phone in the office."

"What was making her sick?"

A shrug. "I don't know."

Julie could see that Rosa had exhausted her fund of knowledge. But a doctor. Julie checked her watch. Almost seven. She was fighting back the sadness that threatened to overtake her. But if she gave into tears now …

"Rosa, bring me the number."

Julie waited, trying to sort through the tangle of thoughts. If Connie had been so ill, why hadn't she said something? And the wedding gown … was this some statement of going to be with Skip? Some crossing over in the same gown she wore in her youth? Some forty years ago? No. This one looked new. But could she be sure? Probably not. The only sure thing was the premeditation. Her death had been planned to the last detail.

Julie quickly looked around the room. Nothing was out of place. There had not been a visible struggle against death—just some sort of quiet giving in. If there had been a life-threatening illness, this would be just like Connie to take control. Do it her way, in her time. Would there be an empty pill container in the bathroom?

"Here is the number."

Rosa held out an open planner. There were two numbers—one appeared to be Dr. Bancroft's home if she could trust the H in parentheses after it. Julie walked to the phone on the nightstand. She picked up the receiver and quickly dialed that one first.

"Dr. Bancroft?"

"Yes." The woman sounded sleepy and a little out of sorts.

Julie explained the urgency.

"Oh no. I sensed this when she was in Monday. I insisted that she begin oxygen, but she wouldn't hear of it. She was so proud. This was so difficult for her but she had planned everything. She was ready; that's the only consolation, the only solace I can give you."

Julie listened numbly to an explanation of leukemia. How Connie had known for a couple months—at most had two or three months left. No, it wasn't unusual for someone to succumb in a shorter amount of time. But the wedding gown, Julie thought to herself. What a bizarre twist. But wasn't it more proof of Connie's being prepared? The impact of what was happening began to sink in, and she felt the tears well up to spill over and run down her cheek.

"I, of course, will order an autopsy."

"Is that necessary?" They always seemed like a terrible invasion of privacy, of person.

"There are a number of questions that need to be answered. Did she, as I suspect, take her own life? Did she succumb to the combination of medicines she started two days ago? We were trying something new—perhaps, she had a reaction. She was very fragile."

If suicide was suspected, an autopsy was mandatory. That, Julie knew. Another body for the OMI. Another suspicious death. Or death of unknown origins. Doctor Bancroft said she would make all the arrangements. Julie was relieved. Suddenly she was drained and it was becoming an effort to think clearly. She thanked Dr. Bancroft and hung up just as Rosa thrust a cup of coffee toward her.

"You need."

"Rosa, this could save a life." Julie felt guilty at her choice of words and looked away. Suddenly, she needed to get out of the room. And where was Wayne? Could he have slept through all the screaming?

She headed into the hall toward yet another wing of the sprawling house. The nearest guest room door was open and the room was very empty. Bedclothes were piled on the bed and half on the floor. But, no Wayne. Had he left in the middle of the night? She hadn't heard anything, but that was not surprising. A few thousand square feet separated her room from this area.

She'd see if his car was still in the circle drive.

It also was gone. She closed the heavy front door but not before she marveled at the streaks of rose that stretched across the eastern sky. No more pale grayness. The sun was now above the mountains and streamed into the foyer from domed panels of stained glass which cast an artist's palette of color across the floor. How could so much beauty exist side by side with death? How could this house, a tribute to so much Connie had done in life, go on without her? Without its inspiration? But hadn't she planned for that? Hadn't she given away this house hoping the pueblo would use it as a museum? A monument that would go on without her.

Suddenly, suicide made perfect sense. Hadn't Connie been planning all along how to get rid of the property? Giving the land back to Sandia Pueblo was her legacy. Julie stood sipping her coffee and watching the sky deepen in color. The rose was now palest peach with pink outlines to every cloud and the sky itself a wonderful, clear deep azure.

And then the thought that had been hovering at the periphery slipped into focus—if Connie had taken her own life, there would be a note or something—some indication she knew the end was near. Julie set the cup on an end table and walked, then almost ran, back to Connie's bedroom.

The fire was barely a pile of embers. Thank God. The heat had been stifling. Quickly, Julie looked at the nightstand, then the desk. She opened a drawer, then another. Nothing. But would a note be tucked away? She didn't think so. She needed to look for something obvious—out in the open.

The fire popped, sending sparks far out into the room.

She needed to put the screen up before a fire started that she didn't want. She looked at the Navajo rugs that dotted the room. Tens of thousands of dollars as floor covering—not something she'd want to go up in flame. As she neared the fireplace, a speck of white caught her eye. Quickly reaching for a poker, she pulled a small leather-covered book from under a burning log. It appeared to be an address book of sorts. She turned it over, back cover and spine were charred but otherwise intact. She'd give this some time later; she slipped it into the pocket of her sweatpants.

What she was looking for wasn't trash to be burned. If Rosa was right and Connie had wanted to be with the angels, there would be some sort of note. Something she'd want others to find. It didn't take her long. Julie reached across the bed to run a hand under the pillows stacked against the headboard, and she stepped on papers under the bed. She bent down and pulled out a bundle of official-looking documents rubber-banded together. The envelope on top had the return address of a law firm in Denver, a large manila envelope and three fat letter-sized ones were underneath it. But it was the handwritten note tucked under the band that caught her attention. Dated yesterday, it began, "When you read this, I will be gone ..." Julie couldn't go on. So, it was true. She knew and had planned her leaving—possibly instigated her own death.

"The hospital men are here." Rosa's voice prodded Julie into action. Quickly she stuffed the bundle under her sweatshirt. Surprised at herself, she started to remove it as she heard voices coming down the hall. But something more than curiosity made her cinch the drawstring on her sweats and secure the papers at her waist. She was the administrative assistant, wasn't she? And she needed a quiet time and place to go over these. Even in death Connie would want some respect and would want the right person looking at her personal papers. Of this she felt certain.

"Ma'am?"

"In here." Three young paramedics came into the room. One gave a low whistle.

"Did you dress her?"

"No. We found her this way."

The young man stood to one side as his two companions flanked him. But not one of them could take his eyes off of Connie.

"She was very ill. Her personal physician is Dr. Margaret Bancroft. I talked to her a half hour ago. She spoke of an autopsy due to her suspicion of suicide."

"Bancroft is Chief of Oncology at UNMH. A good doc. She had the best." He nodded toward Connie.

"When did you find Ms. CdeBaca?"

"Actually, Rosa found her."

"I come at six o'clock on Sundays." Rosa stood by the door and looked lost. Julie motioned her forward. She had no idea how long Rosa had worked for Connie, but it was probably quite some time.

"You came at six this morning?" The young paramedic noted her nod by scratching a quick note on a pad of paper. "What's the first thing that you did?"

"Always, always check on Missy first. She like her coffee very early."

"Were you supposed to wake her?"

"No. Lately, she no sleep and is awake already when I come."

"And this is how you found her?"

Rosa nodded.

"I pushed her veil back. I was just checking for signs of life," Julie added.

The young man nodded. "I'm going to check in with Dr. Bancroft. And then we'll get going. I'll let you know where Ms. CdeBaca will be."

Julie left the room. She needed another cup of coffee so she followed Rosa to the kitchen. She filled a cup and added half-and-half.

"I'll be in my room if anyone needs me. I need to start letting people know what's happened."

"Mr. Byron, he's going to be happy. He never like Missy. And that Cherie …" Words seemed to fail Rosa, but the meaning wasn't lost. Yes, Julie thought, there would be rejoicing in some camps.

The minute she got to her room, Julie undid her sweats and pulled up her sweatshirt. Maybe creased in a couple new places, but otherwise, the documents were intact. She took the address book out of her pocket and put it in her purse. She carried her cup of coffee to the desk, adjusted the blinds and spread the envelopes out in front of her with Connie's handwritten note on top.

Dated yesterday. Julie couldn't stop staring. What had made last night the right time to take her life? Ben would worry he'd upset her by decking Wayne. But that wasn't it. She'd taken the episode in stride. So, what? What turning point? Did she suddenly get sick in the night? Realize what she was facing? That the time was near?

Julie scanned the first page. Connie was well aware of the ravages of leukemia. She had outlined briefly her knowledge of what was happening to her body. The letter contained directions—what documents would be needed.

What needed to be filed. The final ceremony, where and when and how she wanted to be dressed—

"Missy?"

"Yes, Rosa?"

"The men, they leave now. They tell me to get you."

"Thanks. I'll be right there." Julie hastily pushed the papers together and, walking to the bed, stuffed everything between the mattress and box spring. Safe for the time being. She caught her reflection in the mirror above the fireplace. Yuk. No makeup. And there wasn't time to remedy that now. With eyebrows so pale as to be non-existent, she looked a little alien. Maybe a touch of pencil. She dashed into the bathroom and applied a quick feathered line to each brow and a swipe of mascara to her lashes—just enough to keep her from looking dead. Damn. She needed to keep those references from her vocabulary.

The young man she'd talked with earlier was waiting for her in the foyer. She could see the others loading a gurney into the back of the rescue unit parked at the front door.

"I spoke with Dr. Bancroft. She's going to meet us at the OMI. I'm sure she'll stay in touch. Will she be able to reach you at this number?"

With a jolt Julie realized he was asking whether she'd stay here now that her hostess was dead. Would she? She didn't know but thought she would for a few days.

"I expect to be here most of this week but let me give you my cell."

"Good. I'll make certain Dr. Bancroft has this number." He held out a form on a clipboard and she filled in the blanks. Her name. Address. Phone.

He waved from the cab of the ambulance. Somehow

he was just too chipper. She felt drained, and dreaded the phone calls she had to make. She was just closing the front door when she saw the police cruiser turn into the drive and slowly pass the ambulance on its way out.

It looked like those calls would have to wait. She opened the door and waited for Lieutenant Samuels to walk across the circular brick entry.

"That anything I should know about?" He waved over his shoulder at the retreating ambulance.

Julie sighed.

"Then get me the lady of the house. I think we have some things to discuss." His demanding voice irritated her.

"You passed her on your way in."

"Explain."

"Connie died last night. She was terminally ill."

"Shit." He whacked the nearest column with the manila envelope in his hand and turned to watch the ambulance make the turn onto the county road.

"Thanks. Your condolences are accepted." Two could play at bad manners. Julie started to close the door.

"Okay. Unprofessional of me. Let's start over. I came here to arrest Ms. CdeBaca for the murder of Art McNamara or complicity in his death. I can be allowed a little disappointment."

A second cruiser turned in the drive but Julie barely noticed. *Murder?* Connie implicated in the caretaker's death? Julie could only stare. What was there to say? This was so preposterous.

His tone softened. "I'd like to talk. Maybe you can help. If there's an offer of coffee, I'll get rid of these guys and be right back."

Julie nodded. He could have a whole pot. Her morning

could not get any more bizarre.

"The kitchen's back here." It hadn't taken him long to send his backup on their way.

"Great house."

"It is, isn't it? One of the things Connie was most proud of."

"Who gets all this now?"

"The house has been taken care of." She briefly explained Connie's generous gift to the pueblo. "I think it will make a wonderful museum. She and Skip had no children, but there are three children by Skip's first marriage. I'm assuming most things will be divided among the three of them."

"Sounds like she planned things well."

"She had some time. Maybe not as long as she thought."

"But enough to tie up loose ends. Save others the trouble of second-guessing her wishes. There's something to be said for that. My grandmother put notes on everything the year before she died. Pictures, glassware, jewelry—everything. It made my mother's job a lot easier."

Julie knew he was trying to make amends. Offer personal information, draw her in. She'd try to be nicer, too. She was curious about how Connie could be implicated in a murder. As they entered the sprawling kitchen, Julie was almost surprised to see Rosa working at one of the gleaming stainless steel sinks beneath a bank of windows. Julie hadn't been thinking. There was no reason for her to stay. She should have suggested that she go home earlier.

"Rosa. I'd like you to take the day off. This has been so difficult. Come at eight tomorrow and we'll get started sorting Connie's things. I'd appreciate your help."

"Yes, Miss. Thank you."

Rosa's red-rimmed eyes clutched at Julie's heart. She, too, needed a time to mourn but it wouldn't be for awhile. And phone calls. That would be the tough part. She watched as Mark Samuels poured himself a large mug of coffee. He was settling in. She might as well relax; he didn't seem like the type who could be rushed.

"What makes you think Connie had something to do with the letter bomb?" Julie leaned her elbows on the counter after scooting the stool closer.

"Fingerprints. One perfect capture on the tape used to wrap the package the bomb was in. And another on a fragment of a thousand-dollar bill. The package was addressed to Mr. McNamara. I'm betting we can prove the writing's hers."

"There's simply no way Connie could have killed someone."

"Fingerprints don't lie. She's implicated, all right."

"But a bomb. How could she have done that?"

"Not difficult at all. Access to materials and the internet and it's practically done."

"Bomb-making materials? How would she have access?"

"Actually, she's a prime suspect because of the material used."

"I don't understand."

"Ever notice those silver or white boxes usually on a pole beside railroad tracks?

"I think so."

"You'll see more of them in remote areas—on the reservations, for example. The railroad stores leftover explosives there and sometimes forgets about it. It can be there for years."

"Explosives used by the railroad? For what?"

"Explosive-hardened steel is many times more resilient. Rails are often treated after they're in place."

"I still don't see why this would make Connie a prime suspect."

"One of the locked boxes was broken into—three days ago. The box is located about two miles from the edge of Ms. Bigrope's property on the Sandia reservation."

"It still means she'd have to have bomb-making knowledge."

"As I said, easy to pick up on the internet."

"I'm not buying it."

"Why not? The particular type of explosive used is exactly like what's used by the railroad—exactly like the stuff that was stolen."

"I think you're really stretching to make this fit."

"I never rule out an accomplice."

"That's truly ridiculous."

"Can you vouch for her whereabouts every minute over the last few days?"

"No, of course not."

"May I say I've been doing this long enough that I've seen about everything? And I never assume I know someone. Just means you're going to be in for a surprise."

Julie wasn't going to contradict him. It would be pointless. She wondered briefly if he was married. He wasn't wearing a ring. Maybe he'd had experience in one of life's little surprises from someone he'd "known."

"So tell me about this illness that just happened to take her life at an opportune time."

Julie started to protest then thought better of it. It did seem a little opportune, didn't it?

"Her doctor would be of more help. In brief, Connie found out she had leukemia about two months ago."

"Treatment?"

"She apparently chose to forego conventional treatment."

"Any reason?"

"It's my understanding that Connie was faced with four months to live—if she was lucky. There was no guarantee chemo would extend her time by much. Trying to buy an extra month or two didn't make sense to her. Not with the side effects that were pretty much a given."

"I'd say that makes sense to me, too. Who found her body?"

"Rosa, at about six o'clock this morning."

"I understand your letting her go home, but I will have to interview her. Do you have an address?"

"I'll check. But she'll be here tomorrow. Should I just have her contact you?"

"That'll work." He made a note. "Last night was just a regular evening? Nothing unusual?"

"Nothing that pertains to her death. She had a small dinner party and went to bed early."

"Names of those attending?"

"Just Connie and I, my fiancé, and the company lawyer."

"You'll be able to give me those addresses and phone numbers?"

Julie gave him Ben's full name and office numbers, then followed with the same information on Wayne.

"Were you the last one to see her alive?"

Laughing, she said, "I'm beginning to think I need my lawyer present. Is this an interrogation?"

"Sorry." He took a sip of coffee. "Habit, I guess. But something doesn't smell right. Ms. CdeBaca's death seems too convenient. Whether you want to face it or not, your friend was mixed up in something that involved a murder—either of her planning or as a follow-up to her involvement."

"I just can't—"

"I know I'm asking a lot, but I need you to step outside your friendship and be objective. I'm not even factoring in the skull incident."

"What skull?"

He quickly filled her in. "She called it some kind of joke, said it probably wasn't even aimed at her. But a skull with a heart around the bullet hole, a dead caretaker, and now her own death—I don't know about you, but I'm not laughing."

"I can't believe all this. Funny how you think you know someone, been around them all your life only to find out nothing's as it seemed."

"Is there any possibility she took her own life? Knew what she'd face with a murder investigation? And opted out? Especially under the circumstances? Her illness and all."

Julie knew she had guilt written all over her face. "I'm sure of it. That she took her own life. Not that she did it because she feared the consequences of a murder investigation." She slipped off the stool and headed toward the door. "I'll be right back."

She didn't look back, but she knew he was biting his tongue. A suicide under any circumstances would be handled differently. Should she feel guilty about not mentioning the letter of instructions? Probably. But somehow putting

Connie through more—even deceased—was too much. There had to be dignity in death. She knew she wasn't original in that but she believed it, too.

She separated the three pages from the will and took them back to the kitchen. She really had Mark Samuels's attention now.

"She left this."

He took the first single sheet and carefully held it by the edges and looked at it. "Have you read it?"

"Just scanned the first couple paragraphs. Nothing out of the ordinary—she's to be laid out in her wedding gown, and then taken to the reservation. She's Mescalero Apache and will be buried according to her tribe's customs."

He was silent as he read each of the three pages. Then, went back to page two and reread the entire page.

"I thought you said the CdeBacas had no children of their own—the only children involved are from the Senator's former marriage?"

"That's right."

"So, the son mentioned here—mentioned as the sole inheritor of her half of the estate is Ms. CdeBaca's by a former marriage of hers?"

"I'm confused. There was no former marriage. She married Skip when she was nineteen. Connie doesn't have children."

"Oh, yeah?" He held out the second page. "Hold it by the corners."

Julie started to scan the page and then stopped to read each word. "The estate will be divided between my husband's children and my child. I have left a package of instructions as to how I want this to be carried out. The package also contains proof that, in fact, the young man in question is truly my son—raised by others but no less unquestionably of my blood. What separated us in life unites us now without rancor, or duplicity. I will expect every courtesy to be extended to him in this difficult hour."

Julie handed the page back and just sat there. A son? How old? Who was the father? Was he the secret result of a tryst even Skip didn't know about? Wow. She could only imagine Byron, et.al. Talk about being pissed.

"Is this son thing a surprise?"

"Try shock. My mother was her best friend and I know she didn't know."

"So, you don't know the background? Where he is now, how to get in touch?"

"Not a clue. I know as much as you do. There isn't even a name mentioned."

"Where are these papers she mentions—the ones that will prove parentage?"

"I imagine in Connie's private safe in her office at work." Crossed fingers against a probable lie. She was certain they were a part of the envelopes she'd found in Connie's bedroom.

"What's the office address?"

Julie gave him that and both Byron and Cherie's phone numbers. She didn't have particulars for Jonathan.

"Interesting, she wants to be buried in her wedding gown. Her husband died fairly recently. You think that's some kind of togetherness thing?"

"I really don't know what to think. But she was dressed in the gown when we found her."

"This morning?"

Julie nodded.

"Odd. Possible overdose? Dress first then administer fatal dosage."

Did he see her wince? This line of reasoning was just

too painful. "Her doctor didn't rule that out. She'll be present at the autopsy."

"Well, nothing's going to happen today. We won't get results before next week. Look, thanks for the coffee. I'm taking up your time and I know you have things to do. If you could find me some kind of zipper plastic bag for this, I'll be going. Here's my card. Call if you find anything or have a question … hell, call just to say hello." He grinned.

Was that some kind of veiled pickup line? Or was he still just trying to be nice. She couldn't tell. "Thanks." She opened five drawers before finding the storage bags, extracted one and watched him carefully slide the document inside. Then she walked him to the front door and returned to the kitchen. Another cup of coffee was in order. Eight thirty and this was the first chance she'd gotten to call Ben. She fished her cell out of her pocket.

He was shocked and upset that he couldn't help.

"Are you going to be all right? I can't get away until this evening. I don't like thinking of you facing this all alone."

"I'll be fine. I need to make the obligatory calls and put things in order here. I may run by the office later and make copies of the will. I want you back here, too, but I hate to think of you driving so far in one day." What could he actually do anyway?

"Not a problem. I can get back by ten tonight. I'll call you when I'm heading out."

They talked for a few more minutes. Julie shared with him the cop's idea that Connie had stolen explosives and made a letter bomb. Ben agreed with her—there was just no way. Not Connie. But a bomb that killed the caretaker had her fingerprints on its wrapping? How did you explain that? Ben was stymied. A lot of questions without answers.

And they might not ever know now that she was gone. But Julie was to be careful and grab a motel room if she would be more comfortable. Staying in the house alone might be too oppressive.

Oh yes, would he believe that Connie had a son? She was kidding, wasn't she? No. And there were papers to prove it, apparently. Yet, no one knew about this child. Not even Julie's mother. Bizarre. How could things get any stranger? Ben asked that she let him know where she'd be. They said their goodbyes and she slipped her cell back into her pocket.

There was a list of phone numbers for family members beside the kitchen phone. Might as well use the landline. She dragged a stool up to the counter, took the phone off the hook and got started. Cherie first, but it was Sunday morning and she was out. Tough to think of Cherie at church services, but maybe not too farfetched. Still, no one in the family struck her as religious. The day-nanny was sweet and promised Miss CdeBaca would call the minute she got in. Julie hadn't realized Cherie still used her maiden name. She couldn't remember her husband very well and thought that he was a "former" now anyway.

Jonathan's secretary, male and very into himself, offered stilted condolences and would leave a note for Mr. CdeBaca who was out for the morning. Julie didn't even entertain the thought of church—not for Jonathan—more like some hike in the mountains or cycling tour. Only Byron was at home and seemed genuinely upset. Or elated. She couldn't tell at first.

"Do you know when the autopsy will be done?"

"No idea. The police lieutenant thought we'd have results later in the week."

"I have a copy of her will on file at the office. Have you notified Wayne?"

With a pang, Julie realized she hadn't even thought about him—not since checking to see if he'd gone. "No. In fact, I'm not sure I have a number for him."

"I'll give him a jingle. I'm sure there's some protocol he needs to follow to get the ball rolling, so to speak."

Julie hesitated only a second and then decided not to tell him about the will drawn up by a Denver law firm. Some sixth sense said this new one would negate the old and might be very, very different. Ah, this was not going to be pretty. "I'm sorry, what did you say?" She needed to pay attention.

"Just that this is such a shock. No one saw this coming. Do you think that's why she wanted to give the land back? Some last vestige of good will, a grand gesture to secure her legacy?"

"It's difficult to say. I believe she really felt it was the right thing to do."

"Well, that's all moot now, isn't it? We'll have that puppy overturned in no time. Thank God, it was still in the 'nice gesture' stage—nothing official had been done. Nothing in writing, that is. I doubt Wayne had time to draw anything up, let alone get her signature." He paused, "You know, you probably need to secure the house and get a motel for the night. Now don't get the wrong idea, but under the circumstances, nothing should be disturbed. I'll meet Wayne there in the morning to begin an inventory, but I guess there's no hurry. I'd just hate there to be any question of impropriety. Wayne's the executor of the estate. Of course, I'll do whatever he says. But for the time being …"

Julie was furious, but bit her tongue. Maybe he was

right 'under the circumstances.' And she couldn't imagine dear Wayne wanting her around.

"Excellent idea and one I'd planned on anyway. I may run by the office and do a few things this afternoon."

"If it's all the same to you, why don't you let anything that has to do with the business go until tomorrow? I'd like to suggest that there will be fewer questions if a member of the family is present when you're on the premises."

Fewer questions? About what? She'd assumed she was out of a job. But he was making her out to be some kind of threat. "Yes, of course, Byron." She could really learn to dislike this man. But she had the documents in her possession that would rock his world. Moot, indeed. She smiled and took great satisfaction in what he didn't know.

Without further finger-pointing, they made a date to meet at the office around noon and, again, he asked that she convey his deepest sympathies to her mother. He knew Bev had lost a dear friend as, of course, had she. And, did she need help in moving out? He could possibly scare up someone. Ugh! Just posturing. He didn't mean a word of it.

No, she assured him, just a couple suitcases and her computer. *And several envelopes holding your future.*

She was relieved to be leaving, if truth be known. She was rattling around in a house that felt like a shell devoid of Connie's spirit. And there was a tremendous sadness, a feeling she couldn't shake. Julie felt betrayed somehow. Connie hadn't trusted her enough to share her horrendous burden. But Julie admonished herself—why did she feel this way? Wasn't Connie entitled to take her own life? Be in control of the end? Not wait to be hospitalized and give in to a ravaging disease, one that would rob her of beauty and any vestige of life as she had lived it? No matter how many lectures she gave herself on Connie's long life, her accomplishments, her beauty, her wealth—all the things others would lust after, it wasn't enough. She'd gone far too soon. Nothing could make up for that.

Julie would bring the BMW back tomorrow after she'd checked out another rental—surely wanting her out took precedence over any breach caused by continuing to use the car until she could secure another. She'd just deal with Byron if he had a problem with it. The papers would go in the trunk. They were staying with her for the time being. She couldn't wait to go through them. Curiosity and cats— fit her to a tee. Or maybe she just wanted to thumb her nose at Byron. Not very adult, but the truth.

She moved the car from the circular drive in front to the paved strip of asphalt outside their bedroom door. Unlocking the trunk first, she went back into the bedroom and gathered all the papers and took them back to the car. And as long as she was here, she might as well pack. Ben's things were easy—he had most of his clothes with him. Hers were scattered between two closets but she grabbed hangers with coats, sweaters and slacks, piled them on the bed, then did a quick cosmetics pick-up in the bathroom, even remembering the shampoo in the shower.

And then she remembered the designer clothes. There were five outfits that fit her perfectly. Didn't that seem a little greedy? But under the circumstances … she walked to the closet nearest the bathroom. There was a reversible coyote and leather jacket; she carried it, hanger and all, to the bed. Next, a black cashmere dress with dolman sleeves, a midnight-blue beaded jacket, cami and matching wide-legged trousers in silk, a red gabardine suit with silk blouse and the Chanel.

Julie slipped the protective bag off the Chanel dress and jacket and held it up, then walked back to the bedroom and pirouetted in front of a full length mirror. The sun streaming in the overhead skylight picked up the flecks of gold thread, which formed the brocade pattern adorning the cuffs and spiraling up the front plackets of the double-breasted jacket. Stunning. The dress was simple, a low, square neckline, cap sleeves with only the subdued gold brocade around the skirt's calf-length hem. Perfect for her wedding—if she were to get married in the winter. Was this Connie's gentle encouragement to move on with their plans? As she slipped the dress back on its hanger and picked up the jacket, she noticed a slip of paper sticking out of a side pocket. The note said simply, "Check the hatbox."

Julie added the Chanel to the pile on the bed and went back to the closet. In itself a work of art, Julie idly wondered where you had to buy a hat to get such a confection of cardboard and satin ribbon. Inside was a wisp of a circle, white with a sparkle of gold thread—could you call it a hat? The veil, a pouf of net caught by a gold clasp when undone would release a single layer to cover her face at chin length. Perfect. And beneath this, nestled in tissue, was a jewelry case. Julie held her breath and carefully undid the hasp and lifted the lid. She couldn't contain an audible exhale. A bracelet, necklace and matching earrings twinkled against blue satin. Pearls and diamonds set in platinum—settings from the twenties, now popular again. Drop earrings of pearls and diamonds, twists of pearls and diamonds hanging from a chain necklace, links interspersed with bezel set diamonds. And the bracelet, a braided rope of platinum and one-carat diamonds surrounding a mabe pearl in lightest pink. The note read simply,

You would do me great honor by accepting this wedding present.

I wore this set on my wedding day—a gift from my groom. I have no daughter to give these to—but if I had one, she would be just like you!

My love always,
Auntie Connie

Julie couldn't finish the note for her tears. The enormity of the loss washed over her and, clutching note and jewelry box, she slipped to the floor, no longer holding back the wracking sobs.

Finally, she blew her nose, walked to the bathroom, splashed her face with cold water and grimaced when she saw her reflection. She took the time to capture her hair in a scrunchy, put on eyebrows and lip gloss, then, a touch of mascara. There—somewhat more human but no amount of makeup could erase the pain. But she had work to do.

She slipped clothing protectors over the coyote jacket and remaining outfits, carried them to the car, carefully arranging each so as not to wrinkle the garment beneath. Thirty minutes later, the BMW was piled high and ready to go.

She'd contacted the principals—all but her mother. That call would not be easy—for lots of reasons. One being Bev's duplicity in trying to throw her daughter at her former fiancé. But it wouldn't do to put off the call. She pocketed the car keys and walked back to the kitchen. The dregs from the coffeemaker just might give her the jolt of energy she'd need. There was exactly a half cup of very dark liquid left—perfect! A dollop of half-and-half and she was braced. She headed out to the driveway. She started the car then reached for her cell. She couldn't put off the call any longer.

"Mom, do you have a minute? I have the saddest news." Julie quickly reiterated what she knew—the illness, possible suicide, leaving a legacy. Had her mother known Connie was ill? Terminally so? And did she know that Connie had a son? That stopped her mother completely.

"You have to be mistaken. I'd say you were wrong about leukemia, too, but you have the doctor's word. I just know she would have eventually told me. But a son? That's absolutely unthinkable. She wanted nothing more in life than to have her own child. Then to have one and give it away? No. That didn't happen. We never lied to one another."

Julie heard the sound of her mother blowing her nose. She needed to remind herself how difficult this would be for her mother.

"It wasn't as if she lied, Mother. Maybe she needed to hide her pregnancy and maybe there just wasn't time to tell you about her illness. She knew how upset you'd be. Maybe she wanted to spare you. Let the end be shock enough."

"Doesn't sound like her. And what is this about her wearing a wedding dress?"

Julie repeated the instructions Connie had left but again mentioned that she'd been found in the dress. "Uncle Skip died fairly recently. Do you think it was some kind of tribute to him? A final celebration of their long relationship?"

Her mother's harsh laugh startled her. "A tribute to togetherness? Skip and Connie? Oh my, you have no idea how distant the two of them were. There was a loathing of Skip that threatened to erupt every time they spent more than five minutes alone."

"I wonder why?"

"Too many years together—forty-one to be exact—and too many years between them. Skip needed her. Connie got votes—the Hispanic and Indian votes, for certain. She was beautiful—and talented. She fascinated people; they never forgot her—and, by default, him. A politician's dream, wouldn't you say?"

"When you put it that way."

"He was a lucky man. I used to think he knew it. He treated her well, but he had no way to feed her spirit. I guess that's the best way I can put it. She simply withered inside. He kiddingly called her his squaw trophy but I know it hurt."

"That's so sad."

"Well, when a relationship isn't right, that's what happens. And I think an ethnically mixed marriage is doomed." Julie said a silent, "Oh, no" and wasn't disappointed. She knew her mother wouldn't be able to hold back from dragging her disapproval of Ben out … again. "I'm sure you realize that's why I'm so against your relationship with Ben—I see you as ending up like Connie."

"Mom, we've been through this a hundred times. Connie was on our side. I'm sorry we lost an advocate; she was a big fan of Ben's. In fact, it was mutual. They had a lot in common—"

"Well, why wouldn't they? They would be far better suited than the two of you."

"Mom, I really don't want to go there. I'm frankly upset that you didn't tell me you've stayed in touch with Wayne. Who, I might add, made a complete ass out of himself last night. He's juvenile and petty and thinks far too much of himself for us to ever get together. He hasn't changed."

"No mother wants to see her child make a mistake. I don't think you can blame me."

"Not if it stopped there. But I'm sick and tired of your maneuvering."

"I don't ask for a thank you, Julie, God knows, but I would like a little acknowledgement of my caring. I've always put you first. Sometimes to my disadvantage."

"Mom, I don't have time to listen to this. I have a number of other calls to make." A little white lie but she didn't want to be rude. Still, if her mother kept up this anti-Ben campaign, it was only forcing a distance between them—and not one measured in miles. "Will you come out for the funeral?"

"I don't see how I can. Your father's in Los Angeles until the end of the month. They're opening two new branch offices. I'm still on crutches—didn't I tell you about the infection?"

She had, but Julie let her tell the story again. A staph infection, caused by a cat scratch across her big toe, proved resistant to antibiotics. That on top of the two surgeries.

"It sounds awful. I'll be thinking of you. Connie was explicit in her instructions so I won't have much to do. And, the family should be of help."

"I wouldn't count on that. Maybe Byron. I always thought he and Connie worked well together. You know, both shared the same vision."

Julie let the 'same vision' remark slip by. The fact the stepson was going to try to overturn Connie's generous gift of the land to the pueblo negated that. "Instead of flowers there will be a list of charities. Which reminds me, I need to work on an obit. I'll include the list there and make sure

I send you a copy. If you think of anything Connie would have liked me to say, let me know."

After an exchange of "I miss you," Julie hung up. It could have been worse. She'd had yelling matches with her mother over Ben. Would Bev ever change her mind and let the situation alone? Julie wasn't counting on it.

Chapter Sixteen

She checked into the Doubletree downtown, carried clothes up to her room, put the platinum jewelry into the hotel safe, grabbed a bite of breakfast, and headed up Central to Kinko's. The store was almost empty. She chose a machine toward the back beside a table and dumped the envelopes. She was going to copy everything. She wasn't sure why she would need to but she, also, couldn't find a good reason not to. Just in case.

The copier proved to be cranky and it took much longer than she'd anticipated. It was well after eleven when she'd sorted and stapled and put everything back in the trunk. She wasn't reading anything now—time for that later. She couldn't forget to call a rental agency that afternoon and get a car for the next morning. She could probably just leave the BMW at the office after her meeting with Byron.

Ben could pick her up.

She was back in the car heading downtown when it hit her—she'd left Ben's Storyteller clay figure on the mantle in the bedroom. How stupid! If she didn't go back now, it might be a problem to get it after the house had been turned back to family. There would be too much explaining to do. Byron would suspect them of lifting it from Connie's collection.

It took an hour from the center of downtown to get to the estate. But once again Julie was struck by the sheer beauty of the foothills setting. Most trees had lost their color as well as most of their leaves but there were still patches of bright, golden grasses with tasseled heads being stripped of their bounty by flocks of small finches. Idyllic. The beauty, the calm, the space—not another house in sight—only nature and the quiet opulence of Connie's gardens.

She pulled up in front and left the keys in the ignition. This wasn't going to take long. Oh, good grief. The front door was unlocked. Hadn't she set the alarm and pulled the door shut after her? Maybe Byron had run by to check on things—on her; he'd have keys, no doubt. Oh well, she'd check the bedroom door off their room and be more careful this time.

She borrowed a pillow case and surrounded the Storyteller with small throw pillows from the couch. Safe. Perfectly buffeted by cotton batting. She'd return these to the office tomorrow, too. One more look around and then out to the car to secure the figure in the trunk. She walked back to the front door, stepped inside and squarely faced the alarm panel. This time she'd make certain everything was secure.

The jangle of the hallway phone made her jump. The sound was magnified by the emptiness of massive silence. No radios, no TVs, no people talking. She really didn't want to interact with Cherie or Jonathan but probably should. She grabbed the receiver on the fourth ring.

"Oh, thank God I've reached you."

"Dr. Bancroft?"

"Yes, we've just started the autopsy. I don't know how to say this other than just come right out—Connie was murdered. Her death had nothing to do with her medical condition—other than she gave her assailant an easy target."

"Murdered?" Julie felt a slight tremor in her left hand. She swallowed and reached up to steady the phone with her right. But nothing could stop the finger of ice that shivered up her spine. Murder. By someone who knew they were killing the dying? Or didn't have a clue?

"We started to undress her and noticed the stiff collar was covering up evidence of strangulation. Obviously, easy to miss the bruising in that getup. I'll be notifying the police."

"Speak with a Lieutenant Mark Samuels. He's familiar with the situation here."

"All right. And just a word to the wise, I don't think you should stay out there, not alone. Rosa isn't staying the night yet, is she? I'd been yammering at Connie about having someone be there twenty-four-seven."

"No, the quarters aren't ready. And I've already moved out. Just back to pick up a couple things."

"Great. Well, take care. Is there another number where I can reach you if I need to?"

Julie recited her cell number, thanked the doctor

profusely for the warning and hung up. Her legs felt wooden. The shock, no doubt.

Murder. Not Connie. How terrible. Hanging onto life, trying to prolong it only to have it taken by someone. Murder.

It kept repeating, round and round in her head. Connie's murder coupled with the letter-bomb murder … what was going on? She needed to let Ben know where she'd be and share this latest. She didn't expect him to answer but left a message. She knew he'd overreact to the word 'murder' so she just said there were some new developments— information turned up by the autopsy. Give her a call. She'd have her cell handy.

What happened next would haunt her. She'd just placed the receiver back in its cradle when her eye caught movement to her left, from the hallway leading to Connie's bedroom and the living room. She remembered letting out a startled cry and turning toward the figure. It was standing in the shadow of an enormous potted Madagascar palm.

"Get out. Now. Run for your life." The figure leaned forward, familiar. The voice was one she knew, hushed, a forced stage whisper, barely hissing a warning before opening a sliding glass door to the amphitheater beyond the living room and gliding through. She watched as the figure disappeared down the rough hewn stone steps.

Then she bolted, didn't wait, didn't lock the front door behind her but simply ran, jumped in the BMW, turned the key, gunned the sedan up the drive. She felt the power of the explosion even before she saw it in the rearview mirror. Saw the flames billowing upward, followed by numerous secondary explosions and new bursts of fire and smoke coming from different parts of the structure. The house was imploding. She slowed to a stop and watched in horror as priceless art, jewelry, furniture, cars—all turned to cinders.

She pulled her cell out of her pocket and dialed 911 but quickly dropped the phone when she saw the Hummer coming up fast behind her. Where had it been? Her car had been the only one in the drive. She accelerated then barely braked for the turn onto the county road. The Hummer was gaining. The rough, washboard surface made handling even a Beemer difficult at this speed. The first bump jarred her and sent the sedan into a skid. She corrected, kept it on the road but wasn't prepared for the force of the second slam to her bumper. The Hummer rammed her, pushing her forward and over. The BMW left the road and slid down the embankment on its side, tearing out all the scrub oak in its path. The windshield shattered and branches thrust their way inside.

A culvert, anchored by concrete, halted her forward motion so abruptly she struck her head on the dash and was tossed backward to land on the floorboards, partly under the steering wheel. She was aware of her own labored breath but couldn't seem to open her eyes or move her arms and legs. She heard a car door slam, some cursing, more door slamming, and a vehicle accelerating away from her. Then darkness.

Chapter Seventeen

Ben finally stopped pacing and sat on the couch in the waiting room. There was nothing he could do. Nothing he could have done. Hadn't the doctors told him enough times? It wasn't his fault. But if he'd picked up the message sooner, read between the lines, stayed in Albuquerque in the first place—

Eight p.m. and UNM Hospital's ICU was dark. No bustle of visiting hours, no TV blaring from the lounge. Ben stretched out his legs and leaned against the sofa's padded back. He still couldn't believe it. The car accident, the fire. Julie in a coma. He couldn't shake a feeling of numbness, impotence—he wasn't good at sitting and waiting. He looked up as a neatly groomed man approached—pleated khakis, flawlessly pressed button-down blue-checked shirt. Law enforcement. They didn't have to be in uniform to tell.

"Ben Pecos? Lieutenant Mark Samuels, APD." The men shook hands and Lieutenant Samuels pulled up a chair and sat down. "Any change?"

Ben shook his head, "Head injuries are tricky. Too often it's just wait and see. The next forty-eight hours are critical."

"I wanted to say how sorry I am. I keep thinking there might have been something I should have done differently."

"Me, too—speaking for myself, that is." Ben smiled ruefully. "But hindsight is always twenty-twenty."

"Yeah. Sure puts her in the middle of a bad situation. Obviously, we need to talk with her. I think she'll be able to help us with this one." Samuels stood. "I have a box of stuff in the cruiser downstairs. I kept her purse when the ambulance brought her in. Too often things walk away—more like get misplaced. Didn't want that to happen."

He paused. "Took the liberty of opening the trunk before we impounded the BMW. A piece of Indian pottery and some documents from Ms. CdeBaca. She'd taken the time to make copies; I'll leave those with you, but I'm going to help myself to the originals. A murder case always gives me a little legal latitude."

"A murder case?"

"Ms. CdeBaca. You probably don't know but your hostess was strangled. I just picked up a copy of the autopsy. Dr. Bancroft appears to be the last person who spoke with Ms. Conlin. Said she told Julie to get out—didn't have a good feel about her staying in the house."

"Murdered? Are you certain?"

"According to Dr. Bancroft."

"So, Julie was reacting to the doctor's suggestion to leave? The doctor felt Julie might be in danger?"

"It would seem so. She told the doc that she'd already moved, had just come back to pick up some things. Bad timing."

"Julie was maybe a minute away from being killed?"

"I think we can say it's a given. The force of the explosion coming from the center of the house obliterated the entire front. Scattered some pretty impressive pieces of timber and mortar a hundred feet from the door. Luckily, Ms. Conlin was already in the car and on her way out or there wouldn't have been a car to get into."

"Hell of an explosion."

"Understatement. We don't see explosives much, not in this community—a little too sophisticated for the sticks, I guess. And it takes someone who knows what he's doing. It's strange to see two incidents in a week—and, probably related. We'll know more when the lab gets through."

He paused as though he was carefully choosing his words, Ben thought. Then continued, "I realize you'd just borrowed the car and the BMW's pretty beat up, but do you know of any damage—dents or scrapes—before you and Ms. Conlin started using it?"

"Nothing that stands out. I suppose there were some door dings, that sort of thing. It's a couple years old. I think it was Connie's personal car, but she preferred the Land Rover." Ben stopped. Oh my God, he knew what the Lieutenant was getting at.

"What are you saying? Someone deliberately ran Julie off the road?" Ben was standing now. Had there been an attempt on Julie's life, in addition to the explosion?

An intake of breath, a quick exhale. "I won't lie. That's my guess. There was evidence of contact along the back bumper and a crease on the driver's side that wasn't consistent with damage caused by leaving the road. And we have the recording of what took place just after she dialed 911. The sounds suggest her car was being struck repeatedly from behind and the side. Complete with someone checking on her before driving away. Checking but not helping her, I might add."

"I can't believe this. I can't think of anything she might have known that would put her life in danger."

"Maybe she saw the killer or the bomber. They could be the same person. I'm assuming the bombing was to destroy evidence. Something to do with Ms. CdeBaca's death—or it could be something else—we don't know. At this point we don't even know how the bomb was rigged. But Ms. Conlin knows something. We just need her to tell us. I have, by the way, assigned a twenty-four hour guard."

"You think someone may attempt—" Ben couldn't finish the sentence. On what was probably a really tight budget, posting uniforms could be costly. Lieutenant Samuels must be pretty certain Julie was in danger.

"We're back to hindsight again. I'd like to think this is just a precaution. Until we know something, I don't want to take chances. Do you have a place to stay?"

"Julie had checked us into the Doubletree downtown."

"Great. Close by." He pulled out a notebook and wrote it down. "Best number to reach you?"

Ben gave his cell number, hesitated and then gave Julie's, too. He had to think she'd be fine—maybe by tomorrow morning … Normalcy seemed light years away but he had to assume; life had to go on. He couldn't face thinking otherwise.

"Thanks. You want to put that box of stuff in your car or should I bring it up?"

"I'll follow you down."

Lieutenant Samuels pulled his car around and parked next to Ben's pickup. The box wasn't heavy, just awkward. Ben smiled when he saw the wrapping around the Storyteller. He pulled her out of the pillowcase. She wouldn't have withstood the explosion but a less challenging situation like going off the road, and she came through like a champ.

"These are mostly legal papers. I've only taken a quick look-through. And here's a copy of Ms. CdeBaca's note—instructions for burial, that sort of thing. Mention of her son and what she's left him. Her last will seems to have been drawn up recently—by a Denver firm. I'll give them a call. They may want to send a representative down to deal with the family. I understand there are some surprises." He scooted the box onto the pickup's passenger side seat, "Well, guess that does it. I'll be thinking of you. Give me a call if you need anything."

Ben thanked him, watched him pull out and head downtown. The chill in the night air was invigorating but too cold to stand outside for long. He opened the cab and climbed inside. He'd have to admit to being just a little curious about Connie's will. He switched on the interior light and pulled the box toward him.

Chapter Eighteen

A handwritten note had been stapled to the first page of the will. Ben leaned to the left so as not to block the overhead interior light. He noticed the will's date was just three days ago. A fax number had been penciled in the margin next to the name, Arnold Baxter, Attorney, and then in parentheses, Baxter, Butterfield and Morgan, Denver. Interesting that she didn't use, or maybe didn't trust, Wayne. Ben gave in to a smirk before giving his attention to Connie's note.

As directed, I am putting into writing the request I made by phone this morning. I want the entire ten acres which comprises Enchantment Realty to be deeded fully to the Sandia Pueblo. Contact person should be Governor Stuart Paisano. The legal description of the parcel is part of the packet I sent earlier which included the original deed. This land, including my home, the partly completed house and the one just beginning construction will be under the jurisdiction of the Pueblo. All monies including down payments and building costs incurred on the properties under construction will be refunded to the owners by my estate. The estate will not be responsible for any law suits brought by said owners. The risks were spelled out in their contracts.

The pueblo is at will to do with the land as they see fit. I would ask, however, that my home become a museum of pueblo artwork and artifacts. Any admission fees to go to a fund supporting and preserving the museum. Let me reiterate. Under no circumstances should any part of this land be administered to or claimed for any purpose by the CdeBaca children or by my own son. The pueblo is to have sole ownership.

I know the fact of my having a son will come as a shock to friends and members of the CdeBaca family. Not even my closest friends knew and certainly not my husband. My son was conceived out of frustration and disappointment with a twenty year marriage to a man of little emotion. I've included particulars in the attached document.

Ben paused and located three single sheets fastened to the last page of the will. Lieutenant Samuels must be a little obsessive, he'd duplicated not only the print but how the pages related to one another. Ben folded back the pages of the will and smoothed the three typewritten pages of information. The first sheet, some foreign official document attested to the fact that the young man was born March 15, exactly twenty years ago in Barcelona, Spain. Birth mother was one Constance Bigrope. The father was listed as J. R. Mondragon, but there was no address, nor was there any name given to the baby. Odd. But the third sheet explained it—a United States birth certificate issued by the U.S. Armed Services for the adoption of a male child by Colonel and Mrs. Frank Merritt. An address in Barcelona, an Air Force base, was given with a permanent address in Kansas. On this document, the baby was given a name: Robert Emmett Merritt.

"Emmett! Yes!" Ben put down the paper. He felt a rush of excitement and gave the steering wheel a couple firm whacks with the palms of his hands. He'd seen this name before—on medical records and knew without a doubt he'd met Connie's son—worked with him. It explained why suddenly this young man showed up on the doorstep of Indian Health Services in New Mexico. And maybe explained why he so instantly liked the young man, wanted to help him. Hindsight was always foolproof, but there was a resemblance—more than just in looks.

Ben's thoughts came in a random jumble. Emmett's desire for sex change surgery—was that for real? Probably another long story. And where was Emmett now? With Connie's death—how much did he know about her illness? Could that be why he was in Albuquerque? But Connie had been murdered. Where did that put Emmett? Did he know she was gone? How could he? Wasn't he going home to Oklahoma? No, it must have been Kansas. Too many questions. He wished Julie was with him and couldn't wait to share the news.

He'd read enough for the time being. But just as he folded the papers, he saw his name—he and Julie had been named as co-executors of Connie's estate. Oh my God.

Wayne might not ever recover. Actually, Ben caught himself smiling. It made sense. She would need someone who sympathized with her position on the ten acres and would push to see her wishes honored. That certainly wouldn't be anyone in the office. With help from the

Denver firm, he was sure the two of them could muddle through.

He checked his watch; he needed to get back upstairs. Another half hour with Julie and then he'd go back to the hotel and crash. The hospital staff had his cell number. He could get back to the hospital in five minutes if there was a change. And he needed to put these papers in the hotel's safe. He slipped everything back in its original envelope, wedged it under the seat, and locked the truck. Safe at least for now.

A nurse was coming out of Julie's room when he got off the elevator. He watched as she said something to the cop sitting outside the door.

"Any change?"

She shook her head and continued to the nurse's station three doors from Julie's. Ben also nodded to the cop then pushed Julie's door open. The light was low—more a glow from monitors than actual wattage, but he thought she looked better. He didn't really think he could explain 'better,' maybe it was her color. Her eyes were closed and her breathing, assisted by a machine, was regular. The pallor of earlier in the afternoon was gone—no stark freckles against bleached white skin. There was a distinct rose-tan tint to her cheeks and forehead. Even her hand was warm. That had to be good. Certainly attested to improved circulation. And the doctors had been guardedly optimistic; had shared with him that best-case scenario would put her regaining consciousness within twenty-four hours. Best case ... he hadn't even broached worst case. He wouldn't allow himself to think that way.

He sank down into the chair closest to the bed. Suddenly, he was tired. Beat. From driving, from worry, and now from excitement. He knew Julie would be floored. Em … or Emmett, Connie's child. What an unusual twist. He reached in his pocket and brought out Julie's engagement ring. The nurse had given it to him for safe keeping. Thoughtful. He couldn't look at it without seeing the mesa top outside the Hawikuh reservation in the late afternoon sun—the place where he'd proposed. And had been so afraid he'd hear 'no.' Had he been surprised when she said yes? Shocked, even. He hadn't dared to hope.

He'd chosen a wide gold band and asked the jeweler to superimpose a narrow band of inlay—polished slivers of turquoise, coral, obsidian, shell and pipestone with a raised half-carat diamond in the center. All the colors of New Mexico—in fact, that's the first thing she'd said, 'it looks like out here.' He wanted them to stay in New Mexico, but she'd always have a remnant of the land he loved so much on her finger, no matter where they ended up. Once IHS was repaid for his schooling, they were free to go anywhere. He shied away from saying he'd live in New York, but he probably would go anywhere if it meant seeing her happy.

But that was only a part of what he remembered about that afternoon, now over a year ago. He thought of her nakedness, her warmth pressed against him. The granite overhang, a view of the valley below. The wind whistling notes that could have come from the flutes of the ancient ones. And sex. Sweet. Slow. Whispered promises until the heat of the moment turned blindingly red hot. Then it was all hunger, a slippery fever-pitch to satiation, breath coming in gasps, Julie with legs around his waist, finally both of them slipping to the sand, holding, kissing, stroking, saying 'I love you' and 'I'll never leave you' in a wash of emotion and spent energy.

Ben reached out and took Julie's hand. "I love you. Come back to me." He thought he saw a quiver of an eyelid. He stood and leaned over, then mischievously whispered, "Besides, I have some news you won't want to miss. Connie's son—"

The door behind him flew open—a challenge for a hospital door on pneumatic hinges.

"How unthinking … uncaring. My baby is dying and you didn't even have the courtesy to call, let us know." Bev Conlin, one crutch firmly tucked under her right armpit, hopped into the room.

"I think dying is an overstatement. Hello, Roger, Wayne." Ben let go of Julie's hand and faced the visitors. "Julie has a head injury. A massive concussion, if you will. It's a matter of waiting for the swelling to abate." Ben kept his voice down and hoped Bev would do the same.

"We would have appreciated a little heads-up on this," Wayne hissed under his breath, stepping forward. "I understand Julie almost died in the explosion."

Ben didn't correct him and silently noted it probably ruled out Wayne as the one who forced Julie off the road.

"We were called by a police officer. Not her so-called fiancé—an almost-member of the family." Bev sank into the Naugahyde chair Ben had just vacated. "Is this an example of the manners you learned on the reservation?"

"Bev, please. I warned you about *your* manners." Roger looked apologetically at Ben. "She's upset. Ignore what she said."

Ben always wondered how such a mild-mannered, slightly built man could be married to Julie's mother, a too-tanned woman with too-bright red hair and far too much makeup. Of course, Roger traveled a lot, maybe that explained it. Ben always called her 'the Harpy' but always to himself, never in front of Julie.

"Sorry, Roger, I'm going to side with Bev on this. I think Ben owes us an apology." Wayne looked smug. "I've seen mister macho Indian man in action and, quite frankly, he takes care of *numero uno* first."

What did *that* mean? Ben just shook his head. "I got into town an hour ago and am running on adrenalin. It's been a tiring day. If you'll excuse me, I'll be back in the morning."

"Who's Julie's doctor? Can we contact him? What's the prognosis? Has a specialist been called in?" Bev wasn't keeping her voice down.

"That's enough. I can hear you down the hall. Ms. Conlin does not need a crowd. If you are family, you may visit, one at a time. The rest of you, out. There's a lounge around the corner to your left." The nurse stood in the open door, arms crossed. "I mean it. *Now.*" The cop on duty stood at her elbow.

"I'm her mother—"

"Then you can be the first one to visit. Ten minutes and no more. It's late."

As Ben walked past, she lowered her voice, "I'll call if there's a change."

"Thanks."

Ben nodded to Roger and continued out the door. How upsetting. If those in a coma could hear, know what was going on around them, this little show of familial love could slow down recovery. Obviously, the fiancé's rights had been trumped by Mom, but he was leaving anyway. There was no way he was staying with the others there. What rankled was Wayne's presence. Once again, Ben felt the elation of knowing that, not only did Connie *not* call upon Wayne to draw up her last will, she hadn't even named him executor of the estate. Take that, mister macho attorney man. Ben gave a chuckle.

Chapter Nineteen

Ben watched the night desk clerk put the envelope of Connie's papers in the safe behind the counter, along with Julie's engagement ring. There would be plenty of time to go through the legalese later, with Julie. Right now, he was a zombie. But nothing a good night's rest wouldn't cure. Their room was on the second floor and the last thing Ben remembered was sitting on the edge of the bed to take off his boots. He didn't even remember getting off the elevator. When the phone rang, he was still fully dressed, minus one boot.

"Yes?"

"Dr. Pecos. Sally Ornsby, ICU nurse. Ms. Conlin is awake and asking for you."

"I'll be there in five minutes."

Five-thirty a.m. Had he really slept for six hours? It

didn't feel like it. He exchanged a much wrinkled cotton dress shirt for a black pullover sweater, found underwear, clean socks, jeans, jumped in and out of the shower in record time and was out the door. He retrieved one engagement ring and one stack of papers from the hotel safe before heading for his vehicle.

He hadn't parked the truck under a light and now wished he had. Julie would have insisted on it. The passenger-side window sparkled in a thousand scattered pieces on the sidewalk and curb. The hotel was in the heart of downtown. A random act? He was vaguely surprised that the hotel didn't have monitored surveillance equipment, but he hadn't seen any guards walking around.

He pulled open the driver's side door. Someone had littered the floorboards with everything from the glove compartment, under the seats, and the side pockets on the door panels. What a mess. Didn't look like anything was taken. Even his CD collection hanging behind the visor was intact—as was the player in the dash. No, there seemed to be something else that had prompted this break-in, but for the life of him, he didn't know what he had that was of value. And who would have thought he did? He didn't have time now to either report it or worry about it.

+ + +

Ms. Ornsby met him at the nurse's station. "I don't know how to reach the parents but thought you might want some time by yourself anyway." She smiled. "In-laws, never easy."

"Thanks. That was really thoughtful. How is she?"

"Of course, I don't know Julie but I'd say she's well

on her way back to us. Said she was hungry. I always think that's a good sign. All vitals are strong." She patted Ben's arm. "I just know this is going to have a happy ending."

"I think you're right." He smiled, acknowledged the double thumbs-up from the cop by the door, and entered Julie's room.

"Ben, listen to me. Connie isn't dead. I saw her. She warned me to get out of the house right before the explosion."

"Whoa. Julie, easy … you hit your head …"

"I know what happened. I went back to the house because I'd forgotten the Storyteller. Then Connie's doctor called—did you know Connie was murdered? And then the house blew up." Julie had propped a pillow behind her head and was leaning on an elbow. Typical. Ben couldn't help but smile. In a coma or charging along at a hundred-ten miles an hour, he knew he liked this better—even if he sometimes had to run to keep up.

"Yes, to all of the above. But could I interject that I love you? I was scared out of my mind." He put the folders on the edge of the bed then sat down and put his arms around her. "I never want to lose you. This was way too close." He kissed her forehead, tilted her chin up, tenderly kissed her on the tip of her nose, her mouth, then held her. "I don't want to be without you … ever."

Her arms went around his neck and he buried his face in tousled red curls and heard her say the words that almost made his heart stop. "I love you so much. I had to come back to you."

"As to Connie helping you—"

The door opened and the white lab coat announced a doctor before any introductions were made. "Well, Ms.

Conlin, looks like you're on the mend. Nurse Ornsby caught me before rounds. Bruce Barker, here." He moved to shake hands with Ben. "Let me do a quick exam and go over some things … husband, I'm assuming?"

"Almost." Julie held up her left hand and noticed her bare finger. "Oh, no."

"Oops—I almost forgot. Nurse Ornsby thought it might be better off in the hotel safe overnight." Ben pulled the ring from his pocket and slipped it on Julie's finger. "That's better."

"We'll get you moved out of ICU right after breakfast. Three or four days of observation and if things continue at the present rate, you're out of here by the end of the week."

"Way too long. I have too much to do. Give me something for this headache and I'll be fine." Ben was amazed at how good she did look. And patience wasn't a long suit.

"I'm leaving a script for 800 mg Motrin every seven hours in your chart. But I can't dismiss you. There's some question about your safety, let alone your health." Dr. Barker inclined his head toward the guard at the door.

"I'm more of a sitting duck here than at the hotel. I could always walk out AMA."

"Against Medical Advice? I certainly wouldn't suggest it. Insurance companies take a dim view of that action." Clearly, Dr. Barker was becoming perturbed.

"Give us a few minutes to talk." Ben took Julie's hand. "I'm sure something can be worked out."

"I'm sending in the lab team for an update—a round of tests. We'll know more then. But no more wild talk about leaving until we know what we're up against." Dr.

Barker scribbled on the chart and left—seemed relieved to be leaving, Ben thought.

"Not trying out for patient of the year?' Ben couldn't stop a grin from spreading across his face. Julie had never been known for being easy if her opinion differed from others. "A concussion is nothing to mess with. Get through today, find out what the test results say, rest this evening and then if you're still determined and nothing's changed, we'll shoot for release by noon tomorrow. Okay?"

"Okay."

Ben was surprised at the easy victory but knew better than to question it. "We've got a lot of paperwork to go over and we might as well do it here. Bet you didn't know that we're executors of Connie's estate."

"I saw it but couldn't believe it. What happened to Wayne? Or Byron?"

"Don't know. I think Connie chose people she knew would be sympathetic to her wishes. And that wouldn't be your pal or 'the children'."

"I remember the will was new—some firm in Denver drew it up, right?"

"Yeah, and that alone is a slap to Wayne. I'm wondering how much Byron and the rest know about this turn of events."

"We were supposed to meet at the office around noon. Want to go in my place?"

"I suppose I should. I'd like to go through the papers before I enter the lion's den. You eat breakfast, get the tests out of the way and then we'll have an hour or two before I need to meet the ... family. I almost said, enemy."

"I think enemy is closer to the truth."

"Oh yeah, I almost forgot. Want a real teaser?"

"Such as?"

"What would you say if I told you I was ninety-nine percent certain that Em is Connie's son?"

"You're not kidding, are you? You know what? I think you're right." Julie sat up, winced, and leaned back again. "Ben, it must have been Em that I saw. Em in Connie's clothing. He was the one who warned me, told me to get out of the house. But what was he doing there right before the explosion?"

"Good question."

"Just looking at the big picture—God, I hate that term—we're dealing with the death of the caretaker by letter bomb, complete with Connie's fingerprints, Connie's own murder by strangulation, and the leveling of her house." Julie sat up—this time without flinching.

Nothing like a new challenge to bring her around, Ben thought and had to smile.

"What's funny?"

"Nothing's funny. I was just thinking how well you respond to a little mystery." He reached over, pulled her to him and kissed her, but she immediately pulled back.

"Ben, I've been thinking. I don't want to tell the police that I think I saw Em. I can't do that."

"I know, and I don't know what to say. I thought he'd taken off last week. He told me he was going back to Kansas—or home." Ben sat down on the foot of the bed. "Julie, exactly what do you remember about the person who warned you? Like what was she or he wearing? Was she wearing a scarf or a hat or sunglasses—?"

"Sunglasses! Big, sort of wrap-around dark ones. Come to think of it, I'd never seen Connie with a pair like that."

"Hair?"

"Drawn back, dark, maybe in a bun."

"Do you recall the clothing?"

"That's why I thought it was Connie. Remember the outfit Connie wore at dinner—wine velvet pants, cropped just above the ankle? And a big satin shirt in a slightly lighter shade?"

Ben nodded. He did remember. Noticing clothing wasn't his thing but that night, the contrast between his hostess and the woman he loved was stark—the light and the dark, both breathtakingly beautiful.

"Well, that's what the person had on."

"This isn't my category of expertise but isn't that more of an evening outfit?"

"Exactly. But it doesn't rule out Em. And I think the person was barefoot. I know I didn't hear anything until I saw movement—a shadow off to my left. Unless the person wore rubber-soled shoes or was barefooted, those tiles would echo every step."

"Did you recognize the voice? Could you swear it was like Connie's? At least, a good imitation?"

"That's just it. The voice was familiar. But it was hushed, a whisper really. I couldn't swear to anything— only that I'd heard it before."

"Not much to go on."

"Wait. I remember something else. The squash blossom necklace—a huge one."

"The person was wearing a necklace?"

"Yes. Small stones—maybe petit point—but a deep blue, in huge silver castings."

"Had you ever seen Connie wear it?"

"No. But she had a vast collection of jewelry. It seemed old, like something she would own. A collector's item."

"I think we have to tell Lieutenant Samuels. Just what you're relaying now, nothing more."

"You don't think I need to mention Em?"

"Let's not for now. I'd like to try and find him. As an executor, that sort of falls under my duty." But smacks of withholding information—no, not information, speculation. There wasn't a law for withholding that.

"Ben, if Em knew he was her son, he'd know he would inherit at her death. The police might make a case for him being her murderer."

"But she was already dying. It was only a matter of time."

"*If* he knew that …"

"I think he showed up in New Mexico because of Connie—either she contacted him or he was on a parental search of his own."

"The timing is just too coincidental for the search to have been solely his."

"I agree. Let's take a look at what Connie left us. Maybe there'll be answers. I'm not sure what this is but I threw it in." Ben held out the black address book. "It's seen better days."

"The morning Connie died, I found it in her bedroom—in the fireplace. It looked like she'd burned some documents and this was spared." Julie leafed through a few pages. "Looks like an ordinary address book to me."

"In Connie's handwriting?"

"Wow. I wasn't thinking. No, it's not. This isn't her writing. Strokes are too broad, heavy, much too masculine. She had a curvy—almost spidery, sprawling hand."

"Skip's, maybe?"

"I wouldn't know, but it would be easy enough to find

out." Julie thumbed through the book again. "At least, it's alphabetical. Look, under 'C' is Connie's number—home and cell. Not her name, just the number."

"If the book were hers or Skip's, why list her own number? Just for the hell of it, see what's there for 'Rs' or 'Ms'."

"Nothing of interest under R—at least, I don't think so. A lot of this looks like code. Letters, like initials but mostly just phone numbers. Hmmm, there's a penciled note under 'Merritt'—'cl. shrnk for #' and then this number, (620) 845-4343. The number's in ink. Maybe added at a later time."

"Merritt is Em's name. Robert Emmett Merritt."

"Call shrink? Do you think this is the number of the psychiatrist who was treating Em before he came here? Maybe someone got it for Connie—maybe the person who owned this book?"

"Makes sense. I'll see if the area code 620 is Kansas or Oklahoma."

"But whose little black book? And why did Connie have it?"

"I'll give the number a try when I get out of the meeting with Byron. I'd like to think that will give us some answers."

"And you'll come right back here and tell me everything?"

Ben leaned down and kissed her. "I have a feeling my life would be worthless if I didn't."

+ + +

Ben was going to be five minutes late. Traffic, never

a given, had been especially congested, but he doubted anyone would leave before he got there. Lieutenant Samuels had in all likelihood chatted with either Byron or Wayne … or both. With copies of all the papers, he would notify the office—make the documents available. Ben could assume Wayne and the family now knew Julie and Ben were primary players. He took a deep breath. This wasn't going to be pleasant.

Not one CdeBaca family member had called to inquire about Julie. It had been on the news. There was no excuse for knowing … and not responding. These people were so callous. At least Wayne came to the hospital with the Conlins—but there must be a hidden agenda. What was Wayne going to gain by toadying up to Julie's parents?

Ben pulled his truck into the parking lot in front of the office. There were exactly four cars lined up in front of him. Byron, Wayne, Cherie? One appeared to be a rental. Seemed odd. Would Jonathan drive a rental? He wouldn't, as the Jeep that pulled up to his right attested. There was Jonathan in all his scruffy glory. Ben called out a hello as he got out of the truck but was ignored. Jonathan was already heading to the front door.

"I had hoped we'd see Julie here." Byron met Ben in the foyer. "We were all shocked at what happened. Thank God, she was able to escape. Terrible shame about the house."

"Yes, a tremendous loss. Julie was fortunate."

"Will she join us later?"

"No. She's still in the hospital under observation. The concussion is going to keep her grounded for a couple more days."

"Sorry to hear it. Have you met Arnold Baxter?"

Ben shook his head. Why was the name so familiar?—of course, the law firm in Denver. Looked as if they had sent a representative. Byron seemed to be taking it well—only the intermittent twitch along his right cheekbone gave him away.

"Let me present Mr. Baxter, then." Byron stepped to one side and motioned for a short, balding man in an ill-fitting brown leather jacket and jeans to join them. "Ben Pecos, Arnold Baxter."

The handshake was firm even if the man seemed too rumpled to be a professional. Certainly not the same GQ perfection exhibited by Byron and Wayne. Ben had no idea that dress shirts came in chartreuse with a sort of satin finish.

"I've asked to meet with everyone in the boardroom. I'm glad you could join us. My best wishes for Ms. Conlin's quick recovery. This is just all so unfortunate. A truly sad time." Arnold's eyes showed concern and caring.

Acting? Or for real? Ben couldn't tell but felt himself soften toward the man. After all, he represented Connie's interests. Didn't that put him on the right side? Ben knew he'd need all the support he could muster.

Cherie was already at the table along with Jonathan. She seemed intent on reviewing a stack of papers in front of her—scanning one and handing it off to Jonathan before picking up another.

"Well, all principals seem accounted for. We're missing Ms. Conlin, of course, but I will advise her of our discussion." Arnold Baxter pulled several documents from a briefcase behind him. Satchel and jacket matched in color and scruffiness. Ben wondered if the weathered Stetson hanging from a peg by the door was also his.

"Now, I believe all of you know that Ms. CdeBaca named Ben Pecos here and Ms. Conlin as the executors of her estate. I will act as a guide—just to make sure all Ms. CdeBaca's requests are met." Arnold smiled at the group, but any intended warmth or reassurance was lost to the hostility that hung in the air. It was absolutely palpable, Ben thought. But he seemed to be the only one who noticed.

Cherie was withdrawn, and gazed out the window. Her dark hair was mussed—escaping from a wide silver barrette and falling forward across her face. Too bad her line of cosmetics couldn't erase the bags under her eyes. She looked tired.

And Byron? A thin-lipped smile was pasted in place, but his hawk-eyes followed Arnold's every move. Jonathan was no different than ever—grimacing, hostile, chip on the shoulder, distant. What a family. Ben suddenly felt sorry for Connie. He wasn't sure Skip had been the go-between she would have needed.

"Let's start with the land. Each of you has a copy of the deed in the envelopes in front of you. I have contacted Governor Paisano and forwarded a copy to him. The ten acres and attachments now belong to the Sandia Pueblo. I was able to have the deed recorded this morning."

"Can she do this, Wayne?" Byron turned to his counsel.

"Not only can, but did. All papers are in order and the will discussed today is her last will and testament recorded by Arnold's firm in Denver. It replaces the will drawn up at your father's death."

"Can we contest?" Byron seemed to be speaking for his siblings.

"I wouldn't suggest it. Everything's in order. Her life, her money, her decision … I only regret she thought it necessary to hide information from the family, from me."

Arnold paused for other questions, looking from one to the other before continuing. "With the loss of Ms. CdeBaca's home, I have suggested Sandia Pueblo still consider honoring her wish and establish a museum in her honor. Seeing Ms. CdeBaca's Indian heritage and her generous gift, I believe the pueblo will consider it … start with a design agreed upon by the pueblo leaders and incorporate the tribe's needs. The loss of Ms. CdeBaca's collection of pottery and jewelry is a setback, but she kept the more important pieces in a vault off the premises. I believe there will be ample examples for a substantial exhibit."

A look of surprise skipped across Cherie's face and she briefly made eye contact with Byron before asking, "Was any of the collection that was lost in the explosion insured?"

"Not that I know of. It was to be left to her stepchildren. Several of the pieces outside of this grouping were left to her son. But these were in the vault."

"Son." Jonathan spat out the word. "Just who here ever heard of this figment of her imagination? Cherie? Byron?" Both shook their heads. "He doesn't exist. This is some hocus-pocus to steal from us—Dad's rightful heirs."

"I've seen the birth certificate," Ben interjected.

"Just more of her bullshit."

"I don't think so, Jonathan. I'm currently attempting to find this young man," Arnold said. "Military records corroborate Ms. CdeBaca's claim. She gave birth in Spain … Barcelona. I do not believe your father was aware of the pregnancy or birth. It would appear the child was not his."

"Whore."

"There's no call to talk that way. Ms. CdeBaca isn't here to defend herself. It's always easy to pass judgment on a situation we know nothing about." Arnold looked sternly at Jonathan then briefly at the others sitting around the table. "The child was adopted by a husband and wife residing on base in Barcelona. The birth certificate issued by the U.S. is legitimate." Arnold rummaged in his briefcase and then handed a piece of paper to Jonathan.

"So, just what does he get? This bastard son."

"The estate is worth approximately ten million dollars. Five million will be divided among the three of you and five million will go to Ms. CdeBaca's blood offspring."

"And if you're unable to locate this young man?" Byron leaned forward, "What happens to his allotted inheritance then?"

"Of course, he would have to be declared deceased and after the prescribed waiting period, his portion would be reassigned. The three of you would be the recipients."

It didn't exactly put Em in harm's way, but he wasn't in an enviable position either. Declared deceased ... ominous words that didn't give Ben a good feeling. Surely no one in the room, no matter how angry would attempt murder. His gaze strayed to Jonathan. Ugly personality, vindictive, perhaps, but would he ruin his life out of greed? Unlikely. The man was still a professional, an athlete. Angry outbursts seemed the extent of his nastiness. But couldn't someone in this room already be a murderer? Connie's killer? Someone not knowing that she was dying and had engaged a firm in Denver to handle her giving back the ten acres ... Had losing the land been reason enough for murder?

Ben tuned out Arnold's explanation of how the

construction business was structured and who was entitled to what. He'd heard enough and he was feeling the need to find Em—the sooner, the better. Arnold was summing up by saying once again that he would be working closely with Dr. Pecos and Ms. Conlin. He would be staying in Albuquerque until the paperwork was completed. He handed out business cards which included his cell number.

Ben gathered his packet of copies and slipped on his jacket. Funny, in two and a half hours, Wayne had not said one word to him. No apology—but had he really expected one? No love lost. Ben idly wondered if he was still squiring Julie's parents around.

+ + +

"You look great!" And she did, too. Sitting on the edge of the bed eating a bowl of ice cream.

"Mostly because I put on eyebrows. But thank you very much." Julie smiled and tilted her head up for a kiss.

"Hey, chocolate and peanut butter, my fav." Ben licked his upper lip. "You taste yummy." He kissed her again, then picked up the spoon from the tray and took a bite of her ice cream.

"I didn't say you could do that. That's my lunch." She playfully reached for the spoon.

"What'd the docs say? Are they going to turn you loose?" He took another bite of ice cream before relinquishing the spoon.

"They liked your plan. I passed my tests with flying colors."

"Tomorrow at noon? But you're supposed to stay in the hotel room, kick back, watch TV, right?"

"Something like that. I have to come back for more tests on Thursday." The grin said she wasn't taking their suggestions seriously.

"We need to let Lieutenant Samuels know. He thinks security is paramount. Someone tried to …" Ben couldn't bring himself to use the word 'kill.'

"Run me off the road, at least. I can't imagine someone wanting to kill me unless they thought I'd seen something. Maybe the Hummer was the getaway car. I wish I knew the connection between the person who told me to get out, the explosion, and whoever was driving the Hummer."

"You're sure it was a Hummer and it came up behind you in the drive? You hadn't seen the Hummer when you pulled in?"

"The BMW was the only car in the drive. I almost think the Hummer was in one of the garages."

"Didn't Skip have a Hummer? Black, lots of chrome?"

"You know, I think he did. I thought Connie had gotten rid of it. Had only kept the BMW and the Land Rover."

"Might be worth checking on. It should be in a list of assets. I thought I saw one among Connie's papers."

"First, tell me what happened at the meeting. Who was there?"

Ben pulled up a chair and gave her a play-by-play of the entire morning. "I forgot to tell you this morning that someone smashed the passenger's side window on my truck."

"What'd they take?"

"That's just it—nothing—at least, not that I can tell. I think it was random and maybe they were surprised in the act. I need to check with the hotel. I know the Doubletree has security. Maybe their people saw something."

"Are you going to get any work done today?"

"I'd better." Ben grinned. "I've arranged to stay in Albuquerque for a couple weeks—camp out in the basement office. IHS is a little short-handed and Sandy seems glad to have me full-time for awhile. I told him I'd put in a couple hours this afternoon. It'll give me a chance to follow-up on the number in the address book."

"And maybe you could come up with a Lotaburger for dinner?"

+ + +

IHS was literally just a short walk across the parking lot—UNM Hospital was right next door. However irrational, it felt good having Julie nearby. It didn't seem like he was shirking his duty to protect her. He smiled. Now, that was irrational.

In the parking lot, he nodded to a couple docs he knew and hurried up the steps. He'd check his schedule at Gloria's desk, pick up his mail and be ready to give his attention to the search for Em.

"I didn't know whether we'd see you today, so I didn't schedule any appointments. I bet this is a sign that Julie's doing okay?"

"Better than okay. She wants a Lotaburger for dinner."

"That's a good sign. Jell-O gets really old. Keeps me from getting pregnant."

"Jell-O?"

"Um hmm. They make you eat it. Audrey's father smuggled in KFC and look at her now—she plays soccer." Gloria proudly pointed to the picture on her desk. A dark-haired, round-faced girl about ten years old. "See? Corn-on-the-cob, mashed potatoes and gravy—I breast fed and she's strong. The fastest runner on the team. Who knows with Jell-O?" Gloria shrugged and turned back to her computer. Ben guessed that was the end of the conversation. Good to know the evils of Jell-O. He smiled to himself.

He unlocked his office and checked phone messages. Nothing that couldn't wait. He felt an urgency to find Em. Find out, at least, if he went home. And he needed to warn him—no, that was maybe too strong. Ben needed to caution him, tell him what had happened, find out how much he knew about Connie and what, if anything, he knew about his inheritance. If someone had tried to kill Julie, would they hesitate to get rid of a principal player? Someone who was inheriting five million?

A quick check in the phone book revealed the area code 620 applied to western Kansas before turning into 317 about midway through the state. He picked up the phone and dialed the number from the address book.

"Dr. Kaiser's office." A mature sounding woman answered.

Paydirt? Maybe. Ben introduced himself and gave a thirty-second synopsis of why he was calling.

"Just a moment. I believe Dr. Kaiser's between patients. Your name again?"

"Dr. Benson Pecos, Indian Health Services, Albuquerque." A click put him on hold. Not even halfway through Gene Autry singing "Frosty the Snowman"— didn't they wait until after Thanksgiving anymore?—Dr. Kaiser picked up the line.

"Dr. Pecos. Good to finally meet you. Les Kaiser here. I can only hope Robby is well."

"Robby?"

"Oh, sorry, you probably know our young man as Emmett. Emmett Merritt. Is that correct?"

"Yes. I didn't realize he used his first name." Ben was a little put off by the familiarity. The man seemed to know him—expected to meet him. How odd.

A quick laugh. "I can understand the confusion. I'm sure you've found out by now his persona, let alone name, can vary day to day. I realize this must be an emergency of some sort or Sandy wouldn't have shared my number."

"No. I had no idea the two of you had conferred." Ben was feeling a little foolish. It hadn't dawned on him to ask Sandy, his boss, if he knew more about Emmett than what was in his record. Ben had simply assumed he'd been randomly chosen—Ben was the doc with the most free time, wasn't he?

"Sandy and I go way back—in the early days, we were both at Pawnee. I left IHS about ten years ago but have consulted on cases involving Native Americans. When I knew Robby was going to Albuquerque, I called Sandy. He thought you would be perfect—closer in age than the rest of us fogies. I was reluctant to let him loose without knowing he was in good hands."

Ben felt a twinge of guilt. He'd let Robby down. He'd let him slip right through those "good hands." He took a deep breath, "Do you have any idea why I would have found your number in an address book in the possession of Robby's biological mother?"

"I can guess. His mother hired a private-eye to find him. He got my name from the local police chief who conveniently was an old friend. The investigator was aggressive, belligerent. I tried to keep him from contacting

Robby but I'm afraid I failed."

"What's his name?"

"Stan …" Ben heard the rustling of paper. "Here it is, Devon … Stan Devon."

"Do you have a way to contact him?"

"Address and phone. Ready?"

Ben picked up a pen and jotted down the numbers, north valley prefix and a Fourth Street address. Not the most affluent part of town, but it might be a good idea to check in with Mr. Devon.

"You know for certain that he talked to Robby?"

"Yes. That's what was behind his going out your way. Devon told Robby that his mother had hired him to encourage Robby to return to the land of his heritage. I think that's the way he put it. Something romantic sounding which, at the time, had great appeal." There was a pause. "I know I don't have to tell you this; Robby was searching, trying to identify with something—someone. Even I thought becoming a Mescalero Apache, recapturing what had been withheld, might hold answers—help in the gender crisis. An Apache warrior is a pretty strong identifier."

Ben agreed. Somehow he was certain Geronimo hadn't painted his nails. "Did he know his biological mother was dying?"

"Dying? He didn't share that information with me."

"She was in the advanced stages of leukemia."

"I wished I'd known. You use past tense. I'm assuming she's passed?"

"Not under the circumstances I'm describing. She was murdered two days ago."

"Murdered? You're certain someone took her life?"

Ben quickly reiterated the events and the doctor's

conclusion. "It was assumed a suicide at first. She was dressed in a wedding gown—her instructions for burial included this—so, it was easy to think she put on the dress and ended her life. Her hair was done, makeup—it very much appeared well planned."

There was silence on the other end of the line. Then, "Is Robby a suspect?"

"No, of course not. Why do you ask?"

"Because it would be a repeat of something that happened before." There was disappointment, resignation, maybe even sadness in the doctor's voice. "When Robby was sixteen, his adoptive mother was murdered. They had had a tumultuous relationship after his father died when he was eight. His mother was overly protective—the older he got, the more controlling she became. The police were called many times over real or imagined slights to what she saw as her 'duty' as a mother. Throw in religion and the stage was set for rebellion on a grand scale. I was already working with Robby when he came home from school to find his mother dead. A blow to the back of the head, and the murder weapon was never found."

"The shock would have been horrific."

"I don't think he'll ever get past it. Now this."

"But didn't you say this was a repeat of something? So far, the incidents are far different. We don't even know if Robby knows his mother is dead."

"I think he knows. When Robby found his adoptive mother dead, he cleaned up the murder scene, bathed her, fixed her hair and dressed her in her Sunday best. Then he lived with the corpse for eight days."

"And Connie, dressed in her wedding gown—you think Robby did that? Combed and braided her hair?" Ben was beginning to think he was right. "Could something have happened—something that made him angry enough to take her life?"

"Are you asking me if I think Robby is capable of killing?"

"Yes, I guess I am."

"I was one of his biggest supporters. I still believe he did not kill his adoptive mother. But this gives me pause—it's just too coincidental. But what is Robby saying? Is he a suspect? Have the police taken him into custody?"

"That's just it. He's disappeared. He told me two weeks ago that he was going home—to the Midwest—maybe even follow up with his artwork. I don't even know if he ever made contact with Connie. I do know that he's inherited five million dollars and a number of very expensive artifacts."

"Five million. Quite a motive. I'm sure the police will be interested—at least want to talk. To the best of my knowledge, he's not in this area."

"Who knows about the death of his adoptive mother? I mean Robby's part in it—the laying out of the corpse?"

"Stan Devon for one. I'm sure he uncovered Robby's record. His friend with the local police wouldn't have overlooked that. I tried to get it sealed, his being a juvie and all. I'd like to think I understood the gesture, understood where Robby was coming from, and I didn't want it to follow him."

"Sounds like exactly the wrong person to have the info. Mr. Devon appears to be an opportunist of the worst sort."

"Couldn't agree more. I don't trust the man. He'd be the type to try blackmail. Or take payment to set Robby up."

Ben made a note to look up this Stan Devon. As quickly as possible. "I'm not sure you gave me a definitive answer earlier. In your opinion, do you think Robby might have had something to do with Ms. CdeBaca's death?"

The pause was so long, Ben thought for a moment that he'd lost the connection. Then, "I've been thinking of that. Honestly? And I never thought I'd be saying this—I don't know. The stage was set for a repeat—if you can believe he was involved the first time. Abandoned again. Too late to save his biological mother, to spend quality time with her, discover their common roots." Another pause, "How do you know she didn't ask him to help her end things?"

Now it was Ben's turn to pause. Interesting twist. Farfetched? Actually, not really. In fact, it made sense at a certain primal level. And didn't it make sense that Julie had seen Robby? Dressed in Connie's clothing, his hair pulled back, dark glasses … He looked like his mother; his voice would be familiar. But there was something brutal about strangulation—could he have done that? Ben really doubted it.

"I just heard a knock. Must be my three-thirty. Listen, if I can be of any help, please call. And keep me informed. I care about that young man. I hope there's an explanation for what's happened."

After exchanging contact information including cell phone numbers, Ben promised to give Les's best to Sandy and hung up. A lot to think about. But just that much more reason to find Robby, who apparently was still in the area. He'd like to get Sandy's take on all this, and a quick call to Gloria confirmed that Sandy had a break. Second opinions never hurt.

+ + +

Ben had learned that having a chat in his boss's office meant clearing his own chair. The office never changed. Not one of four chairs, presumably for patients and colleagues, was clear. It was sort of a specialized filing system. So, when Ben picked up the two open books and four-inch pile of papers on top of the chair nearest Sandy's desk, he gingerly put everything on the floor. Nothing was disturbed. He'd be able to replace the stack in exactly the same order as when he removed it.

"What's up?" Sandy closed his laptop and sat forward. "I'm assuming Julie's still doing well?"

"Better than well. Can't wait to get out. If you have the time I'd like to run some things by you. Concerning Emmett, alias Robby, Merritt. For starters, I just got off the phone with Les Kaiser. He says, 'Hi'."

"What led you to Les?"

Ben filled him in on the little black book and private investigator.

"When he referred Robby to us, I supported Les in his request to keep his part of Robby's history under wraps," Sandy said. "These cases are sensitive. I don't have to tell you that. Most of the time you feel like you're flying by the seat of your pants. Sometimes you just don't know how things are going to go. I think Les wanted to compare notes—once you'd spent some time with Robby—and not influence you one way or the other. Finding out you were available to take the case put us both at ease. We both felt you would be a terrific role model. Fair and non-judgmental. I hope you don't feel I let you down—needlessly kept you in the dark."

"No, not at all. Thanks for the vote of confidence. But I've lost contact with Robby. I don't feel good about that."

"Didn't he tell you he was going home?"

"Yes, but I have every reason to believe it was a lie or something changed his mind." Ben paused, "Were you familiar with the circumstances surrounding the death of Robby's adoptive mother?"

"More or less. I know he was cleared of any wrongdoing."

Ben quickly shared the circumstances surrounding Connie's death, ending with the fact that she was his biological mother.

"That's an interesting twist. I suppose he stands to inherit a part of the estate?"

"Around five million."

"Making his portion greater than what the senator's natural children will get?"

"Yes. They will divide five million three ways. Which hasn't made him popular. Let alone simply the shock of finding out he exists."

"I can imagine." Sandy absently chewed the end of a pencil. "You think it was Robby who warned Julie right before the explosion? Was dressed as Connie?"

"And, the night before, laid his mother out in her wedding gown. I admit because of his history, it's possible. Guess I'd change that to probable."

"But you don't think he killed her?"

Ben shook his head, "I'm not sure the cops will agree with me."

"Well, at least, the fact that Ms. CdeBaca's death was murder hasn't been leaked to the press ... yet." Sandy opened the *Albuquerque Journal* and turned the front page so Ben could read it.

"Local philanthropist, wife of New Mexico's longest serving senator, dies after short illness." That's as good as anything for now, Ben thought. Probably kept Robby safe. The picture looked recent. "Mind if I take this for Julie?"

"It's yours." Sandy picked up a pencil and absently rolled it between thumb and index finger. "How fragile do you think Robby is? Under the circumstances, after the loss of two mothers? Leaving murder out of the equation, if he did dress Ms. CdeBaca and then dressed like her, we're seeing signs of a possible disturbance."

"I agree." Ben watched Sandy tap the pencil against the desk's edge. Nervous habit. Annoying, but not something Ben wanted to mention.

"The risk of suicide is fifty percent higher in gender-variant children. How old is he now?"

"He'll be twenty-one in March."

"He's a bit past the danger years. Still, without transgender support or counseling … did you know he'd been on hormone blockers throughout most of his adolescence?"

"We hadn't gotten that far. It's not in his records."

"I should have made that info available. What is it about hindsight?" Sandy looked sheepish. "He was on them until just a few months before his sixteenth birthday. For all of the research—about twenty years worth—we still don't know how it affects brain growth. There's some indication there's a delay in emotional maturation."

"I've read the research, but the treatment seems a little extreme. I'm assuming both parents agreed to it?"

"According to Les, the father was fit to be tied—his child dressing in his wife's clothing before kindergarten even. The mother appears to have been the supportive one. Then the father was lost—very traumatically, struggling with cancer over a number of years. To keep from upsetting the father, Robby was forbidden to engage in any transgender behavior in front of his father for over three years. Apparently, his mother condoned the behavior in secret."

"I'm not sure you can just turn that sort of thing on or off at a whim. Masculine in front of father, feminine in front of mother."

"Exactly. He was not quite nine when his father died and more than a little disturbed. I think the mother, unable to face losing anyone else dear to her, sought help and was willing to try anything. The possibility of pre-pubescent suicide was a very real threat."

"But instead, puberty was delayed with hormone blockers?"

"Regulation of gonadotropin-releasing hormone— which puts puberty on hold."

"It couldn't have been legal ten years ago."

"Internationally, the treatment is well known and recommended. If I remember correctly, Ms. Merritt sought treatment outside the States. It seemed to have bought her six years or so of calm."

"And then?"

"Robby chose to end treatments and the onset of puberty was immediate. Complete with the acting out of a normal teen. A normal teenage boy, I might add. Which didn't sit well with Ms. Merritt. As with so many parents of teens, she lost control—"

"A control that had been drug-induced for six-plus years. Was she more upset that he apparently chose the male gender or was just a problem teen? It would be interesting to know what part of Robby's gender conundrum was natural and how much was due to the power of suggestion. Or out and out control."

Sandy paused, "What an interesting question. Funny, it didn't dawn on me when I was reading his records. Les couldn't have said it better; there's a lot to be said for a new set of eyes."

"There's always been something not quite believable about Robby's gender crisis."

"How so?"

"He was always so … not sure how to put this … over the top. And I realize that can sometimes be a part of the profile of transgender behavior but with Robby it was an act. I'm almost sure of it."

"Then why continue the act here? It would seem New Mexico could have offered him a fresh start. Become a part of his tribe, establish roots, learn to know his mother—"

"And maybe that was it. The only mother he'd known had, perhaps, made her love a condition of gender. Could he have thought this mother might also? He's still a teenager with marked chemically induced, arrested, emotional development. We can't rule that out."

"It could play into some deep-seated anger … possibly give a motive for the murder of his adoptive mother. A bizarre type of sexual abuse, perpetuated over several years, only to have the subject retaliate."

Sandy was silent. Then, "He must have jumped at the chance to meet his biological mother, to reconnect with his people, get out of a situation in a small town that must have been intolerable." Sandy sighed. "And then to find out his mother was dying. His life was crumbling. Would he have felt cheated? Abandoned, again? Was this just one more disappointment out of his control? Would the anger make him do something rash—?"

"I need to find him. I don't think he's acting or reacting rationally but I don't want to judge him prematurely. And I don't want him found first by the cops."

"Keep me informed. Let me know if there's anything I can do."

+ + +

Five o'clock. He could just make the six p.m. Jell-O run at University Hospital if he hurried, and still get the truck in for a window replacement. He'd have a rental dropped off at the hotel and catch a ride from the garage. But wasn't he supposed to bring food? Damn. Was this a Lotaburger night? Or Powdrell's Barbeque? He'd gotten so caught up in Robby's history that he'd blanked on supper. No, it was definitely Lotaburger. With fries. And don't forget the ketchup.

He ducked into his office, gave a credit card number and used the "doctor" moniker to have a blue Ford Taurus delivered to the Doubletree—keys left with the concierge. Always nice to have a degree come in handy. He rifled through a stack of files in the first drawer of a gray, prison-issue, file cabinet and pulled out Robby's paperwork. No phone, but a downtown Albuquerque address. He copied the info onto a sticky note and put it in his billfold. He didn't hold out hope that Robby was there—still, a place to start.

He quickly locked up and then delivered the truck to Monty's Glass: Repair or Replace. The shop was on

Lomas just a few blocks from the hospital. Easy for pickup the next day. He made it before they closed and caught a ride downtown with one of Monty's techs. There was the Taurus under the Doubletree's front canopy. He was impressed. He still had time to grab a couple Lotaburgers and get to the hospital, almost on time.

He knew, the minute he walked into her room with the distinctive red and blue sack, the choice had been the right one.

"I was beginning to think I'd goofed in turning down the green stuff," she joked.

"Never give up on me."

He spread out the feast on the ubiquitous wheeled hospital tray and sat on the edge of the bed.

"You just missed Mom and Dad."

"How are they?" He leaned over and kissed her cheek.

"Keeping busy. Helping me with Connie's funeral plans. She left instructions for a reception, a celebration of her life to be held at her home. Obviously out of the question now, but Mom and I thought the Pueblo Indian Cultural Center might be a good choice or somewhere on UNM's campus. What do you think?"

"I like the Cultural Center idea. I would guess a reception would be well-attended. What's the timeframe?"

"Mom and I both feel it's too close to Christmas to do something now; the Center is booked until mid-January. But that might be a good time. Get past the holidays."

"Where will she be buried?"

"Connie requested her body be sent ahead to the Mescalero reservation. The body will be released tomorrow. Gloria helped me contact the right people. But Connie had already written to the tribal leaders of her wishes—

probably accompanied by a handsome gift. I've set up transport and Mom and I will accompany her. The docs here have given me the okay to travel."

"That's probably not a bad plan. You won't have protection, but I'll feel better if you're with a group." Even though the cop was still on duty at the door, Ben had a feeling Julie was no longer the killer or killers' object. If Julie hadn't told Lieutenant Samuels anything in two days that had sent the cops their way—whoever they might be—then her assailants probably figured she didn't know anything. Not knowing was often the best guarantee of safety.

They ate in silence for a few minutes before Julie spoke. "Ben, let's get married. I've had time to do some thinking and Connie's right. There won't ever be a good time. Certainly not according to my mother. We can put it off and put it off and gain nothing. Originally we'd said Christmas. Let's stick with our plan."

"I have approximately a month to get cold feet." Ben grinned. "I like the idea. Might be the right thing to involve your mother in the planning."

"Already thought of that. Give her a chance to redeem herself if she sees it's going to be a done deal."

"Pick a date and I'll make sure we can get the chapel at the Tewa Pueblo."

"Mom can help me with a lot of things … invitations, reception. I think she'll give in to the excitement. Besides, her best friend picked out my dress." She quickly explained her find—the note, the jewelry, and the dress—probably several thousand dollars worth of vintage Chanel. Perfect for a Christmas wedding.

Ben got up and kissed her on the mouth, lingering,

ignoring the overriding taste and smell of ketchup. "I'm going to call it an early night. Seems like I remember both of us being up at the crack of dawn this morning. I'll check with hotel security about my window and then hit the sack. I'll be here for breakfast."

"I don't suppose there's any way you could bring me a burrito from Garcia's?"

Ben laughed, but nodded. He'd do anything for this woman, his almost wife—burrito delivery was the least of it.

Chapter Twenty

Ben slid behind the Taurus's steering wheel. He missed his truck already. He wasn't a family sedan type, but he'd chosen it because of its anonymity. He'd just be another car on the road—hopefully, one that wouldn't draw attention and would be difficult to remember. Just in case he was still of interest to whoever broke into his truck. But before he went to bed, he was going to run by the office of Stan Devon. It was past eight, but if luck was with him maybe the investigator would be working late.

Traffic into Albuquerque's North Valley was sparse. He drove through the edge of downtown, taking Lomas west to Fourth and then heading north. An older part of town and cheap land prices had encouraged the proliferation of junk stores and fast food chains. The fact that Mr. Devon's office was in this neighborhood made prejudgment almost

a given; Ben hadn't needed Les Kaiser's take on the man—
the surroundings said it all.

Ben waited at the light at Griegos and Fourth then
pulled forward on the green and made an immediate left
after the intersection, turning in beside a Lowe's grocery
and a two-story building which had seen better days. He
scanned the directory, a wooden sign board that looked as
old as the building. If 1A was any indication, Mr. Devon's
office would be on the first floor. Ben pulled into the first
available space in front of a hand lettered notice with an
arrow that announced an AA meeting was taking place on
the second floor. Judging by the cars in the parking lot, it
would seem well attended.

And based on the fact that 3A was straight ahead of
him, logic put 1A either to the right or left. Guessing right,
he was surprised to see police tape across the door. Yeah,
this was 1A—and it was absolutely empty. He stepped up
to the plate glass entry and looked inside. An open safe
at the back, a folding chair, metal desk, and that was it.
Obviously, Stan Devon was long gone.

"I swear Mr. Devon is just as popular now as he was
before he disappeared. You another cop?"

Ben turned to see what was probably a custodian/rent-
a-cop combination leaning against the building to his left.
No gun visible, but he did have a nightstick in a leather
carrier strapped to his belt.

"No, not a cop. I'm just looking for Stan Devon." Ben
leaned forward to take another look at the room.

"You and about a dozen others. You a client?"

"Nothing like that. I have a couple questions for Mr.
Devon, that's all."

"Well, he had some pretty hoity-toity clients. You know

that senator's wife? The one that just died? She came here. Lied to me about her name, but she sure was a looker. You think they got her age wrong in the paper?"

"Ms. CdeBaca?"

"Yeah, that's the one, only she said her name was Bev something or other. But it was the same woman—those big dark eyes, hair down to her ass. I'm not going to forget that."

Ben wasn't going to get into a discussion of Connie's beauty. Somehow the man made it seem tawdry.

"Know what happened to Mr. Devon?"

"Wish I did. He skipped out owing rent and never told anyone where he was going. He sure pissed off the landlord."

"I bet. But that doesn't explain the police interest. What do they think he's done?"

"Well, for starters, murder." The man took a conspiratorial step closer and lowered his voice. "The cops were around here matching up fingerprints. Seems he delivered a package to some unsuspecting fool up in the mountains, only it was a bomb. You know, a letter-bomb made to look like a package of money. Guess our man here played a little trick and instead of bills, the package held paper—cut to look like bills. He pocketed the real stuff. Now, get this, some of the papers had his letterhead, guess he thought they'd blow up or burn up once the bomb detonated. But no such luck for Mr. Devon. He led the cops right here to his office. Now that's a reason for cutting out."

"Any idea how much cash Stan was delivering?"

The man cleared his throat and took the time to look to his right and then the left. In even more hushed tones,

"Judging by the couple trashed bills they found, the package was made to look like it held forty-eight more. Least that's what I heard." He straightened up and leaned back against the door frame.

"Fifty thousand." Ben said it more to himself. The package that had Connie's prints on it. She had hired her PI to make a delivery to the caretaker at the old lodge. But, fifty thousand? That was hefty. A payoff? But why to the caretaker? Only to be double-crossed. In all likelihood, Stan knew she was dying. He'd been sent to ferret out her son. Would he have known why? Probably. So, pretty untraceable. Steal from the dying. He'd know that Connie wouldn't be in a position to do anything about it. Especially if it was payoff money. Ben idly wondered where his source got his info but didn't have to wait long.

"My boss wouldn't want me running my mouth like this. Cops even dragged him in to see if there was a connection. Luckily, he's a golfing buddy of the mayor's. They leveled with him pretty quick about what was going on."

Ben thanked him for his time. He hadn't found Stan, but just maybe he'd ended up with some pretty valuable information. Trouble was, he just didn't see how this piece fit into the puzzle.

+ + +

When he pulled into the Doubletree's parking lot, he drove through, turning left onto Tijeras. He parked the Taurus next to a service entrance in a short alley—under a light and directly below a surveillance camera.

"Dr. Pecos? If I could have a minute of your time, thought you might want to see this. I'm Richard Healy,

Chief of Security for the Doubletree." Ben had just walked through the revolving double-door entrance of the hotel.

Ben shook the outstretched hand and followed the man around the front desk. "I was going to stop by before turning in. This probably has to do with the break-in this morning." Ben was carrying his CD collection, ice scraper and a box of Kleenex. No use leaving anything for someone to steal.

"First of all, my apologies. We're usually well staffed, but last night we had one of our guys call in sick. And then there was a trashcan fire on the north side of the building started by a couple transients. By the time we got it quieted down, someone had taken out the window of your truck. We did catch some of it on tape. Don't know how much help it will be; it's hard to tell anything in the shadows. If I could make a suggestion, park under or close to a light from now on. Makes all the difference."

Ben leaned over the monitor as his truck came into view. Grainy black and white film, not helped by the shadow of the building and taken at a distance across the entire parking lot. He really did need to pay attention to where he parked from now on. A figure dressed in hooded sweatshirt and baggy pants leaned against the tailgate. He probably stayed there for five seconds before moving to the passenger side of the truck and ducking down. Another wait and then an upraised dark hand—must be gloved—brought a tire iron down swiftly and with force. Ben's window exploded. The guy was quick, opened the door, rifled the glove box, disappeared from view, presumably while running a hand under the seat. Then, empty-handed, he abruptly closed the door and bolted. It had only taken seconds. Maybe ten.

There was a vehicle at the edge of the frame— "There.

Can you stop the tape? Looks like he's being picked up."

Ben watched as the back and side of a Hummer came into view, slowed and picked up the vandal. The Hummer looked to be black, a solid dark color, anyway, on tape. Could this be a coincidence? Two different black Hummers wreaking havoc on their lives. Ben very much doubted it.

"Could you make a copy of that for me? I'd like to share it with Lieutenant Samuels of APD."

"I'll have it ready for you in the morning."

Ben thanked the man and headed toward the elevators. The message light on the phone beside the bed was blinking. Ben pushed the play button and started to undress.

"Doc, it's Lieutenant Samuels here. We need to get together. What's your time look like in the morning? I'll be in my office." He left a number and hung up. The next message began, "Ben, this is Arnold Baxter. Any possibility we could touch base sometime tomorrow? Use my cell; I'll be running around all day. See you soon."

That was it. The cop and Connie's Denver attorney. The machine whirred and then clicked off after a recording thanked him for using the hotel's services and reminded him the messages would be saved until deleted.

Ben finished brushing his teeth and sank into the bed. He put his cell on the nightstand. Julie would use that number if she needed anything. He propped up a couple pillows behind his head and leaned back. He always liked to run through the cases of the day. When working with patients, many a night's review turned up something he'd missed earlier. But tonight his eyes closed before a rational thought formed.

The cell's shrill ring startled him awake.

"Hello."

"Help me."

Two simple words, but they cut through the sleep-fog like a knife. Ben propped himself on an elbow, tucked the phone under his chin, and checked the time. Green luminescent numbers cast a glow in the room. Two-fifteen. He watched the numeral sixteen pop up.

"Where are you? I'll pick you up."

Silence.

"Emmett—Robby, talk to me. Where are you calling from?"

"How do I know you'll believe me? How do I know you want to help me?"

"Because I say I will."

Something that sounded like a laugh, then, "Someone's trying to kill me. It's dangerous to know me."

"Who?" Ben sat up and cursed the 'unidentified' caller that showed clearly on his phone. He needed to know where Robby was calling from. A number, anything. "Let's talk. I can keep you safe." Stupid thing to promise. The minute it was out of his mouth, Ben wished he could take it back.

"I don't know where to go."

"You called me. You must think I can help."

Ben waited. The silence was so complete that he thought Robby wasn't there.

"Hello?"

"Okay."

"You'll let me help." Ben made it sound like a statement. "I'll pick you up. We'll decide what to do. Tell me where you are."

"About two blocks from you."

"How do you know where I am?"

"I followed you. I saw you leave the hospital."

"Why didn't you just come here?"

"I'm being followed."

"Are you safe now?"

"Maybe."

"Robby, where are you?"

"Meet me in the alley behind the library."

"Main Library? Corner of Fifth and Copper?"

"Yeah."

"I'm in a Blue Taurus, give me five—" The phone went dead.

Ben was getting pretty good at pulling on socks, jeans, boots and turtleneck in record time—maybe not *Guinness Book of World Records* time, but pretty damn fast. He grabbed his jacket, felt the pocket for the Taurus's keys and the room's keycard and was out the door. Was he being watched? Taking the time to get a rental might just be paying off. The last thing he wanted was to lead whomever Robby was afraid of right to him. He punched the elevator's 'down' button and didn't have to wait. He quickly stepped in, a quick jab at L, a muffled whir of machinery, and the obligatory chime announced his arrival at the lobby.

He paused as the elevator doors opened, checked their closing with a hand to the steel casing, and took a quick look around. From his vantage point, the first floor was empty other than a man in hotel livery sitting at the concierge's desk. So far, so good. A hallway leading to the restaurant and kitchen was half a dozen paces to his right. Even though it wasn't quite three, he knew the kitchen, which began room service at five-thirty, would be manned. Or ought to be. He should be able to walk through to the alley without being noticed by more than a couple people.

A bleary-eyed head chef barely acknowledged him as Ben pushed open the back door—about two car spaces to the left of the Taurus. Again, a quick look around didn't turn up anything unusual in the alley, and Ben 'beeped' open the car and got in. He literally was going about five blocks. Not a great distance, but a huge one if he put Robby in danger.

He backed out, pulled forward and stopped at the edge of the drive before turning onto Marquette. There wasn't a car in sight. He leaned against the steering wheel and waited. He wasn't even sure for what. Maybe the truck's being broken into was a random act and no one was watching him. More than one person owned a black Hummer. Yet, the attempt on Julie's life, Robby's running scared—didn't do much to calm his jitters.

The street, shiny from rain, mirrored lights spreading like an oil slick into the darkness. Too chilly already for street people; no one was warming stiff limbs over a steaming grate or slumped drunken in a doorway. The quiet of a downtown asleep was surreal. But all the better, he guessed. He turned left and accelerated.

Ben remembered that the book drop was to the side of the library, on the north, opposite a loading dock for an adjoining business. There was space enough to park three or four cars—spaces reserved for a CEO and other company dignitaries. But, importantly, the area was not a dead end; the alley was a through street connected with Fifth. He could go around to the back, pull in, pick up Robby and continue back to the hotel, because wasn't that what he thought would be the safest? Take him back to his room?

He didn't see Robby immediately. Not until the lanky figure in leather jacket and jeans threw open the car door, tossed a paper bag on the floor, dove onto the back seat and slammed the door shut.

"Did anyone see you turn in here?" Robby stayed stretched out on the floor behind the front seat.

"Not that I know of." Ben pulled forward toward Fifth. He paused and looked up and down the street before pulling out. A vagrant jaywalked in front of the library, pushing a grocery cart spilling over the sides with what looked like blankets. He disappeared up Copper trailing one large plaid blanket wrapped around his shoulders. There were no cars and no other pedestrians.

"Looks clear." Ben turned north, accelerating to catch the green light at Tijeras.

"Where are we going?"

"I thought you'd be safe with me—at the hotel."

Silence, then, "Probably."

"Do you need anything? Need to stop by your apartment?" Ben realized that the address he had in his billfold was a short two blocks from where they were.

"Moved out. The day after they stole my truck. Everything's in here."

Ben assumed that explained the paper bag. He was curious as to where Robby had been staying for the last few days but guessed he'd probably find out in due time. Robby's appearance surprised him—close-cropped hair, long on top, trimmed clean and short at the hairline, still had the mustache, only one earring, left ear, simple silver hoop, small and unobtrusive. Model handsome. Had a corner been turned? A gender choice made? Now was probably not the time to go there.

Catching every light, they made the trip back quickly. A space, three down from the hotel entrance, was empty and Ben pulled in.

"Can we sit here a minute? Then you go in first and I'll give it, maybe five minutes, and follow."

Overly cautious? Ben wasn't certain it wasn't overkill, but it would be easy enough to comply. "Sure. I'll meet you by the elevator—to the left of the reservation desk." Ben counted off another couple minutes before opening his door. "See you inside." He'd kept his head down so someone watching wouldn't catch the movement of his lips. God, the kid had him running spooked now.

Ben pushed the 'up' button the minute he saw Robby hit the revolving front door. "We're on second." Probably a stupid thing to say since Robby had just watched him press two. But there didn't seem to be any conversation forthcoming. Ben found himself glancing at the numbers above the door. When the chime announced two, Robby touched his arm and motioned toward the hall.

"How far down to your room?" The whisper was barely audible.

"Next door, first room on your left."

"Good. You go first. When I hear the door open, I'll be there."

Ben nodded, stepped out of the elevator and moved to his left. There was no one in the hall. Ben inserted the keycard and opened the door.

"This is nice." Robby walked past him to the window that opened onto Second Street. "Could we leave the light off a minute? I'd like to take a look at the parking lot."

"Sure." Ben had been about to switch on a desk lamp, but watched Robby carefully draw back a corner of the drapes and look below.

"Nothing. It's dead out there."

"Who's following you?"

A shrug. "Who knows? Somebody in a black Hummer. Windows are too dark to tell."

Ben sat forward. The ubiquitous Hummer—Julie, his truck, and now Robby. And no one got a license number. Still, it was information for Lieutenant Samuels.

Robby turned and sat down on the bed nearest the window. "This was a good idea."

Again, Ben just nodded and switched on the lamp. He wasn't sure whether Robby was referring to his calling him or Ben's bringing him to his room, but guessed it didn't matter. Robby picked up the copy of the *Journal* Ben had tossed on the bed and folded it to look at the feature article. Ben watched as Robby sat looking at Connie's picture.

"I killed her." Robby's index finger pointed to Connie. He looked up at Ben. "I killed my mother."

Chapter Twenty-one

How did you do that, Robby?" Ben took a deep breath, pulled out the chair behind the desk, sat, and leaned forward.

"She needed a bone marrow transplant. I would have probably been a good match. I don't think she had any other relatives to ask." Robby paused; he was tentatively stroking Connie's picture, index finger tracing the outline of her nose. "She asked me if I'd do it—save her life. And I said I'd let her know." He looked up at Ben, tears spilling over. "I put her off. I was pissed that after all this time she only wanted something from me. But I think maybe she just wanted to be with me—live long enough to try to make things right." Now tears, unchecked, streamed down both cheeks.

"You had no way of knowing how seriously ill she was.

How little time was left."

"But I disappointed her. She put her faith in me. I know that now." He snuffed loudly, reached for a Kleenex and blew his nose. "Do you think she suffered?"

"I don't know." Ben had a decision to make. Unless he was watching Oscar-worthy acting, Robby did not kill Connie. And Ben was going to level with him. Tell him the truth and see what his reaction was. "Robby, when did you last see Connie?"

"Two days ago at her office. It was the first time we met … face to face."

"Had you ever been to her house?"

"Yes, but not really inside. I performed a ceremony for her outside in the garden. And then one night I thought I'd go in. I went around to that door off the driveway, but I ended up in your room. I left right away."

Ben pulled his chair around to face Robby. "Robby, Connie didn't die from her illness. She was murdered."

Black eyes quickly looked squarely into Ben's and held. The paper slipped to the floor. "How do you know? Why would someone …?" His voice trailed off. "But it wasn't reported in the papers."

"It was covered up … literally … and only discovered when an autopsy was performed. Connie had requested that she be dressed in a wedding gown, her hair braided with pearls—"

"And that's how she was found?"

"Yes, with a high-necked dress that covered the marks of strangulation." Ben noted the slight shudder that the word, strangulation, produced before Robby abruptly stood and walked to the window.

"If someone knew my history, they would suspect me."

"No one should know. I know your history only because I've had access to your medical files." A little bit of a lie, but he wasn't going to mention Les's name quite yet. "I would assume those records are sealed because you were a juvenile."

"Stan Devon got them … at least the police records."

"Are you certain?"

"Yeah. He threatened to tell Ms. CdeBaca. I paid him five thousand dollars, but I think he told her anyway."

Slime, Ben thought. He took Robby's money and then double-crossed the caretaker and walked away with almost fifty. And God knew how much Connie had originally paid him.

Neither of them spoke for a few moments, then Robby broke the silence, "Do you think someone is trying to set me up? Make it look like I killed her?"

"I hadn't thought of that." If a person knew the history, it was a perfect setup. A great diversion for the real killer or killers. Ben had wondered about Robby's innocence, had even questioned Les. He could only imagine what a cop would do with the information. But nothing had been reported. Over two days. "You need to be careful. I have an idea how we could keep you safe—send you to the reservation."

"Which one?"

"The one you belong to. Julie and her mother are accompanying Connie's body to the Mescalero Apache reservation in the morning. I'd like you to go with them. I'll make some inquiries, get you a place to stay and maybe some muscle to protect you." Ben thought he had just the contact, a man he'd treated before, an elder of the tribe.

"I'd like to go to the burial."

"I think she'd be pleased that you were there."

"You know, my father is half Mescalero."

"Did she tell you who your father is?"

"Yeah, Jose Rodriguez Mondragon."

"You're kidding. The poet?" When Ben had read the birth certificate, he hadn't connected J.R. Mondragon with the poet. This was great news. What a pedigree!

"I guess. You act like he's someone famous."

"Well, in New Mexico, he is. A combination of Indian and Hispanic heritage, a child prodigy, a professor at UNM by age twenty-five, his poetry celebrated worldwide. But if I remember correctly, he disappeared when he was only thirty."

Robby reiterated Connie's story of a summer in Spain, a love affair between the thirty-year-old and the disconsolate forty-year-old, a pregnancy and a murder. A murder set up by Skip CdeBaca and carried out by his henchman. But with his wife's fingerprints on a gun that gave him control—a lifetime of leverage. Ben was quiet. Murder. It made sense. The henchman had come back to collect. Probably threatened exposure and, under the circumstances, that was the last thing Connie needed. She attempted to buy the murderer's silence. Fifty thousand dollars worth. And then this caretaker or henchman—McNamara—gets blown up by an even greedier villain. What was it his adopted mother used to say? There's no honor among thieves? But didn't Mac get what was coming to him?

Ben kept coming back to Joe Mondragon's son. The name alone would get Robby into circles that would be the envy of most artists. And what a story! Complete with the kind of mystique that would garner a following. "You know, you have relatives from your father's side on the res.

A few years back, I met your grandmother. I would like to involve her. I believe she would be thrilled to know about you."

"Will she believe you?"

Ben chuckled. "She'll only have to look at you. From pictures I've seen, you look very much like your father." A shy smile from Robby, and Ben knew he was doing the right thing. What must it be like to think he was all alone, then discover his birth mother—only to have her die—a grandmother and a tribe who would honor him and would give him roots. Then, with a pang he thought of his own life. How very parallel to Robby's.

"I was adopted. My mother died when I was young and my grandmother thought giving me up would give me a better chance to achieve—I didn't really get to know my grandmother or my people until I was grown."

"Really?" He had Robby's attention.

"Yeah, really. It's difficult for people to understand what it's like being from two worlds." Robby nodded. "It's not easy. I honor my grandmother's decision, but I know now what I've lost." Another nod. "So, tomorrow at this time you'll be a part of the Mescalero Apache. How does that sound?"

A smile and a nod was all Ben needed. He realized how much he wanted Robby's story to have a happy ending. "Good. I suggest we get some sleep—tomorrow's going to come early."

+ + +

At quarter 'til eight Ben left Robby, with a tray loaded with scrambled eggs, pancakes, juice, coffee and slices of sugar-cured ham, to tell Julie of his plan and pick up his truck with new window in place. He wondered why parents of teens and young adults didn't go bankrupt. There was no way he could put away that much food let alone afford to do it on a regular basis.

Ben was anxious to get Julie's reaction to turning Robby over to his grandmother, but first things first. He left the Taurus sitting in Monty's lot on Lomas and called the rental company to retrieve it. Slipping behind the wheel of his truck felt too good. He was glad to get out of the sedan. Five minutes later he was at the hospital.

He knew he could count on Julie's enthusiasm, but he was surprised at how excited Bev was. Robby was going to be among friends. Somehow this piece of Connie in the guise of a son seemed to make accepting her loss a little easier. And he couldn't rule out mothering instincts. Julie had undoubtedly told her mother Robby's story—the loss of both mothers. He sensed that Robby would be taken care of. He called ahead to the IHS clinic in Ruidoso from Julie's room. An explanation to the administrator, a tribal official, and he was assured that Robby would be protected and introduced to his family.

Ben waited until Bev and Julie had been picked up by the limo driver who would follow the hearse. They would swing by the Doubletree, pick up Robby, and be on their way. A call to Robby, who promised to be ready, and Ben could relax. He'd suggested an overnight at the Inn of the Mountain Gods might make the trip less stressful for the two women. He was still a little worried that Julie was trying to do too much, too soon. Typical, but dangerous.

A night at the hotel would mean more rest and Julie could rent a car and drive back at her leisure in the morning.

He thought Bev had liked the idea—because the Inn had a casino? Probably. He remembered she liked the slots. He checked his watch. Nine-ten and he already felt like he'd put in a day's work. But as long as he was downtown, he might as well check in with Lieutenant Samuels.

Parking downtown was never easy so he left his truck at the Doubletree and walked the short two blocks to the station. The November day had turned decidedly chilly with a biting northeast wind. Winter could come early. Ben jogged the last half block before taking the steps up to the double doors two at a time. He made a mental note to dig out his sheepskin jacket.

"Hey, doc, glad you showed up. I was about ready to put out an all-points." Ben smiled but had the distinct feeling Lieutenant Samuels wasn't exactly kidding. "I've got a couple questions and I think you might be the one to answer them."

"I'll give it a try." Ben took the proffered metal chair to the right of the officer's desk. Not comfortable but it wasn't meant to be, he guessed. Lieutenant Samuels was staring—not necessarily unkindly, but not necessarily friendly, either. Ben waited, watching the man steeple, then separate his hands and crack his knuckles. The waiting game—first one to speak would be the loser. But of what? Ben had no clue.

"You're acquainted with the family's counsel, Wayne Stanford?"

"Yes, I've met him."

"Might that be an understatement? I have a copy of a restraining order here in front of me, taken out day before yesterday following what was described as an unprovoked attack on his person."

What a weasel. Ben was furious but kept his cool. "I

defended myself when physically assaulted." Ben leaned back in the chair and met the Lieutenant's stare. "I don't really expect us to be buds—he's my fiancée's former."

"So, according to you, nothing serious. The lawyer started it?"

"Yes."

"Nothing that would have any bearing on Ms. CdeBaca's death?"

"None whatsoever. Wayne made a derogatory remark to Julie, I suggested we step outside, he took a swing, and I defended myself."

Lieutenant Samuels nodded but didn't appear to believe him. "Speaking of Ms. Conlin, Mr. Stanford has postulated that she was the last person to see Ms. CdeBaca alive."

"I suppose we both were."

"According to Mr. Stanford he went to apologize to Ms. CdeBaca for the dinner disruption and heard Ms. Conlin having a heated discussion with the deceased."

"What time was this?"

"Precisely one-forty-five in the a.m." Lieutenant Samuels opened a folder on his desk and appeared to double check the time.

"Impossible. We were asleep. I'd set the alarm for four-thirty so I could get an early start. I was due in Gallup by nine."

"And Ms. Conlin never mentioned her yelling at her hostess—a confrontation which, heard through the door, appeared not only heated, but threatening?"

"No, of course not. It never happened."

"Your word against his. And, might I add, if you were asleep you can't really speak for Ms. Conlin."

"She would have told me."

"You don't think a bump on the head might have altered her memory?"

"We talked before I got on the road and then later—before the explosion. Julie simply did not meet with Connie—let alone confront her." What was Wayne talking about? Why was he trying to implicate Julie? No one had really stopped to wonder about his leaving the house unannounced. Could a retainer by the family include getting the land back at any cost? No one knew Connie had filed to make the gift legal.

No, he couldn't think that way. He might not like Wayne, but he refused to think the man was a killer.

"Mr. Stanford is pretty convincing. But I'll stop by the hospital later this morning and see what Ms. Conlin has to say."

Damn. The one thing Ben didn't want was to alert anyone to Julie's whereabouts—not with Robby in tow. But he couldn't lie. He realized he'd paused too long already. The stare was palatable and suspicious.

"Julie's being released this morning. Maybe not something I totally agree with, but she's persistent." Ben managed a rueful grin, but there was no understanding smile returned.

"I'm assuming she'll be at the hotel?"

"I don't know. Her parents are here and I imagine she'll spend the day with them."

"Will you be in touch?"

"Yes."

"Then I expect you to tell her to call me."

Ben nodded and briefly felt he'd dodged a bullet. He was not prepared for what Lieutenant Samuels handed him next—a police report from Haskell, Kansas. More exactly, the police report and a copy of the local DA's notes. The one who went after Robby. Ben bought time before he'd have to comment by leafing through the notes. Vendetta came to mind, the sort of Indian bashing, witch-hunt he'd seen before by prejudiced authorities who used their power to ruin lives.

"Don't expect me to believe that you haven't seen this before."

"I haven't. I know the contents; I've been treating Robby. This is part of a juvenile record that should have remained sealed. How did you get it?"

"It was sent to me … print-free, of course … but I can assume by someone who feels as I do. Robert Emmett Merritt is the prime suspect in his mother's death."

"Based on something that happened four years ago?"

"Ever hear that there are no coincidences in my line of work? We know he'd moved to the area—you just admitted you've seen him. I know what he stands to inherit. I'd say all the motives are there, let alone any mumbo-jumbo his shrinks can provide as to his state of mind. In my book, you do something once, it's likely you'll do it twice—especially if you get away with it the first time."

"You're wrong."

"Oh? And what are you basing your opinion on?"

"Mumbo-jumbo from his shrinks." The term rankled and Ben was getting more than a little pissed at the Lieutenant's short-sighted conclusion.

"No need to get bent, doc. Just calling it how I see it. But I've put out a warrant. I'm assuming you know where he is?"

"Patient-doctor confidentiality prevents me from any further comment."

"Give me a break here, doc. Don't push me. I'm not above slapping your ass in jail on a charge of aiding and abetting."

"That won't be necessary. You have the wrong person."

"I disagree. I'd suggest you reconsider your refusal to help. I'll be contacting your supervisor."

The trump card—the old 'I'll tattle on you and get you in trouble' ploy. Thank God, Ben could count on Sandy. He knew Sandy would support him. But he felt he'd been dismissed and rose to go.

"One more thing." Ben turned back when the lieutenant spoke. "I don't suppose you have any ideas on the skull."

"What skull?" Ben was truly baffled but waited as his face was scrutinized. Apparently deciding that he was telling the truth, the Lieutenant filled him in on the gift Connie had received. Ben sat back down. Who would send a skull with a heart around the bullet hole? The killer, who else?

Suddenly he was beginning to put things together. The skull would have told Connie that the assassin, Skip's henchman, was back. And she had to have known the skull she held was that of her lover—the father of her child. Didn't Julie see her talking to a man at the lodge? So, the payoff was to keep this man quiet? Probably. Ben took a deep breath.

"There are some things you need to know—maybe you know them already." It took ten minutes to fill in the gaps—the discovery that Art McNamara was back, the killer, set up by the senator—the cuckolded husband. Art, who would have had the skull, the hiring of Stan Devon to find her son, then deliver a payoff to the caretaker, the double cross by Mr. Devon, and lastly, the name of

Robby's father. A couple questions by Lieutenant Samuels and then silence.

"I know the cops were onto Stan Devon delivering the money and the fingerprint tie to Ms. CdeBaca. I wasn't sure you knew the connections."

"Not everything. You're saying the skull is Jose Rodriguez Mondragon?"

"I'd bet on it."

"And somewhere there's a decapitated corpse." Lieutenant Samuels leaned back in his chair. "Ever been to UNM's History Museum? The entire second floor is filled with boxes and bags of remains—bones found on the desert, in car trunks, suitcases, lunchboxes. Some mummified. There are bags of teeth, femurs, skulls—stories, all stories that seldom get told. And all part of the OMI's four hundred or so bodies that have never been identified."

"Grim. And a lot of closure that would help some families heal."

"I doubt we have a body that goes with the skull, but a name is a start and matching it with remains surfacing twenty or so years ago—who knows? We may get lucky. New DNA programs can be valuable."

Ben got up and walked to the door. "I'll stay in touch."

"You know, doc, I like you but I was serious about you hiding the kid. We need to talk to him. For the time being, let's just call him a 'person of interest.' I'm sure he can clear himself if he's innocent."

Ben wasn't so sure but he nodded and continued out the door. He'd seen too many overly zealous law enforcement officers, wanting to wrap up a high profile case, name a plausible suspect and stop there—leading to the wrong person rotting in prison. He wouldn't let that happen to Robby.

The wind, if anything, had become more biting. He jogged back to the Doubletree. He'd grab a heavier jacket and then put in a day at IHS. He'd just stepped into the lobby when he saw the headlines. *Socialite Murdered—Son Implicated.* He put fifty cents in the slot of the nearest newspaper dispenser and pulled open the front. This time there was a large picture of Connie and the story was three columns—above the crease. That hadn't taken long. He wondered how the paper had gotten the information. Probably the same way Lieutenant Samuels had. He tucked the paper under his arm and continued to the elevators.

In the room, he spread the paper out on his bed. A lot of the article was just reiterating what had already been reported—but now the ominous word 'murder' was the attention-getter. Ben was curious as to how much of Robby's former situation would be revealed. The revelation of Connie's having had a son was referred to as "… a best kept family secret." Robby was named as R.E. Merritt and the history of his adoption was included, noting that both adoptive parents were deceased—the mother being a murder victim.

Then the clincher: "Because of the mysterious circumstances surrounding both women's deaths, comparisons have been drawn between the two murders." Ben kept reading, expecting to find the bizarre laying out of the corpses. But nothing. Only the one line about drawing comparisons. This could have been worse. Did this mean the article's author knew the truth but had chosen not to print it?

On impulse, he dialed the *Journal.* He was not familiar

with the person named in the byline, Sally Johnston, but was curious as to her source. He hadn't expected to find her in but was pleasantly surprised when he was immediately put through.

"Sally Johnston."

Ben introduced himself as executor of Ms. CdeBaca's estate and trustee of Mr. R.E. Merritt's interests. He complimented her on the feature and then asked her source.

"Actually, an anonymous phone call. Someone left a message suggesting that I check the Haskell, Kansas *Republic*'s coverage of a similar story just four years ago involving a son who possibly murdered his mother. Once the OMI released cause of death, Ms. CdeBaca became news again. A Lieutenant Samuels confirmed that R.E. Merritt was, in fact, the same young man in both situations."

"I admire your constraint. You could have implied a killer."

"My boss thinks I'm missing a chance to sell some papers ... KOAT-TV is describing Mr. Merritt as a 'person-of-interest' but I promised your fiancée I'd give it forty-eight hours."

"Julie?"

"We go way back. Worked together five years ago. I trust her judgment; she has me convinced this kid didn't do it. And after what happened to her, I think there's a bigger story."

"I agree, but I'm not sure forty-eight hours is enough time."

"Best I can do. I keep reminding my boss that he doesn't want to make apologies. People never forget when you're wrong."

"I forgot to ask … was the caller male or female?"

"Difficult to tell. The voice was distorted but I'm guessing male."

Ben thanked her again and hung up. Forty-eight hours. No time at all but at least Robby was safe. More proof that someone seemed to be setting him up. He wished now that he'd questioned Robby about where and when he was followed—what did the person or persons in the black Hummer do? Had someone tried to hit him with the vehicle? Robby had been frightened; that was obvious. Ben should have asked. He kicked himself at how hindsight, once again, was flawless.

He tucked the cell into the pocket of his jacket only to bring it out again a second later on the first ring.

"Ben, Arnold Baxter here, glad I caught up with you. I'm hoping Miss Conlin is doing well?"

Ben had forgotten to return the attorney's call, but didn't get the sense the man was upset with him. "She was released this morning."

"Good to hear. When she's feeling up to it, I have a little job that needs tackling. Perhaps, it's one for the two of you. I took the liberty of sifting through what was left of Ms. CdeBaca's house and putting anything salvageable into storage. A lot was lost but there were some things the family might want. Boxes of old photos, for example, some of which had been in the garage. Turned out to be the safest place on the property."

"How soon does this have to be done?" Ben added that Julie and her mother were accompanying Connie's body to the reservation. He omitted Robby's name. The fewer people who knew where he was, the better.

"Oh, some time this week if you can. I don't think

there's anything of real value. I would suggest you officiate when you invite the family to divvy things up. Could be a free-for-all, but then again, they may not be interested. I thought I'd drop off the combination to the storage unit at your office. I need to go back to Denver for a few days, but I'm only a phone call away if you need me."

Ben thanked him. Sounded like a job for both Julie and Bev. Already he was thinking that the three of them should take a look first.

Chapter Twenty-two

The limo was too comfortable. Julie wryly admitted to herself that she could get used to this. The three and a half hour drive was light years more decadent in a limo than bouncing along in a pickup. She settled back against the dove gray leather upholstery—a nicer grade of leather than her favorite coat, she had to admit. A wisp of a headache hovered behind her eyes and she pulled down the blind that covered the window beside her and reached in her purse for a Motrin. She really was feeling better—maybe not one-hundred percent, but close. And she was enjoying watching her mother interact with Robby. Bev had brought a photo album from home, thinking Julie might want early pictures of Connie for her article. It turned out to be the perfect thing to share with Robby.

"Your mother was seventeen here." Bev was pointing

to a school picture that showed the two of them at a football game. "We fought over who was going to wear the heather gray cashmere sweater. It was my sweater, but I owed your mother a favor and that's what she wanted for payment. It all seems so frivolous now, but we didn't speak for a week. That explains why we don't look very happy. And, you know, with her coloring the sweater looked so much better on her."

"Did she date a lot?"

"It was a girls' school but we had exchanges with two boys' schools in the area—holiday dances, that sort of thing. We were really well chaperoned. Children today can't even imagine how strict the rules were—and how well enforced." Bev was pensive for a moment. "You know, there never was a steady boyfriend. Lots of dance partners but never dating just one individual. She was only a year out of high school when she married Skip."

"Were you surprised?"

"About as shocked as I was to find out there was a you." Bev playfully patted his arm. "For a long time it put a wall between us. I went on to school, dated, traveled. Skip was controlling, didn't want us seeing each other, thought Connie had obligations that didn't include an unmarried friend."

"That's not fair. Couldn't she have stood up to him?"

"Not to Skip. If she had, I always got the feeling there would have been repercussions—I don't know what, exactly, but life would have been made unpleasant." Bev paused as if thinking about what she was going to say. "I always thought she could have done better. Oh, not where money was concerned. Skip always had plenty of that. Or prestige—a senator's wife put her in an enviable position socially. But he was just too old for her. He wanted her for all the wrong reasons—to parade her beauty, to make himself look young. Toward the end they could barely tolerate each other. There's no doubt in my mind that your father was the love of her life."

"And me? Do you think she was happy about me?"

"I believe she loved you unconditionally. I can't imagine the anguish of giving you up—having to give you up. She wanted children so badly. And then to conceive but have to keep it a secret … she must have been devastated. I can't even begin to imagine losing your father in such a heinous way. How did she even survive the suffering she went through?"

Robby turned away and was staring at the landscape rushing by. Julie couldn't help but think this was good for him to hear. He'd lived his life not knowing. This was truly a gift of "roots," if nothing else. Gave definition to his life.

"If you loved your friend and she was Indian, why do you hate Dr. Pecos just because he's Indian?"

The magazine Julie had just opened slipped to the floor. She saw her mother blush and then stammer, "I don't hate him and certainly his ethnic background has nothing to do with my feelings. Well, not really."

"You don't want him to marry your daughter."

Who had told him this? But then, Julie thought, it wouldn't take a lot to figure it out. Her mother had been especially curt to Ben as they were getting ready to leave.

"I don't want my daughter to suffer. I don't want her to give up her career and get caught in some one-horse town—someplace in South Dakota or Oklahoma. She's worked for national media firms, for heaven's sake—she could replace Katie Couric someday."

Julie tried not to roll her eyes. She was finding her mother's discomfort amusing. It was about time Bev was taken to task by someone other than her daughter.

"I guess I think that's Julie's decision to make—not yours. I think your friend's life would tell you what it's like to live in a loveless marriage. Dr. Pecos loves your daughter. Why don't you just leave them alone?"

This last wasn't really said unkindly—more in wonderment—and Julie's first inclination was to burst into applause. But she could see how uncomfortable her mother was—chastisement of the in-control Bev was not an easy accomplishment. Julie only hoped she'd listened.

Robby turned to her. "Do you have a time and place yet … for the wedding?"

"Christmas Eve afternoon in the Tewa Pueblo. The ceremony will be in the Mission Church."

"That will be beautiful. Can I come?"

"I would be very disappointed if you didn't."

"Do you have a dress?"

Once again, Julie described Connie's gift. "It's so perfect. You'll see what I mean. I couldn't have found something that I liked better. I thought I'd decorate the Mission church in all white poinsettias with white roses around the altar. I'd like huge white velvet bows with smaller bouquets of roses at the end of each pew—"

"Who will stand up with you?" Bev interrupted.

"I've already asked Sally Johnston—remember her? I worked with her at the *Journal* and then stayed in touch when I moved to the TV station. And Carol Finley, another reporter friend. I'm just not sure about their dresses. I'd thought of a fitted sheath, with a neckline like the one on my dress and cap sleeves—but what should I do about color?"

"I like your all-white theme, but a touch of red might be perfect. In keeping with the season." Robby offered.

"I agree with Robby. Why couldn't their dresses be a deep red velvet, for example?"

"Red might work but velvet is too heavy, Mom. Carol will throw a fit. I know her. She'll think of added pounds."

"What might work better is a midnight blue—maybe even embossed—taffeta or another material that has body. The cap sleeves should look like bells. And something dark would be slimming. Your friend would thank you."

"Robby, that's a great idea. Carol's a blond—she'd look stunning. If we can find the right material, the dresses can be plain—let the cut and the material be the attention-getter." Julie was truly impressed. Robby had a wonderful knack for color and materials. She looked at him—close cropped black hair with a forelock that dipped almost to cover one eye, strong jaw, tall, sinewy, not skinny—a handsome kid with just the hint of something feminine, maybe the dark smoldering eyes with long lashes. But what a far cry from when she first met him. She willed herself not to look for hints of nail polish.

"I bet Bev and I could pull this thing together for you. There's not a lot of time. What do you think?" Robby turned to Bev.

"Well ... yes ... of course, we could." Bev first looked startled, then beamed and exchanged high fives with Robby. Julie hadn't seen her mother this animated and outside herself for a long time. She owed Robby big time—just maybe her mother had turned a corner. But less than a month. Not a lot of time to be successful.

The sirens interrupted any further wedding talk. Julie lifted the blind on her window. Three, no four, patrol cars pulled alongside then passed them, but she could still see at least one behind the limo. Was the senator's wife important enough to get an escort? But then, she felt the limo slow, pull onto the shoulder and stop. Had the hearse been pulled over, too? She couldn't see.

Robby and her mother were seated facing her with the exterior door in between. Julie leaned forward, scooted off the seat, pushed the handle down and forced the door outward.

"Those exiting should do so with hands in plain sight." Was that a bullhorn, or whatever those things were called?

"Oh, for God's sake, what is going on here? This is a funeral procession." Bev pushed in front of Julie and stepped to the pavement.

"Ma'am, that means you. Hands where I can see 'em." Now, Julie could see the cop—actually four of them. All with guns drawn.

"Ms. Conlin?"

"Which Ms. Conlin do you want?" Indignant, Bev stood on one foot, sans crutch, shielding her eyes against the sun.

Julie crawled from the limo, "I think Lieutenant Samuels is referring to me. To what do we owe this pleasure?" Did that sound snide? Probably. And probably she knew why they were stopped. Their 'person-of-interest' was just stepping out of the car behind her.

"I'm here to take Robert Emmett Merritt into custody on suspicion of murder."

"Murder?" Julie thought Bev was about to faint. She leaned back against the limo and propped herself up, hands splayed against the limo's side. "That's ridiculous. Just who was murdered?"

"My mother." Robby added, "They think I killed Connie."

"But you didn't … couldn't have … this is all some mistake. We are escorting the body of his mother and my dear friend to her home to be buried."

"Minus one mourner." Lieutenant Samuels stepped forward. "If you're innocent, I'm sure we'll find out soon enough. You need to come with me, son. There'll be time later to pay your respects."

Julie hit Ben's number on speed-dial. No answer. He seldom had his phone on during work but did regularly check messages. "Ben, Lieutenant Samuels is arresting Robby and returning to Albuquerque. Could you meet them when they get in? They should be downtown by one-thirty. There's probably not a lot I can do, so Mom and I will continue to the res. I'll call later." She knew Ben would be pissed. But she also knew he'd meet Robby— maybe arrange bail, but on a murder case, that might be impossible. Would money help? There was five million dollars with Robby's name on it, and he probably wouldn't have access to it until the paperwork had cleared the courts. Who said timing was everything?

She watched as Robby was ushered to the lead patrol car—cop on each side, cop in back. Only then did Lieutenant Samuels place cuffs on him before pushing his head down as Robby slipped into the back seat. What were they afraid of? That he'd run? Jump out of the car? Wire mesh and double locks made that a little difficult. Robby seemed resigned. But she knew she could never forget his expression when he looked back. It was more than resignation. A mix of bitterness with fright? All of those and maybe a touch of defiance.

+ + +

Ben played Julie's message twice. One o'clock. He'd been heading out for a late lunch—he was glad he'd checked messages first. He wouldn't tell Robby this, but his first thought was—at least he'll be safe. The murderer was out there—or was it murderers? Plural. Did the person who killed the caretaker also kill Connie? And try to kill Julie? Had someone hired Stan Devon to get his hands dirty? Who would stand to benefit from those particular three deaths? Family. It all came back to family. And he knew exactly who would benefit if Robby disappeared. Three people who would become five million dollars richer.

So maybe Stan Devon hadn't taken the money and run. Did he stick around for yet a bigger paycheck? Connie's death might prove to be a family thing. Why not a hire? Done before anyone realized that she'd already deeded the ten acres—and was dying *and* had a son. Then the same guy who had come up with a letter-bomb was paid to obliterate any evidence of murder or possible new wills by leveling the house. But running Julie off the road? Afraid she'd seen something? And breaking into his truck? All this on top of threatening Robby? Who would gain from all this? Big question marks, but what Ben knew for certain— Robby had nothing to do with any of them. All Ben had to do was convince Lieutenant Samuels.

Chapter Twenty-three

He'll be housed separately, if that's a concern."

"One of them." Ben had snagged some time with Lieutenant Samuels after Robby was booked.

"I didn't appreciate the lack of a call. I remember having a little chat about aiding and abetting. I had to put two and two together when I realized where the body was going."

Ben didn't comment. None was needed; the good lieutenant was obviously feeling pretty smug.

"So, you think you have your man?"

"I'm not a shrink, but even a layman can draw some conclusions. It's just too coincidental—adoptive mother and biological mother murdered and laid out."

"Robby says he was never in the house—at the house, but no farther inside than a room to the west of the garages."

"Shame we can't even check for prints."

Did that sound a little snide? What did he mean? Was he trying to link Robby with the explosion? That was absurd.

"I'll know more, of course, once we've had a chance to chat. If he has alibis, well, he has nothing to worry about."

"I think you're going to have a tough time coming up with a motive. This isn't a kid motivated by money."

"I don't think you can say that for certain."

"He didn't have any idea that he was in the will."

"Oh, I would think he could assume as much."

"He has an adequate trust from his adoptive parents. He'll get the bulk of it when he's twenty-one—more than enough to see him through school and support him in the process."

"Then, we play the psycho card."

"And that is?"

"Stopped taking his meds, went berserk, felt abandoned—struck out."

"Tough one to prove, don't you think?" Ben hoped so, at least. If the transgender behavior came out—no, Ben couldn't even go there. Lieutenant Samuels wouldn't exactly be understanding, he'd bet.

"Can't be ruled out."

"You have four instances of criminal activity—death of the caretaker, death of the benefactor, bombing of her house, threat on Julie's life—are you treating each separately?"

"For the time being. Until we find the thread that connects."

"Any word on the whereabouts of Stan Devon?"

"That's kinda interesting. Granted, he had a head start but he didn't fly out of here. Looks like he cleaned out his office and just went *poof*. It doesn't make sense, but I'd swear he never left."

"You think he's still in the area?"

"Can't prove that he left. But why would he stay around? Fifty thousand in his pocket should be reason to take off. He has no criminal record—until now. And he's got to know we're after him."

"Was he licensed?"

"Perfectly legit. Been a PI for twelve years, before that a military career."

"Had he been in Albuquerque long?"

"About eighteen months—California transplant."

"I wonder how Connie found out about him?"

"His surroundings wouldn't have given a clue, but he had some real hotshots as clients."

"Such as?"

"Your pal, the lawyer, for one."

"Wayne Stanford?"

"One and the same. The name of a good PI probably comes in handy if you're a lawyer. Mr. Stanford gave a user endorsement in an ad in UNM's *Law Review*."

"Well, it explains why Connie would have trusted him with fifty thousand."

"You know, he could have just stolen the money … took it and disappeared. There was no reason for murder. No reason to even show up at the mailbox with an altered package."

"But he wouldn't want the caretaker to come after him or even go back to his client, for that matter. Murder was much neater. Put him in the driver's seat."

"But why? He would have known the consequences all too well. Another reason it doesn't make sense that he didn't just take off. He knew Ms. CdeBaca wouldn't—maybe even couldn't—do anything about it." The lieutenant paused. "If I allow as how your patient didn't kill his mother, who's next in line?"

"Let's go back to Stan Devon for a moment first. I agree with everything you said—it makes sense that he would take off but as you've pointed out, it looks like he's stayed around. So, what if the fifty wasn't enough? What if he had an opportunity to make more? Probably, a lot more."

"By?"

"Hiring out to kill Connie. You ask who's next in line for wanting Connie killed? There are three possibilities."

"The CdeBaca children?"

"Exactly. As far as standing to gain, I know for a fact that no one knew Connie had already recorded her gift to the Sandia Pueblo. Nor did anyone think he or she would be sharing their inheritance with a half-brother they'd never heard of. And no one knew of her illness."

"Stan Devon did. Why wouldn't he tell the CdeBacas? It's my understanding that they wouldn't have had long to wait. And there would have been no blood on their hands."

"Unless Stan's finding Robby—the one bone marrow donor who could have saved her life—might have changed things. If he was aware of her illness, he was aware of why finding Robby was so important. That and the promise of a handsome paycheck."

"Okay. Let's say that's one theory. Do you have any profiles on people who strangle?"

"You mean like bed-wetting, fire-starting, torturing small animals?"

"Yeah, something like that."

"The dysfunctional family, of course—which is becoming ever more difficult to distinguish from what's considered normal."

"Your boy would fit the dysfunctional part."

"But there's just no way he could strangle his own mother. Strangulation takes a lot of strength and anger. If you could have seen his face when he found out his mother had been murdered … you'd know why I can say that."

"Pity I wasn't the one to tell him."

Ben ignored the jab. "He's been trying to belong, all his life, to find the heritage that would give his life definition. His only regret is that he didn't tell his mother he'd take part in a bone marrow transplant. He's convinced he could have saved her life."

"Easy to say after the fact. You really think he would have offered?"

"I have no doubt."

"I'm telling you your business, doc, but I think something set him off. I think there's something we don't know—something we missed, maybe. I think the anger on his part could have been there."

"I don't know. I didn't see it."

"You gonna be in earshot if I need to touch base after my chat with our boy?"

"You've got my cell number."

+ + +

The cold air blasted him with a mixture of ice particles and rain. Why did they keep government buildings so warm? Ben pulled up his collar and buttoned the sheepskin jacket's top button before shoving his hands into pockets lined with shearling. He didn't feel like going to work and he still needed to get lunch. He should probably just grab a sub and head back. Walking away and leaving Robby incarcerated was eating him up. He felt like he'd failed the young man, but he should have known he couldn't hide Robby forever. But interrogation? He had no idea how Robby would handle it.

At two forty-five, there were no lines at the sandwich shop. Had meatballs and melted Swiss ever smelled so good? Chips and a drink and he was headed to work. He picked up the combination for the storage unit from Gloria along with a stack of mail, unlocked his office and, trying not to tip his soft drink, put his lunch on the desk. He'd ignore the blinking light on his phone until after he'd eaten. But after busting open the bag of salt and vinegar chips, he picked up the receiver and punched in his code.

"Ben, I'm worried sick about Robby. Maybe I can't do anything, but I'd rather be there with you. I called Dad and he's meeting Mom at the Inn of the Mountain Gods after the service. I think that relieves me of any babysitting duties. I'll pick up a rental in Ruidoso and come on back tonight. Should get there by five-thirty or six. See you at the hotel. Love you."

That was the best news he'd had all day. Only another couple hours. He could finish a few evaluations he owed Gallup IHS, check the paper for a movie, and have the offer of a fun evening all planned.

But it didn't turn out that way. And he should have known, the minute he shared that Arnold Baxter had left the combination to a storage unit holding more of Connie's things, the cat and curiosity collided.

"I'm sure it won't take us too long. Maybe we could catch a late movie?"

"Yeah, maybe. But it means not reading everything, and, God forbid, not organizing." Ben laughed and pulled her to him. "I've never thought of you as a cheap date. Have things changed?"

"Aren't you curious at all? We both know the family. We need to do this—take a first look before we call them. For Robby's sake, at least. There might be family things—pictures of Connie—he would want." She pecked him on the cheek and stood back. "After all, we are the executors. That comes with some responsibility. It'll be fun."

A lot of things struck him as possibly being more fun—a stick in the eye or a pie in the face. But Ben did have to admit, his interest was piqued. He didn't have his hopes up that there would be anything of value, but one never knew. And value was in the eye of the beholder. Julie had made a good point about keeping Robby in mind when they looked through things. It served him right for telling her right away—he could have waited.

The salad bar at the hotel was fantastic. It quickly cleared his conscience of any lingering regret over the meatball sub. And Julie ate like the condemned. After her third helping of pickled beets, Ben was hoping he didn't need to be worrying about birth control, or the lack thereof. They were being careful—maybe it was possible a person could just love pickled beets. He watched the beet juice tint the dollop of cottage cheese at the edge of her plate. Pink food. Not an Indian thing. But it was great to see her looking so healthy and back to her old self. As much as he might have wanted to see a movie and relax, watching her get so excited was worth it. This was therapeutic. A movie could wait.

Chapter Twenty-four

Temperature control, track lighting on a rheostat, indoor/outdoor carpet—he had a number of patients who didn't live in anything half as nice as this storage unit. He supposed the estate was picking up the tab but then, why not? There were funds for incidentals. Ben was surprised anything had been salvaged from the house. A lot of the boxes were water-stained and the air, though purified he imagined, was still tainted with the acrid hint of smoke. It would be difficult to know where to begin.

One wall was lined with hat boxes, handbags and shoe racks—a sorry mix of mismatched and mangled leather. Another held boxes of kitchen implements, mixers, coffee makers. Then came rows of file boxes—the kind you put important papers in—and lastly, the center of the room was packed with furnishings—broken, twisted lamp stands, what was once an ornate desk, a display case with not one bit of glass intact, a stained glass shade, huge and a quarter of it missing. But if it was a Tiffany, would it be worth repair? Ben guessed so.

His first reaction was "what a mess." But Julie was amazed so much had been saved. As he pointed out, "saved" was the questionable word here. He stood back, reluctant to get started—what actually were they supposed to do? Julie, with pen and pad, headed toward the personal articles. His cue, he guessed, to start on the file boxes.

"I can't understand this. This is the fourth hat box I've opened only to find it empty. Are you sure we're the first to look through these things?"

"Yeah. I think Arnold hired some muscle to move everything here and then had to go back to Denver."

"Well, someone's gone through things. There's no way Connie would have stored a bunch of empty boxes."

"You haven't met Arnold, but it's really difficult for me to imagine him popping open a few hatboxes to maybe confiscate some wispy confection with sequins or feathers."

"Well, someone did."

"Why are you assuming it happened after the explosion?"

"Oh my God, I never thought—" Had there been time for someone to go through Connie's things between the time she died and the explosion? Hadn't Julie been there most of that time? And guards had been hired afterward to oversee the house—the house in ruins. Supposedly, there hadn't been a time it had been exposed, open to vandals. Other than the couple hours when she had left to make copies. The person she'd seen—she thought might have been Robby—had that person been in the house long enough to take things?

"Maybe the boxes were just tossed around and Arnold put the tops back on."

"Not exactly a manly thing to do—I can't see some guy picking through the rubble to match up tops and bottoms to hat boxes."

"Me, either." Ben didn't say anything, but the first file box he opened had been picked over. Files were out of order unless the alphabet started with M and zigzagged back and forth from O to B back to N.

"Ben, look." Julie was holding a locket dangling from a heavy gold chain. "If this is what I think it is, it will have been worth coming out here for." The locket was large, an inch and a half in diameter and made of heavy gold. The flowery initials interspersed with diamonds were CB & JRM. Inside, a smiling Connie and beaming Professor Mondragon snuggled for the camera. Beautiful people caught in time. They looked perfect together—both dark, both incredibly handsome. Julie turned the locket over and opened the back compartment—a lock of hair less than an inch in length, very fine, dark—unmistakably baby hair. "It was in an envelope in the lining of this makeup case."

"This will mean a lot to Robby." Ben stood looking at Connie with Robby's father. Happiness could be so fleeting. Time borrowed but not paid back. Stolen, really. He wanted Robby's life to be different. He thought it would be if they could just connect him with relatives on the reservation.

"Look at all these picture albums. They're hardly scratched." Julie held up a leather bound book about three inches thick and eight-and-a-half by eleven. There appeared to be three boxes holding identical albums. "They must have been in the garage. I hope there are pictures of Connie. Mom shared an album of school pictures with Robby—I think he really appreciated it." Julie dragged a chair cushion missing the chair over next to the box, adjusted the lighting, and sat down. "I hope I'm not wasting my time. I can't imagine any of Skip's children interested in pictures of their stepmother."

Julie leafed through the first album. Skip as a boy, Skip in uniform, Skip with mother and father ... Julie put the album to one side. The second seemed to pick up with Skip and the mother of his children. According to the labels, Helen was homecoming queen, a cheerleader, and president of her college class. Then Helen married, had several wedding showers, got pregnant, had several baby showers, delivered three children and took pictures of them in wagons, on tricycles, in tree houses ... ad nauseam. None of this was what Julie was looking for. Then with the next to last album—paydirt!

The very first picture was of a gangly Connie hugging the neck of a spotted pony. From there, the pictures graduated to Connie as barrel racer, roper, State Fair Queen and Miss Indian America. Someone looking at the young Connie and Robby would never question the family tie. It was amazing. Julie carefully set that album to the side.

The last album was entirely Skip's children. The pictures continued with them after high school. Byron as valedictorian of his college class. Cherie receiving some kind of award—Julie couldn't tell exactly what, and Jonathan at boot camp. She was getting ready to put it back in the box when a caption caught her attention. Jonathan, it seemed, had been an EOD Specialist—Explosive Ordnance Disposal. Explosives. Coincidence?

Julie read the citations. Decorated for his work and there was a picture of his squadron. Julie ran down the list of names and glanced at their pictures. All gung-ho young men from some twenty-odd years ago. Then a name stopped her. McNamara, Arthur N. The same name as the caretaker. The man who had been killed by explosives. If it was the same man, then an EOD Specialist had been killed by a letter bomb. The very kind of thing he'd been taught to disassemble. Some sort of poetic justice? Or just not possible? Would someone trained in the field reach into a mailbox to extract a bulky, maybe suspicious, package? Doubtful. Even if he was expecting it?

She sat up a little straighter, leaned over and ran her index finger across the group picture until she reached Private McNamara, but the tiny and now fuzzy full-front photo was of little help—there were no really distinguishing features. If she could trust his standing in the back row to indicate height, then he was at least six foot three or four. And thin. Lean long face—a string-bean frame that hadn't filled out at nineteen or twenty. But on the next page was a photo of Jonathan and Art together. Buds standing in front of a bus, duffle bags at their feet, in a couple king-of-the-mountain poses that shouted, 'don't mess with us.' Testosterone on the prowl. Art was a good four inches taller than his pal and she knew Jonathan was six foot.

She felt the shiver of excitement that meant she'd found something important … really important. If her hunch was right, Art McNamara was very much alive and Stan Devon very dead. And possibly, just maybe, his long time buddy, Jonathan CdeBaca was an accomplice—not in the letter bomb but the explosion that leveled Connie's house.

Lieutenant Samuels should be interested in two munitions experts, both with stakes in the CdeBaca fortune.

"Ben, if an investigation is still underway, will the OMI keep a body—not dispose of it?"

"Not sure, but I think they have to. Why?"

She explained her suspicion and showed him the pictures. "Is there anyone we can call?"

"Probably not tonight but first thing in the morning."

They spent another three hours opening boxes, cataloging contents, organizing what was left by useable versus non-useable—one pile against the north wall, one the south. It was ten forty-five before they were finished and Julie was beat. But she had a locket tucked away in her purse and a picture album that just might explain some things. Were they closer to naming Connie's murderer? Just maybe.

+ + +

Alarm? No, phone. Ben checked his watch. Nine o'clock. Shit. They'd slept in. But if he could use getting his bones jumped as an excuse—it had been worth it! He grabbed the receiver over Julie's shoulder.

"Yeah?"

"Just thought you'd want to know your boy made bail. Called his lawyer and walked." Lieutenant Samuels sounded far from happy.

"He doesn't have a lawyer."

"Well, he did this morning. That family lawyer—the one that loves you."

"Wayne?" Now Ben sat up and saw that he had Julie's attention, too. She'd rolled on her side propped up on an elbow.

"When?"

"About a half hour ago."

"No idea where they were going?"

"None. But I want to know if he gets in touch." The click of the disconnect seemed loud, Ben thought, or just final.

"Our pal Wayne just got Robby out on bail."

"What do we do?" Julie slipped out of bed and headed for the bathroom.

"Wait 'til he calls or maybe try to contact Wayne. Do you have his number?"

"I think so. All the work-related numbers are programmed into my cell." Julie rummaged through her purse, pulled out her phone and tossed it to Ben. "Give him a try while I shower." Leaning back around the bathroom door, she added, "Don't forget we need to get hold of someone at the OMI."

Ben sat on the edge of the bed and scrolled through the numbers. There it was. He dialed using Julie's cell thinking Wayne would be far more likely to pick up. Six rings and voicemail—a very business-sounding Wayne assured the caller he'd get back quickly. Odd. If he just sprang Robby why would he have his cell off? Or maybe he was one of those who hated being tied to a phone. But practicing law was competitive, why would he risk being out of touch?

Ben tossed the phone on the bed. He had other things he'd rather think of. If he dropped his clothes now, he just might have time to join one beautiful woman in the shower.

Chapter Twenty-five

N ext of kin?"

"No. Executors of the estate where this man was killed." Ben wasn't sure this was going to get him the information, but it was worth a try.

"Wait. Didn't I see you at the site? With Ms. CdeBaca?" The lab tech turned to Julie. "I'd pulled bag duty that day and helped scrape this guy together."

She flinched inwardly at his terminology. "Yes, I thought you looked familiar."

"So, what is it you guys need to know?"

"General information. Height, weight, age—that sort of thing." Ben breathed a small sigh of relief. He wasn't certain how protected this kind of information might be.

"That's easy enough. Want to sit over there?" The tech motioned to a desk and chairs to his left. "Give me a minute and I'll bring up the info." He turned on the computer and the three of them waited. Tough to make small talk in a place like this, Ben thought.

"Here we go. Let's see. Identification was made by jewelry and clothing. Arthur McNamara, estate caretaker. Didn't get a dental—guy took the blast in his face. General mass at weigh-in would indicate 200 to 210 pounds. One femur in pretty good shape used to estimate height at five-feet-eight inches. Age estimated somewhere in early fifties."

Julie had scooted to the edge of her chair. "Are you positive about height? I mean you couldn't be off by five or six inches? Or more?"

"I could be off an inch—more like three quarters, but not more."

"Could you get prints?" Ben knew that a PI and an Army Specialist would have prints on file within easy access.

"Not available. There wasn't a lot left. He leaned down, probably hands in front, reaching inside to get the package … guess you guys know the particulars. Surprising the ring survived intact."

Not really, Julie thought. Not if it was planted later. The one bit of evidence that would prove to Connie the body was her caretaker.

"Thanks this really helps." Ben looked at Julie, "Anything else?" She shook her head. "Guess that does it." A couple quick handshakes and they were out the door.

"I knew it. This changes everything." Julie hopped up into the truck's cab and turned to face him. "We have to talk to Lieutenant Samuels."

Ben agreed. But would the cop listen? Would he think he needed to broaden his search—expand the number of suspects? They'd know quickly enough.

"Why don't you try Wayne again? I know we're going to be asked if we've heard from them."

Julie snapped open the case of her cell, rolled through her contact list and tapped Wayne's number. Again, nothing. The sixth ring and voicemail. This time Julie left a message. "Wayne, there are some new developments I think you'd be interested in. Give me a call." She left her cell number and hung up. "I wonder where he's taken Robby?"

"Maybe to stay with him? But I don't see that happening. I'm frankly surprised that Wayne met bail, was the one to go to all the trouble to get Robby out. I don't feel any better about his safety."

"Me, either."

"You know, Lieutenant Samuels could be right—Robby could have called him. Used Connie's connection. Maybe Wayne would have felt obligated to help a family member?"

"Or he was just curious. Or he was setting him up."

"Hey, I don't want to think that way. Let's stay positive." Ben wasn't going to admit it but that's exactly what he was thinking.

This time he found a parking place at the curb, a short half block from Samuels's office.

"Mind walking? At least the wind has died down."

"It'll feel good." She turned and smiled, leaned across the seat and kissed him. "I like being with you. Just tell me Robby's going to be all right."

"I wish I could. But what's going to be all right is your being with me, Mrs. Pecos."

"Mrs. Pecos? Aren't you rushing things?"

"I wish I could."

Chapter Twenty-six

So many things dimmed in importance with the light of day. Conviction could turn to speculation, an overheard comment to hearsay. Suddenly, Julie had doubts. So, two men were friends and both explosives experts. So what? It was a long time ago. It didn't make them killers. Experts might blow up a house, but it didn't put either of their hands around Connie's neck. Yet, both did have a lot to gain.

And could one femur really attest to height? Unequivocally so? And age … fifty-something or forty-something could be close. Still, this was not proof of anything. Who's to say Stan Devon didn't accidentally blow himself up? However, Mac was the only one who could have planted the ring and left his shirt. Then the question became, why?

Why did Mac want to, or even need to, slip into anonymity? Was all this reason enough to ask questions? She was hoping Lieutenant Samuels would think so. She opened the photo album and nervously pulled several pictures and two articles from beneath the yellowing plastic protection. Lieutenant Samuels was in a meeting and it gave them time to get prepared—and have second thoughts before he appeared in the doorway and summoned them into his office.

"So, what do you have for me? More coincidence?" Lieutenant Samuels was the only person who laughed. He put a handful of papers on his desk and sat down.

"Actually, yes." Julie handed him the articles and pictures. "I think we might be getting closer to who could be behind the use of explosives."

The Lieutenant quickly scanned the articles, "This doesn't necessarily prove—"

"I know. And you're going to use the word 'coincidence' and it is."

"It's more than that." Ben moved to stand behind Julie. "We can pretty much prove that Stan Devon is dead, and Art or Mac McNamara is alive. We can't prove he killed Mr. Devon, but he did exchange places with him." He quickly reiterated their findings at the OMI. Now, they had the lieutenant's interest.

"Must have had a reason to disappear."

"That's what we think."

"And you believe this McNamara is behind the death of Professor Mondragon? Behind the gift of the skull?"

"Yes, I believe Robby's story. I think an audit of Skip's accounts will show a yearly payoff to Mr. McNamara. And I believe there's a gun somewhere with Connie's prints."

"And they needed to blow up the house to cover their tracks?" Lieutenant Samuels leaned forward, elbows on the desk, hands clasped.

A tap on the glass panel in the office door interrupted any further speculation.

"Excuse me for a minute." The lieutenant stepped into the hall and closed the door behind him.

"So, what do you think?" Julie asked.

"I think we have his attention. Not sure what he'll do with the information."

"It's a start."

"We've got a little problem here." Lieutenant Samuels stepped back into his office. "About an hour ago, a jogger reported a car on fire. Sandia foothills, not far from Tramway. Belongs to that lawyer fellow, your friend, Wayne." The lieutenant turned and sat on the edge of his desk. "I'm sorry about this, but he was found dead in the car."

"Burned?" Julie asked a little breathlessly.

"No. Thanks to the jogger, the fire was put out before it did very much damage. Preserved the scene of the crime."

"How was he killed?" Ben just had a feeling, but he wasn't sure he wanted the answer.

"Strangled. Guess I don't have to use the word coincidence, do I?"

"I think you're stretching things."

"In my line of work, people use guns and knives and fireplace pokers—I don't see a lot of strangulation. So, when I do and it's the second instance in a month on the same case, suspicion mounts." He paused, looking first at Ben, then Julie. "Do either of you know where I might find Robby?"

"You were the one who told us Wayne had bailed Robby out. We haven't heard from him."

"I know I don't have to ask you to call if he gets in touch. And I mean it. You may think you know this young man, but be aware that you may be in danger if you try to help him."

+ + +

The wind had picked up, and blowing snow swirled around them. The walk to the truck meant heads tucked into raised jacket collars, obscuring vision. Talking was impossible with less than six inches between them. Ben started the truck the minute they were in, cranking the heater up full blast. A fine dusting of snow slipped across the warming windshield to clump on the wipers. Would there be a white Christmas in three weeks or was this shot winter's best? Ben knew New Mexico's weather was unpredictable. He'd never lived in a state where the TV weathermen were wrong fifty percent of the time. Or so it seemed. He turned on the wipers to clear the windshield but didn't pull out. This was as good a place as any to sit and talk. And a plan was half forming …

"Wayne bailed Robby out, but we don't know where he was taking him. Then Wayne and his car ended up in Sandia Heights, sans Robby, with Wayne dead of strangulation and the car on fire. The car was found less than three miles from Connie's property—three miles from the lodge. If Mac is indeed alive, he doesn't know that we know. He won't be taking any extra precautions like staying under cover. And my guess is he's been living at the lodge."

"Are you suggesting we look?"

"Why not? There's got to be a reason this Mac wanted to remain 'dead.' He could be doing the dirty work for the family—killing Connie, destroying evidence—now maybe his aim is to kill Robby."

"Wouldn't it be a little dangerous for us to just show up?"

"Cold feet?"

"Never! Let's go."

"I'd contact Lieutenant Samuels but I don't think he's ready to hear a theory that doesn't include Robby as perpetrator. And I don't want us to look like idiots, getting the cops involved in chasing down some half-baked hunch. We really don't have any evidence. So, I'd like to think a ride out there would be innocuous. We don't even have to leave the car. We can tell by the snow if anyone's driven in or out. *Then* we get APD involved—hope they'll send someone out to check."

"And if we suspect Robby is being held?"

"We call for help. No heroes in this truck ... got that?"

Julie nodded. "I just can't understand why Wayne would be killed and not Robby. The two of them were together. It also makes no sense to kidnap Robby. Unfortunately, Robby is only good to the family if he's dead. There should have been two bodies in that car, according to our theory."

"Unless the family's had a change of heart and wants to welcome their sort of half-brother into the family fold. Which I doubt. Or, we can believe like Lieutenant Samuels—Robby killed Wayne."

"That's ridiculous."

"I agree." Ben added, "You know it's possible Wayne had already dropped Robby someplace."

"That would be great, but where? He doesn't have

an apartment, or car … I can't imagine where he would go. And why does it look like Wayne was on his way to Connie's? Or the lodge?"

"Maybe he was supposed to meet with members of the family. Wayne and Robby. Robby could have talked him into letting him skip. And maybe, just maybe, Wayne's death is a fluke—a random robbery, make it look like a body burned on the mesa. Happens every day."

"Why am I not convinced?"

"I know. Me, either."

They rode in silence. Ben needed to give all his attention to a road that was getting slick and snow packed. He'd had a new set of Michelins put on at the end of the summer and the truck had four-wheel-drive; still the driving was quickly getting dicey. The flakes were big and round and coming faster now. It was all the wipers could do to clear a path across the glass and then do it again, wiping even more snow to the side two seconds later.

"It's beautiful if you can get past the danger."

"The snow? Yeah, I'm just afraid we'll miss our turn."

"There it is. The street beside the 7-11."

"Looks like they're getting ready to close." Ben saw the outside lights blink off. "Guess the storm is giving merchants a respite." Of course, he reminded himself, this was a city that closed down if an inch stuck to the ground. Every year, kids were still in school in June to make up for the many snow days.

Ben slowed, put on his blinker, moved to the far right lane and turned. The truck sashayed, then gained traction and began to climb. There would be pavement for about two miles and then the county road, packed gravel, would take them the last mile to the lodge. In these less-traveled areas, the snow had stuck and even drifted in spots. Ben shifted into four-wheel-drive. The mountain seemed to pull them into its whiteness, wrapping them in a fleecy blanket. Trees bowed with snow leaned over the road, forming a tunnel that offered some protection from the relentless storm.

They passed the turnoff to Connie's house and followed the road as it veered left.

"It's still so sad to think that there's no house at the end of the lane. It was so beautiful. It would have made a perfect museum."

"I'd like to think the pueblo will follow her wishes—even if they have to build something. A museum would help everyone."

The road leveled and Julie could see the spot where the mailbox had been. So many reminders on this road of such horrendous acts—her own near brush with death included. She couldn't suppress a shiver. "The road to the lodge connects with this one in about a quarter mile on your left. Then it's maybe another quarter mile to the front door. The road starts curving to the right almost as soon as you turn onto it then back to the left."

"No other way out?"

"I don't think so. Connie never mentioned one. Unless this road cuts back to the county road farther up the mountain."

Ben slowed and turned onto the road leading to the lodge. It was marked on either side by Colorado blue spruce. All about fifteen feet tall, all snow-laden—it was like turning into a fairyland inhabited by Christmas trees.

"Do you get the idea you're in a winter wonderland? I know Bing Crosby's around the next turn—I think I hear sleigh bells."

"Stop. I'm trying to squelch the Frosty the Snowman refrain that's been repeating itself in my head, as it is. But I'm not having any luck."

"I could start whistling a pretty good rendition of Jingle Bells."

"No, don't." She laughed. "I don't know which would be worse."

"I don't see any tracks. If someone came in earlier, they stayed in. The storm is so intense that someone coming in a couple hours ago would have his tracks completely covered. I bet they'd be wiped out in less than half an hour."

"And, of course, we could be wrong. The lodge may very well be empty."

The afternoon sun was only a glow obscured by clouds, and a near white-out wall of snow blew on a slant to blanket the ground. The wipers were almost useless, losing the battle against the heavy wet stuff. And maybe that's why the sudden appearance of the black Hummer coming straight toward them seemed to explode out of nowhere. Black against white, a colossal giant with snow flying from wide hood and fenders. Julie screamed as Ben yanked the wheel to the right and slid sideways, slipping backend-first to rest half on and half off the road. The Hummer didn't even slow.

"Are you okay?"

"Yes."

"Good, because I want to follow him. But it might be dangerous. I want you to hike into the lodge. It can't be far from here. See if there's any sign of Robby. I'll call Samuels and he can have this guy picked up. But I don't want to lose him. This could mean getting Robby off the hook."

Julie already had the door open. "Be careful."

"I should be back within the hour. Make sure your cell's on. Take the flashlight." Ben reached under the seat and handed over a fourteen-inch silver cylinder.

She grabbed the flashlight, slipped to the ground, pushed the door shut and stepped back. The rear wheels spun then caught on the gravel substrate, popping the truck back on the road and headed the way they'd come. Ben accelerated and the truck fishtailed, then straightened. Julie watched until the taillights disappeared.

She had a stab of angst about missing the fun and getting left in the snow. But she knew he wanted her to be safe. It wasn't as if she wasn't dressed for it. And she could do a thorough check of the lodge on her own. She fully expected to find evidence that Mac had been working with explosives or had held Robby captive. She idly wondered if Ben would find Robby in the Hummer being spirited away against his will.

She pulled her goose-down hood over her head, snapped the down coat closed to mid-calf, and retied the scarf at her neck. Her boots were rough-out leather lined in shearling and laced to her knees. She felt like she was about to do "one giant step for mankind" but she was comfortable; she was prepared for the snow and cold.

There was no getting lost on the spruce-lined path. The wet snow made it slow going, but she probably wasn't in a hurry. She had a feeling the Hummer contained exactly who Lieutenant Samuels was looking for and maybe the evidence he'd need to put one Art McNamara away. She only hoped Robby was safe. And Wayne? Was she upset? Yes. But not broken up. More shocked and sad—sorry that someone had cut his life short. She couldn't think he'd been caught up in any wrongdoing but could she really speak for him? She'd realized she didn't really know him anymore—maybe she never had. She honestly couldn't say what he was or wasn't capable of. But still, murder ...

The going was easy if she stayed in the Hummer's tracks. She could just see the outline of the lodge ahead. The snow was still a curtain, a gossamer one that shifted from something almost solid to shimmering, see-through gauze. In this half-light, the lodge looked ethereal. The snow gave it a majesty that the light of day would take away. No worn boards with peeling paint were noticeable; no ugly spans of roof with chunks of missing shingles. It looked serene, at peace, no longer the home to hunters fresh in from the kill.

Julie stopped at the base of the porch steps then lightly held onto the banister to better balance in the ice and snow. The massive front door was ajar and a small mound of snow was building up just inside the threshold. She pushed the door open then turned and, with the toe of her boot, flicked the gathering snow back outside. Judging from the black stained hardwood flooring next to the door, this wasn't the first time water had found its way underneath. Caulking and weather-stripping were the first things to go in old buildings like this.

But where to look first? She switched on the flashlight and scanned the foyer. The floor was covered in prints of someone coming and going. In fact, she'd be very surprised if the prints were from just one person. She bent down and found a couple clear sets—one a dress shoe with smooth sole and one a hiking shoe or boot deeply grooved along the instep, toe and heel. There was about an inch difference in length and because of size, both male, she guessed. So, one thing was proved and they had been right—the lodge had been occupied.

Did the one pair of shoes belong to Robby? He'd been wearing hikers the other day. The tread pattern was showing so clearly that she surmised the shoes were new—she remembered Robby's had that just-out-of-the-box clean look. She scanned the area but saw no other prints. Two men. Should she take heart that the prints seemed to indicate Robby was alive? She really needed more proof he'd been here, but she had a hunch.

She straightened and walked through an archway on her right. A gigantic stone fireplace and mantel was the centerpiece among well-worn leather couches and chairs in the gathering room. Rats and other rodents had not done the Indian rugs any favors—most were in tatters. Likewise, the trophies. A large bull elk was missing an eye; several antelope had bare spots where hair should have been. A rogue's gallery—certainly one which had seen better days. The flashlight only made the animals appear menacing, looming outward, casting weird shadows. The gloom would be better. She switched it off and moved to the next room.

Once-polished plank tables filled a large alcove off the great room and served as a dining area. Somewhere along the way, someone had broken up a couple, maybe to use as firewood. The fireplace in this area was part of a see-through with the one in the great room, but it was missing stones from its hearth. And someone had put the proverbial cigarette in the mouth of the elk's head above the mantel. She never understood how anyone could find that funny.

The next room in her path was the kitchen. She remembered it ran the length of the lodge across the back.

Floor-to-ceiling china cabinets, now empty, seemed to waver above her. She chided herself for having an overly active imagination. But she couldn't shake the feeling of sadness. Or was it a foreboding? Wasn't the structure doomed to be razed? It seemed like such an ignoble ending. She remembered the lodge from her youth when it was vibrant and comfortable, offering a great vacation for her family. There wasn't a time when a cauldron of Skip's famous elk-meat chili wasn't simmering on one of the Chambers wood stoves. Was tequila really his secret ingredient? Now those stoves were gone and three blackened and greasy holes remained in the adjoining counter space.

The Coleman camp stove sitting on the oak island was a poor replacement—but once again proved recent occupancy. A wastebasket filled with empty Hormel chili cans attested to diet. A battered saucepan with stuck-on brown sludge sat in one of the utility sinks. What a mess, but why did she expect squatters to wash dishes? Turning, she almost fell over a knee-high bar fridge sticking out from the edge of a counter. She pulled the door open—a six pack of Budweiser, a jar of olives and a stick of butter. Not exactly the condiments she'd choose to accent a bowl of canned chili but maybe she was missing something. She supposed the beer was the right touch, though.

She walked to the back door. It looked like the smokehouse was still in one piece, just off the deck, a few steps from where she stood. Skip had offered full services for any game killed on the premises—he could have the animal quartered and wrapped, then frozen, smoked or dried for jerky. He could have meat packed in dry ice for fresh delivery to anywhere in the states. Pheasants, ducks, and geese were dressed, ready for the oven; duck and goose pâté would be packed in separate containers. It was little wonder his 'retreats' as he called them were so popular. She moved to the hallway and admonished herself to stick to the task. A nostalgic tour wasn't why she was here. She needed evidence in addition to empty chili cans that whoever was living here was also up to no good. An understatement considering murders and bombings.

The gloom now invaded the corners of the rooms and seemed to float down the hall ahead of her. It was no longer possible to see clearly without light. She switched on the flashlight again and swung it in an arc. She distinctly remembered a cloak room opening onto the hallway. Yes, there it was, complete with double barn-style doors. She opened the top one, pushed it inward, leaned against the shelf counter, and pointed the flashlight at the back wall. Rolls of house plans, some leaning, some stacked on the floor, filled a quarter of the tiny room. Connie's house? Spec houses? Maybe someone rigging an explosive would need blueprints but finding plans wasn't proof of anything. This was disappointing. No Robby, no explosives—

"Finding everything all right?"

Julie dropped the flashlight and whirled toward the voice. He was standing on the bottom step of the stairs about twelve feet to her left. An arm casually thrown around the pineapple carving of the balustrade. Even in the near-dark the picture taken twenty-five years earlier could have been taken yesterday. Arthur 'Mac' McNamara hadn't changed much. There was still the bravado, the mocking half smile that seemed to curl his lip more than express emotion. And the eyes—hard, piercing and more than anything else, angry.

She swallowed, "I'm Julie Conlin. I don't believe we've

met. I'm executor of Ms. CdeBaca's estate. Her lawyer asked me to inventory all holdings on the property."

"That's bullshit, Sweetie. I don't want to waste time pretending. Something more like curiosity brought you here. You know and I know I'm supposed to be dead. You were with the squaw princess the day Mr. Devon went to his reward."

"With your help?"

The laugh was harsh. "Hardly. He was an idiot. He blew himself up." Again, that guttural laugh. "I did help myself to what was mine, however, and traded places. The squaw princess owed me. I don't think she ordered me killed—I think that was the PI's bright idea."

"But you killed the golden goose—that doesn't seem too bright."

"The squaw princess? Sorry, not my work."

"But the cover up?"

"Taking her house out? Now, you're getting warm."

"I could have been killed."

"You weren't supposed to be there."

"Who warned me? He probably saved my life."

"I think you know."

What did he mean? Did she know? Had it been Robby all along?

"Where's Robby?"

"Son of squaw princess? Hey, sounds like the title of a book or a bad sitcom." More laughter. "Can't tell you that. Never seen such a family for half-breeds and bastards. Ol' Skip's flipping in his grave."

"You can't tell me where Robby is? Or don't know?"

"Same difference, isn't it? But that's for you to find out."

"Was Wayne just in the way? Knew too much maybe?"

"You could say that. Ever know a lawyer to respect boundaries? Know when enough was enough? This one couldn't even follow directions." He straightened and stepped down to floor level. "The question is, what do I do with you? I wasn't planning on company."

"My fiancé just dropped me off. He'll be back in half an hour."

Mac stepped to the door and, only briefly taking his eyes off of her, opened it a crack. "I doubt that. No one's going anywhere in that mess and not up this road. But I bet he's going to be surprised to find that the driver's a CdeBaca. He'll probably figure out you've got company up here. He'll try to play the hero." Mac was frowning, obviously not liking the situation.

"So, you're in this mess with your old Army pal?"

"You could say that. Jonathan doesn't want to see this place ruined any more than I do."

"And that excuses killing?"

"You do what you have to do." He looked out the door again, then shut it firmly. "Looks like it's just me and you for the evening. Isn't that cozy? Shall we adjourn to the soft furniture?" He made a flourish of clicking his heels, coming to attention and slightly bending forward at the waist, holding his arm outstretched.

She hesitated. What was she going to do? Should she bolt and run? Could she outrun him? Doubtful she could even get past him and out the door—front or back. And near white-out conditions ... could she make it to the road? How disorienting was the storm?

Suddenly, her cell began a rendition of a Sousa march. Ben. She quickly dug the phone out of her pocket. And just as quickly Mac struck it from her hand.

"I'll keep this." He picked it up off the floor and let the ringtone finish. Then he snapped it open, turned it off and dropped it in his pocket. "Don't want any temptations lying around. Now, how 'bout a little drink by the fire? Oops, forgot there's no firewood and no liquor."

He grabbed Julie's arm and twisted it behind her, forcing her to walk in front of him.

Chapter Twenty-seven

Ben looked in the rearview as he drove away, but Julie had already disappeared in a curtain of white. He hoped he was doing the right thing by splitting up. It certainly seemed the safer thing to do. He was going to have to push it to catch the Hummer and that would be dangerous. The snow was at least four inches deep and continuing to come down—faster and thicker. It was like driving into a wall. He had maybe a car's length of visibility and the truck was struggling to maintain traction.

It hadn't dawned on him that the lodge might not be open, but Julie would be smart enough to break a window or seek shelter in one of the outbuildings. He'd be back within the hour. She was dressed warmly. He reached for his cell, flipped it open and dialed Lieutenant Samuels, but he had left for the day. He ended up telling a dispatcher what was going on, where he was and that he needed the Hummer intercepted. He tucked the phone back into his jacket pocket and was thankful he'd freed up two hands for the steering wheel as the truck glanced off the side of a large rock and slipped precariously close to the opposite edge of the road. An eight-foot embankment would have taken him out quickly. The snow had buried several pitfalls, and he was driving from recent memory with crossed fingers.

He rechecked that he was in four-wheel-drive and then he accelerated. Twenty miles an hour seemed like a hundred. Rounding the first turn, a gust of wind cleared the air for a second and he could see the Hummer's taillights. He had to acknowledge that Mac was a good driver or maybe the Hummer really was the better vehicle for these conditions. He was doing at least five miles an hour faster than Ben. The trick now was going to be keeping him in sight and not losing him when they got to Juan Tabo Boulevard.

They passed the turnoff to Connie's and now were covering the last mile of downhill paved road, which intersected with the major thoroughfare. The 7-11 was dark other than security lights that offered a pale gold glow at the corners of the building. Then it dawned on Ben— the Hummer wasn't slowing down. There was no way the driver could keep it under control on the icy incline unless he slowed now.

Ben began to brake but was mesmerized by the vehicle in front of him. Suddenly its brake lights burst on at the same second it started to spin, careening wildly left, back right, and then in a three-sixty, it flew onto Juan Tabo going sideways across traffic. Ben didn't need to have the window down to hear the sickening scrunch of metal as the Hummer plowed into a pickup, pushing it into a guardrail.

Ben parked at the edge of the convenience store's parking lot and sprinted onto the boulevard. Another car had stopped, putting on its flashers. Ben reached the driver's side door on the Hummer and pulled it open as Jonathan CdeBaca slipped sideways from behind the wheel. Ben caught him and lowered him to the ground. He checked for a pulse and used a rag from under the Hummer's front seat to slow the blood gushing from Jonathan's hairline. Ben wound the cloth tightly around his head and tucked the ends. Makeshift, but the flow seemed to be slowing. He appeared to only be knocked out, but paramedics would make sure.

He left Jonathan to check on the driver of the pickup. The man was already out of his truck's cab and inspecting the damage. Ben introduced himself and told him help was on the way. A few scratches but the guy seemed all right, just mad. His truck was totaled.

The shock of not finding Mac McNamara didn't register until Ben had pulled himself up into the Hummer on the passenger side to see that it was empty. Jonathan had been the only occupant. Ben heard sirens as he walked back around the Hummer to stand beside Jonathan who was making noises of coming to.

What had Ben done? Thinking she would be safe—safer than riding with him—he'd put Julie squarely in danger. Big danger. There was no doubt in his mind Mac was at the lodge—maybe Mac holding Robby hostage. He'd never felt so impotent.

He pulled out his phone and dialed Julie's number. It rang seven times and went to voicemail. He banged his gloved fist on the Hummer's fender. Damn it. What if it was too late? All his strength seemed to drain away—

do something, he kept saying to himself, you're wasting time, you have to go back. Move. He didn't see Lieutenant Samuels until the cop was standing in front of him. Ben quickly told him what had happened and the danger he suspected Julie was in—maybe Julie and Robby.

"Shit." Lieutenant Samuels stood looking across Juan Tabo and up the county road. "There's no way you're going to get a vehicle up there. We've closed all major arteries and when those go, the side roads including the county are off limits. There's at least eight inches on the ground with a lot of drifting and deeper snow at higher elevations. We're going to have to hike it."

"We?" They both stepped to the side as the paramedics strapped Jonathan to a gurney and prepared to wheel him to the emergency vehicle.

"Can't let you do this by yourself. I think you could be in real danger. Let me make sure this guy's held after treatment and then we'll take off."

Ben felt the minutes like stings to his conscience. He had to stop thinking they wouldn't be in time. They simply had to be in time. Ben watched as Jonathan struggled to get out of the constraints and a uniformed officer stepped into the emergency vehicle and closed the door.

"Looks like stitches and then he can be taken downtown. Don't think he's happy about it." Lieutenant Samuels was pulling on goose-down reinforced gloves. "Ready? Let's hit it."

Ben fell in behind Samuels as both jogged across the street and began the incline past the 7-11. It wasn't going to be easy; already the snow swirling from the east was blinding them. And they'd be walking into the storm the whole way. Ben slowed to take a scarf out of his pocket and wind it around his head, covering mouth and nose. Ben accepted the offer of a police-issue billed cap and watched the lieutenant snap his down jacket's hood in place and pull the drawstrings to snug it up to his chin.

The first mile was hard; the second brutal. There was no pushing it. In a white-out, attempting to keep their bearings meant losing something as simple as the road. Time and time again they found themselves almost waist deep in snow, obviously having slipped off the road and into a ravine. Climbing back to where they should have been meant falling more than once. Their footing on the second mile of pavement was treacherous at best. The temperature drop of an hour earlier had formed a layer of ice, now covered with blowing snow. They quickly learned not to speed up just because the wind had cleared a patch of concrete—that was a recipe for a nasty tumble.

Trees which had seemed romantically beautiful before were now all but obscured. Darkness had fallen and even the lieutenant's flashlight worked poorly. Ben wanted to check his watch. He did stop once and hit redial on the cell but again got voicemail. Of course, it could just be the storm, a problem getting a signal, but he couldn't shake the feeling of foreboding. He'd never forgive himself.

"Isn't there a shortcut?" The lieutenant had to cup his hands and yell literally in Ben's face.

"I think we can get back to the house in a straighter line by going left where the mailbox used to be. The road levels there. But it's going to be easy to miss."

"Have you been that way before?"

"No."

"I'm not sure I'm comfortable trying something new when there's no visibility. It'd be easy to get lost.

Disoriented. I know we won't be able to see the lodge."

"We know we can stay on the road but it'll be about thirty minutes longer—if not more."

"It's your call."

Ben hesitated. Could he gamble getting there quickly against not getting there at all? "Let's play it safe."

Chapter Twenty-eight

They sat opposite each other in front of the fireplace on moldy-smelling overstuffed chairs. The leather was cracked and peeling and snagged Julie's coat sleeves. The snow from her boots puddled on the hardwood floor and melded with other black stains too numerous to count. The room was far from its glory days. She pulled her coat around her. The wind seemed to find every chink in the log exterior and whistle in. And the downdraft from the fireplace attested to an open damper or no damper at all. It was better than being outside, but just barely. They were now in almost total darkness with the only sound being Mac's drumming his fingers.

Was she setting Ben up? Yes—with no way around it. No way to warn him. The minute he found out Mac wasn't in the Hummer, he'd be frantic. If he couldn't drive back up to the lodge, he'd walk in. She knew him and he was beating himself up for leaving her, insisting she'd be safer here. But there had been no way of knowing—knowing Mac's accomplice was his old Army bud. And she wasn't sure how far Ben had to chase Jonathan. Had he been able to get a hold of the cops and get help? He might have ended up so far away it would take hours to reach her. She fought a feeling of dread. She just might be in this by herself.

"Is Jonathan coming back?"

"He was going to the 7-11 for supplies. Don't know what's going to happen with your boyfriend chasing him. But Jonathan can take care of himself. If I were a betting man, I know how I'd place my money."

That wasn't what she needed to hear. Would Ben even be able to get back to the lodge? If there had been a confrontation, Jonathan may have been armed. With Connie and Wayne dead, and probably Robby, what was one more? Or two? She couldn't let herself go there, but she knew too much and was in the way. At least they had told Lieutenant Samuels about Mac switching places with Stan Devon. And there was proof. Mac's cover was blown. Somehow it wasn't very comforting to know he probably wouldn't get away with anything. She'd really like to be around to make sure.

She needed to think. Her best chance, maybe only chance, was to get away. But Ben? Shouldn't she wait? He would come back ... if he *could* come back. She would need to warn him. No. Sitting here didn't improve her chances of survival or his. She simply couldn't take a chance and wait for Ben. She hadn't seen a weapon but then this was a man who preferred strangulation or explosives—or both. A hands-on kind of murderer, so to speak. So, she'd just have to out maneuver him. How she was going to do that, she didn't have a clue.

She could use the old bathroom ruse. There was a utility room off the kitchen complete with tiled floor, a drain in the center, and two deep double-sided utility sinks separated by a long granite counter—a place to clean the kill before it was brought into the kitchen to be dressed or taken to the smokehouse. Because skinning and gutting was anything but neat work, Skip had outfitted the room with a shower. And later turned it into a full bath the kitchen help could use by adding a commode.

She remembered large windows across the back of the room to the west and two on the north. At certain times of the day the natural light was perfect; Skip had often used the area to tie flies or clean his guns. Earlier, when she'd been in the kitchen, there had been a decided breeze coming in around that door. She'd bet anything a window was broken out.

If she had the time, one minute or two, she could get out the window and run for it. Definitely a figure of speech because she doubted there would be any running. She would go south, breaking for the trees as soon as she was off the deck. And then? The best bet would be to double back to the road and follow it to civilization. If luck were with her, she might intercept Ben.

"I'm going to the bathroom."

"What?"

"Bathroom. I have to use the bathroom." Julie got up, turned her back on Mac and started toward the kitchen.

"Not so fast." He moved like a cat. He grabbed her arm before she heard him leave his chair.

"I don't need company. This is something I can handle by myself."

"And you think I was born yesterday? Come on, you're not going anywhere."

"I have to pee. I'm going to the bathroom." She turned to confront him, defiant, hoping if she stood her ground and insisted he'd either have to let her go or show his hand. And somehow she didn't think he was ready to make that decision. Was he waiting for Jonathan? That made the most sense. No killing unless there was a consensus of opinion.

"I'll be outside the door. Don't lock it."

She continued around the corner and into the kitchen—with Mac at her side holding a flashlight in front of them.

"May I borrow the flashlight?"

"No. You can figure it out in the dark."

"Thanks."

She was right about the draft coming in around the utility room door. She could only hope Mac wouldn't put two and two together and realize that there might be a ready-made escape route. She quickly opened the door just enough to squeeze inside and then bang it shut.

"Don't take all day."

She didn't answer. The gray light merely outlined the contents of the room, too dim to distinguish anything other than shapes. She immediately bumped into a table on her right but missed a packing crate on the floor in front of her. She was walking bent over with arms sweeping as detectors out in front. There had to be an easier way. She moved sideways until she found the granite counter. She could follow it along the wall and stand upright, checking windows.

At first it didn't register what she'd found resting on the edge of the counter until she'd examined it with both hands. A fish scaler, a knife used to scrape scales, serrated on one edge and sharp and smooth on the other. Only this tool was rusty, its tip dulled, and sharp edge pitted and split. Still, it was something. She quickly slipped it into the top of her right boot.

She needed to concentrate and hurry. Find the broken window and get out. Each howl of wind outside the room's split-log siding sent a gust of cold air across her face. The broken window was on the north at the back. She slipped and grabbed the counter. The floor was treacherous; tile, once slick from draining blood and guts, still had a coating of the industrial soap used to wash the offal down the drain. And now a dusting of snow covered everything. It was worse than walking on greased glass.

The window was on the corner. Long icicles of broken glass caught in the frame moved with the wind. She would have to break the shards free before she could get out. And that would mean noise. There was no counter underneath this window. She would have to hoist herself up and over the sill and then jump or fall to the ground. She didn't remember the deck extending around this corner. It was probably six feet to the ground. The snow would cushion the impact to some extent but not a lot. Not pretty. She was bound to cut herself going through the window frame. But she kept reminding herself of the alternative.

"What's taking so long?"

"Hey, give me a break. I just found the john."

She needed the packing crate that she almost fell over. If it would hold her weight, it would make getting out the window so much easier. She backtracked, working her way along the wall opposite the counter. Her toe hit it before she saw it. Quickly she grabbed the nearest slat and pulled. The scummy-slick floor made moving it easy and the howling wind muffled any sound. She had it in place in record time.

But would it hold her? She was going to find out.

She slipped off her heavy down coat, turned it around, thrust her arms in the sleeves and with the back protecting her front, the collar covering most of her face, she stepped onto the crate. She felt the slat under her right foot crack and she quickly moved her foot to the outside edge—an edge probably reinforced. That was better; it was holding. Standing on the crate put the bottom of the window at her waist. With both covered arms raised she struck at the glass and pushed outward, hearing rather than seeing the remnants of the pane break free. Glass pelted her head and her coat sleeve ripped. Behind her the door from the kitchen exploded and Mac leaped into the room, only to flip ass-over-teakettle when his boots hit the slippery tile.

Go. Go. Go. It was now or never. In one arcing jump, she pushed off of the sill and tumbled free of the casement. She struck the ground, arms splayed, more of a belly-flop than a tuck-and-roll, but she was free. Gulping for air, she scrambled upright, silently taking inventory of moving parts. Everything seemed to work as she begged her legs to run. There would be bruises but the alternative … she had to remind herself of that … made a little black-and-blue amount to nothing.

She started to her right, struggling to get her arms free of her backwards coat, when he struck. She hadn't even heard him—only sensed, more than saw, his shadow at the last second. He'd lunged, knocking her flat. She pulled the scaler from her boot and twisted onto her back to face him, bringing the knife down with two hands on the handle. Surprise was on her side. The point of the knife gouged his eye and the serrated edge cut deeply across his cheek and along his jaw line. He screamed, sat back holding his face then blindly reached out to grab her but only got a handful of coat.

Julie wiggled out of the coat and scooted backwards. She turned, hurriedly half-crawled on all fours, then stood and ran, plowing through the snow that was now more than a foot deep. She saw the smokehouse looming in front of her and, dodging a stack of alder, she ran for it. Would the door be open? Would it lock on the inside? Then she saw a better opportunity. The latticework skirting along the side of the deck nearest to her had a segment missing—just big enough for her to crawl into.

Wouldn't it be better to hide than stumble blindly on, waiting for Mac to overtake her? Her coat was gone and adrenalin was keeping her warm—but for how long? Wasn't shelter of any kind better than the blowing snow of the open forest? She didn't waste time, quickly dropped to the ground and wiggled between broken slats to pull herself under the deck. And then backward, inching away from the opening toward the foundation of the lodge. She put her hand on something furry but very stiff and swallowed a scream.

Okay. She had to be realistic. She just might not be the only occupant under here—dead or alive. She could rule out spiders, thank God—wrong season and the altitude was too high for snakes … what did that leave? Rodents? No, most of them hibernated or she thought so anyway. Probably rabbits, and those she could handle. She willed herself to stop the mental babbling and concentrate.

Chapter Twenty-nine

There was no talking—just one foot in front of the other—and progress was slow, at best. At the quarter mile mark, where the county road was met by the evergreen-lined lane to the lodge, Ben felt a burst of adrenaline. Close. They were close. He could only hope the choice to go the long way would pay off. Lieutenant Samuels paused until Ben was next to him to give a thumbs-up. Then both men stepped up their pace, made difficult because they were now directly facing the storm. But the moment the lodge came into sight, Ben sighed in relief.

Fifty feet from the front door, approaching the lodge from the side, Lieutenant Samuels motioned Ben to move closer.

"I think we need a plan. Are you armed?"

"No."

"Maybe the question should be, can you shoot?"

"Yeah."

"Okay. Here's my boot gun. It's not going to stop an elephant, but it could keep you from getting killed. You gonna be all right?"

Ben nodded. The twenty-five was a lightweight and he hoped he wouldn't be in a position to have to use it. The best scenario would be to find Julie taking a nap, just waiting for his return. But gut-level told him it was wishful thinking. He was straining to see any light in the lodge. Wouldn't Julie have left the flashlight on? At least as a beacon of sorts? Maybe propped it in the window?

"One of us needs to take the front, the other the back. Any preference?"

"No."

"Too dark to toss a coin. I'll go in the front and give a yell if it's clear. Go around to the back. Don't come in the house until you hear my shout. Got that?"

"Roger."

Ben tucked the gun in his jacket pocket and started out. He'd stay close to the building and follow the driveway to the back. Snow was piling up on the north side of the lodge; the going would be slow. And what would he look for? Tracks were out of the question. Hearing anything would be a miracle.

+ + +

Julie pulled her knees up to her body and willed her teeth not to chatter. The lack of a coat was rapidly becoming a problem. And it had dawned on her that hiding under the deck was not the vantage point she'd need to warn Ben.

How would she know if he were even near? And Mac …
would he figure she hadn't gone far? Figure she'd play it
safe and stay close?

Suddenly she froze. Someone walked across the deck,
then turned and stepped off using the three steps just to
the right of her hiding place. The person was probably two
feet from the opening in the broken lattice. She stretched
out full length and, on elbows, pulled herself toward a huge
support post. It was two feet square and the indentation in
the earth around its base might be deep enough to hide her.
She kept her head down and held her breath. The beam of
a flashlight rotated Klieg-like from one corner to another.

Then it stopped. The owner was pulling back,
standing, and walking back up the steps, turning toward
the smokehouse. Mac. She'd just dodged a bullet—maybe
literally. She slowly let her breath out and tried to calm the
pounding of her heart. She was safe. He hadn't found her.
He would not look under the deck again. Now, it was a
matter of waiting and hoping—

"Juuuu-lie." The first syllable was drawn out and
carried on the wind, the second fading only to drop away
in the storm. It was Ben. He was coming up the steps at
the north end of the deck. She had to warn him. Mac was
in the smokehouse but wouldn't be for long. She wiggled
forward, through the opening and raced up the steps
nearest her.

"Ben. Here."

The arm coming around her neck nearly pulled her off
her feet.

"Not so fast."

Mac snugged her against him and held the barrel of
a gun to her forehead. Julie watched as Ben continued to

come toward them, hands in front of him, palms up to show he wasn't armed.

"Let her go, Mac. All this can stop now. It doesn't need to go any further—not with more bloodshed. There's been enough."

"Stop right there. Don't come any closer. I'll decide what needs to happen."

"I wouldn't think you'd want another murder on your hands."

"You can't prove anything."

"All the more reason to let her go."

Then all hell broke loose. The back door flew outward, and as Mac loosened his grip to swing the gun in that direction, someone yelled for Julie to get down. She slumped, making Mac stumble, trying to keep her in front of him. But the blast blew him backward, his gun discharging harmlessly, as Julie sprawled on the deck. Ben picked her up, slipped his jacket around her, and told her everything would be all right. And just held her.

Lieutenant Samuels was standing over Mac but there was no doubt—with most of his brain splattered over the smokehouse wall—he was permanently out of commission. Fast—it had happened so fast. But she was safe. She buried her face in Ben's warmth and just held on.

+ + +

It was almost midnight before a snowplow could reach them, clearing a path for emergency vehicles and two squad cars. The storm seemed spent. Wreak havoc and move on—wasn't that New Mexico's trademark? Snow like hell and all gone by noon the next day. Bad weather seldom stayed. Logs of alder burned brightly in the great room and Julie slept on the couch, too tired to mind the smell of mold. By two a.m., reports had been completed and Mac's body placed in the emergency vehicle for the trip to the OMI.

It was decided she and Ben would meet with Lieutenant Samuels at one o'clock the next day to notarize their statements. The only question left was Robby. Had he been killed with Wayne, his body carried out on the mesa? Maybe there simply hadn't been time to do the same with Wayne. Or Mac, maybe Mac and Jonathan together had been interrupted. Only the interrogation of Jonathan could bring closure.

By the time they got to Juan Tabo Boulevard, the sand trucks were out; major roads were snow-packed but passable. Lieutenant Samuels dropped them off at Ben's truck and helped them scrape windows and brush away the foot of accumulated snow. The trip across town to the hotel took them more than an hour.

Never had a bed looked so good. Julie began to strip the minute she stepped into the room.

"Don't you need music for that?"

She hit him with a pillow. "Instead of being a smart ass, why don't you check the phone messages?"

Ben lifted the receiver, punched in the 2-digit code for voicemail, listened and sat down on the edge of the bed laughing. "Here, you've got to hear this." He started the message over and held the receiver out.

"Julie, it's Mom, give me a call the minute you get in. We're in a quandary here. Robby wants silver accents for your attendants' dresses, but I distinctly remember the accenting trim on your dress is gold—am I right? I just think the dresses should match yours—in all but color, of course. I guess it's not a big thing—we're having a wonderful time. Your Dad and I are so thankful that Robby took a bus to come all this way to help. He is an absolute dear. Well, that's all for now. Call as soon as you can. Oh, I almost forgot, could you call the florist in the morning? I still couldn't get him to confirm fifty white poinsettias by the twenty-fourth. I hope the storm isn't going to cause us problems."

+ + +

They slept in until eleven, ordered room service, showered, made love as if the world might end by evening and still got to Lieutenant Samuel's office by one. Barely.

"You know, when one partner's dead, it's easy to blame him for everything. According to Jonathan, it was Mac who killed Ms. CdeBaca, bombed her house, and killed Wayne. We couldn't even get a straight answer as to why Wayne was killed. Somehow he got in the way. I don't think he was supposed to have dropped Robby off at the bus station. I think Wayne suspected Robby might be a sitting duck if he took him up to the lodge. He lost his life because he saved one."

"Mac had nothing to gain by killing Wayne. I suppose no one really did unless Wayne knew some dirt—maybe knew Mac was alive and had killed Connie." Julie was pensive. It bothered her that some things just weren't making sense—nice and neat—no unraveled edges.

"Mac thought he had a reason to kill Connie," Ben added. "He was double-crossed—or maybe he felt she owed him more money and she refused to pay. He could have thought she'd set up Stan Devon to kill him. Bombing the house was more than likely done to cover up the killer's tracks—if Mac was the killer. Yet, why would he kill the golden goose?"

"My take is that the family hired Mac to do their dirty work. There was a lot of anger over Ms. CdeBaca's giving up the family inheritance. I think bombing the house was done to destroy any documents concerning the will. But thanks to Julie, the pertinent information was saved and Ms. CdeBaca had already hired a different law firm and made her wishes known. Proving their involvement is going to be difficult."

"Have you talked with Cherie or Byron?" Julie was curious how the siblings would react.

"They swear they don't know anything. Byron passed it off as Jonathan's hotheadedness—act first, think later. But he was quick to add that he knew his brother could never truly harm anyone. The sister's one half-step from being a nut case. Seems obsessed with her business—something called Lavender and Lilacs—and with contesting the will. I don't see her as a player in murder."

"What's going to happen to Jonathan?" Julie wondered if blaming a dead man could exonerate him.

"We're a little low on proof. He may walk. He's already hired a local hot-shot lawyer."

Did she care? Julie was probably a stickler for a person paying for his indiscretions … still there had already been so much sadness, so many irretrievable actions set in motion. But Connie had left her son a legacy—reunited him with his true heritage and family and guaranteed that his life would be easier than it had been to date. Connie would be pleased. Perhaps, it would be best to just dwell on the positive.

Chapter Thirty

The three weeks before the wedding flew by. And now she was down to her last four hours as a single person. Julie laughed. She couldn't be more ready to give up that status. But it was nice to have some alone time. A leisurely shower, time to do her hair. Her bridesmaid and maid of honor were picking her up. Bev and Robby had gone ahead to the church. They were consumed with details. Finally, someone to out-obsess her mother. But they worked well together, and everything had come together. It was hard to believe but dresses, flowers, a cake—all was ready. A knock at the door made her turn.

"Door's open. But it's bad luck to see me before—" Julie caught her breath. Dark hair drawn back, sunglasses— the sunglasses she remembered—Connie's leather jacket. But this woman was not about to save her life. Not this time—not if Julie could believe the .38 in her hand.

"Cherie, I don't understand."

"You stole my jewelry. I wouldn't even have known if that lawyer, what's-his-name Baxter, hadn't included the set in his estate inventory. My father gave his bitch wife my grandmother's diamonds and pearls on their wedding day. They were never supposed to leave my family. My grandmother promised them to me. 'Cherie,' she used to say, 'these will be yours someday'." She took a step toward Julie. "You have no right."

"I don't expect you to believe me, but it was Connie's gift. I didn't just take them. They're a wedding present. But I don't think it requires a gun to ask for them back."

"Do you have any idea how much they're worth? Nineteenth-century platinum, over fifty one- to two-carat diamonds in the necklace alone, nine- and ten-millimeter pearls. A French designer made those pieces for my grandmother. Over two hundred thousand dollars!—yes, that's what they're worth. Don't try to tell me you didn't know. They're family heirlooms."

"Then they're yours." Julie walked to the bedside table, picked up the velvet bag containing necklace, earrings and bracelet and held it out. Cherie didn't move.

"You've already told them, haven't you?" Her face was flushed and there was spittle at the corners of her mouth.

"Told who? Told them what?"

"That I took the ring."

"Cherie, I really don't know—"

"Yes, you do. You've been looking for it. You and your money-grubbing mother. I saw how everything in the storage unit had been picked over." Cherie was absolutely wild-eyed.

Julie shook her head. She had absolutely no idea what the woman was talking about. Another piece of jewelry? "So, whatever it was, it's gone. And I don't have it."

"I know you don't have it. Weren't you listening? I have it." Cherie shifted the gun to her right hand and held her left hand in front of her, fingers spread. "Here. Remember?"

The huge diamond sent multi-colored flecks of light bouncing outward. Connie's engagement ring. She seldom wore it, but Julie remembered it from when she was small. And the last time she saw it? The night of the dinner party. The night Connie was killed.

"She *owed* me. She promised to invest in my business. To pay my debts and help launch the new line. But then she decided not to. Said there was something else happening in her life. She couldn't commit at the moment. Don't you understand? She promised. I believed her. I expanded on that promise, borrowed money—money that was going to be paid back a month ago. I didn't use a bank. I trusted Jonathan to find some Vegas money—that's what he called it. Use people who bet on a sure thing and offer big, short-term loans with big interest. But when I couldn't pay them? They were threatening to *ruin* me. Take away everything that I am—make a laughing stock out of me. Maybe even kill my family … I had to cancel with Martha Stewart for God's sake."

"You killed her. You killed Connie for your inheritance? And you didn't even know that all you had to do was wait."

"That inheritance was supposed to include the CdeBaca family land. Our land wasn't a gift to some Indians just so they could go out and pick flowers. And the remainder? Divided unfairly with some bastard child. My father would have killed her if he'd known."

And almost did, Julie thought. They had all been so wrong. Assumed Mac was the one—the only one capable of killing. But hadn't Wayne said he heard a woman arguing with Connie that night? He'd assumed it was Julie.

"Do you know what she said to me? 'I think you're my angel—my angel of death.' And then she begged me to grant her one favor—let her dress in that wedding gown and help her fix her hair before I killed her. Do you believe that? Isn't that the most bizarre request?"

"But you did it."

"It kept her quiet. It made killing her easy—she didn't even struggle."

"I suppose she considered it a favor. She had very little time to live and would never have wanted to be a burden."

"I didn't know she'd already given things away ... had drawn up a new will."

"Cherie, I don't care about the jewelry. It's yours. This is my wedding day. I need to dress."

"You're not marrying anyone, let alone that half-breed. And speaking of dress, isn't it bad luck to marry in something you stole?" Cherie was pointing to the Chanel carefully laid out on the bed. "I'll just take that while I'm here."

"Am I intruding? I thought maybe you could use some help." Sally Johnston poked her head around the door.

"Sally—"

As Cherie turned, Julie dropped the jewelry bag and jumped, throwing her weight into Cherie's torso, reaching for the hand holding the gun. Cherie maybe outweighed Julie by fifteen pounds and was an inch taller—but it wasn't an unfair advantage. Julie's anger gave her momentum. The two of them toppled, hitting the edge of the bed. Cherie recoiled as the shot exploded, splintering a bedpost, then regained her concentration as they hit the floor. She tried to lower the barrel and aim at Julie's forehead. Julie dug her nails into Cherie's wrist, pushing the gun away while trying to shake it loose. She drew her knees up to deflect any kicks, then quickly rolled to straddle Cherie before she knocked the gun to the side.

"Get help." Julie had no idea if Sally heard her above her own screams. But suddenly there was silence—only the muffled sound of feet running on carpet. It felt like a hundred years before a security guard kicked the gun out of Cherie's reach and helped Julie to her feet.

Cherie was handcuffed, sullen, and uncooperative. My God, what a family, Julie thought. It took over an hour but Julie gave a statement, corroborated by Sally, and finally she was alone to shower and dress. At last. Wow, how many people had wedding days like this one?

Epilogue

The afternoon was clear. Snow had melted off the roads but stuck to trees and mounded on the tops of fence posts. The Jemez Mountains were resplendent with white mantles sweeping across their peaks and sliding down their sides. Pueblo rooftops were edged with sugary icing and looked like gingerbread cutouts, not real dwellings. Julie smiled as Sally parked the car in back of the chapel. She could not have chosen a more perfect day for her wedding. Christmas Eve. Evergreens beside the chapel twinkled with colored lights underneath each branch's cap of white. A huge Christmas tree took up almost all of the tiny chapel's foyer and was covered in natural ornaments—popcorn strings alternating with ropes of cranberries, fat tallow candles in tin clip-on holders, and bows of white velvet. Simple, but breathtaking.

She carried the Chanel in a dress bag; Sally followed with shoes and the hat box. The platinum jewelry bag was safe in her purse. It was still an hour before the ceremony, but curiosity got the best of her. She peeked through the curtain that screened the rectory from the pulpit and was amazed—already the chapel was filling. Friends from her studio days sat toward the back. Gloria from IHS was halfway down on the right with her family. Two docs from IHS were acting as ushers. Thank God. It promised to be a full house.

"You need to get dressed." Sally motioned her toward a sitting room, now a makeshift dressing room. "Let's do a little work on your hair."

Julie dutifully slipped on her dress and draped the bed sheet she'd borrowed from the hotel over her shoulders, wrapping the ends around her mid-section. She'd die if she got makeup on the dress. She would leave the matching jacket in the dressing room until after the ceremony and only wear it for the reception. It really gave her two outfits. She dug hair brushes and makeup out of her bag and sat in front of a large mirror brought in from the hallway.

Sally deftly pulled Julie's hair straight back without a part, smoothing the wad of curls under at her crown. She positioned the hat at an angle, gathering the veil into a knot on one side, securing it under a white rosebud and slip of greenery from her bouquet. All this with three bobby pins, two hat pins, and a rubber band. It wasn't how Julie had envisioned it but it was right. Somehow it looked more modern and lost the look of a '50s pillbox. Blusher, mascara, lipstick, a light dusting of powder to set it. She looked in the mirror. Perfect.

The jewelry was the last touch, and, again, perfect. Sally

excused herself to get dressed, walked out the door then leaned back in. "Break a leg, kiddo."

Twenty minutes. She could hear strains of Christmas music from a quartet in the loft above the congregation. Her father's gift. Only live music would do and she agreed with him. The chapel's acoustics seemed to separate, yet accentuate, each instrument's interaction with the others, blending the notes beautifully. She and Ben preferred only instrumentals, no soloist.

A knock on the door and there was her father—could it be time to go already? They would have a brief walk outside in order to come in at the back of the chapel. Father Emerson, the groom, and his attendants must already be in place. Julie got only a glimpse of Sally in the midnight-blue dress whose cut mirrored her own. Very plain, classic lines. She looked beautiful. Robby had worked with a seamstress in Albuquerque and proved to have a real talent for design and execution.

The two ushers held open the double doors to the sanctuary. The strains of the wedding march sounded and everyone stood. This was it. There were people crowded into the foyer and lining the back of the pews. Her maid of honor and bridesmaid had taken their places. Sandy Black stood next to Robby who was next to Ben; Father Emerson beamed in the center.

If there was one thing she'd remember all her life it would be Ben's smile. He never took his eyes off of her, even when her father was declaring his love and stating that he and her mother blessed this union. Ben smiled and squeezed her hand. Robby discreetly pointed at her hat and gave a wink and a barely concealed thumbs up. The rest of the ceremony was a blur. The exchange of rings went smoothly and only once did she falter and have to repeat a vow. Then it was over. She and Ben kissed and walked down the aisle to the applause of the congregation. She stole a look at the narrow band of diamonds and inlaid turquoise, pipestone, coral and obsidian. She was, indeed, Mrs. Benson Pecos.

Thank you for taking the time to read *Fire Dancer*. If you enjoyed it, please consider telling your friends or posting a short review. Word of mouth is an author's best friend and is much appreciated.
Thank you,
Susan Slater

+ + +

Watch for *Under A Mulberry Moon*, Book 5 in this critically acclaimed series!

Get another Susan Slater book FREE when you visit Susan's website at http://susansslater.com and sign up for her free mystery newsletter and a chance to win some very cool stuff.

Contact Susan: susan@susansslater.com
(note the middle S in her name)
Follow Susan on Facebook